DON'T SPEAK

DON'T SPEAK

A JADE HARRINGTON NOVEL

J. L. BROWN

This is a work of fiction. All the characters, organizations, and events portrayed in this novel are either products of the author's imagination or used fictitiously. Any resemblance to actual persons, living or dead, events, or locales is entirely coincidental.

Printed in the United States of America.
For information address JAB Press, P.O.
Box 9462, Seattle, WA 98109.

Cover Design by Damonza
Library of Congress Control Number: 2015918331

ISBN 978-0-9969772-1-0 (paperback)
ISBN 978-0-9969772-0-3 (ebook)

First Edition: January 2016

To Audi, for everything

If we don't believe in freedom of expression for people we despise, we don't believe in it at all.

- Noam Chomsky

PROLOGUE

Ten Years Ago, Chattenham, Pennsylvania

I WAITED BEHIND THE corner. The wind bit into my face as I glanced up at the wintry sky, clouds obscuring and then revealing the moon. Kyle would be wrapping up the evening broadcast. Always the last one to leave, he departed the radio station at 10:10 p.m. every day. So predictable.

Five minutes later, Kyle came out the back door right on time and walked toward his car. Bereft of lights and usually full when Kyle arrived for his 7 p.m. show, the lot was now empty except for his beat-up Honda in a far corner, alone, underneath a large, leafless elm tree. As I knew it would be.

Silence.

Kyle paused. Maybe he sensed me. I'm not sure. I stayed where I was, not moving, not breathing. He continued walking, fishing in his pocket for his keys.

I took long strides toward him, not trying to mask my footsteps.

He turned.

I smiled.

He smiled in return. "Hey, man, what's up? I thought someone was sneaking up on me."

I pulled a baseball bat from behind my back, the wooden handle smooth and comforting in my gloved hand.

Kyle's eyes shifted toward the bat, a frown starting to crease his forehead. His eyes searched mine. "What are you—"

Kyle raised his right arm to block my swing, and the sound of wood meeting bone was like a two-base hit to center field. He screamed. His arm dropped and dangled by his side. He tried to throw a punch with his left, his weaker arm. I side-stepped and as he spun around, I struck his kidney next. Kyle staggered, then fell. I stood over him, cocked the bat back, and swung for the cheap seats. A sickening thud echoed as the bat's sweet spot collided with Kyle's head. He grabbed his head, curling into a fetal position.

I struck him again. And again. And again.

I stopped, my breaths heavy and visible and loud. I had thought I was in shape, but now I wondered. I scanned the parking lot and surrounding buildings to make sure my actions hadn't been observed. My hands shook; I was nervous after all. Letting go of the bat, I bent and tilted my head. I studied Kyle, but didn't touch him.

Yet.

His dark blond hair was now matted with blood and brains and bones and other matter. His eyes stared back at me, unseeing. Triumph surged through me in the silence. The taste of victory, sweet and satisfying.

I glanced at the bat and grimaced. What a mess.

I took out a knife I bought recently, the blade gleaming in the darkness. Kyle's lips were parted, waiting for me. I opened his mouth wider and tugged at his tongue, pulling it out as far as it would go. I laid the sharp edge of the knife against the organ and began to saw. This was harder to do than I thought. It was my first time. They say you never forget your first time.

After I finished, I willed my fast-beating heart to slow.

Crickets chirped, but otherwise the night was quiet. Peaceful.

I needed to leave. The campus police patrolled this area and would be by soon.

I checked to make sure I didn't leave any evidence. Something shiny lay on the pavement next to what was left of Kyle's head. I peered closer.

A penny. Heads up.

My lucky day.

I already got my wish, though; I would never have to hear one of his broadcasts ever again.

PART I

CHAPTER ONE

Present Day, Arlington, Virginia

JADE HARRINGTON STARED down at her opponent. He was four inches shorter than she but built like a linebacker. For this Tae Kwon Do testing, she had already defeated six opponents—all men—and at one point, took down two fighters simultaneously. At the beginning of this final match of the day, a few onlookers stood outside the ring. As the match progressed, however, more spectators from around the arena gravitated from other contests to observe this fight between two highly ranked competitors.

Jade pushed up the front of her protective headgear, which had inched down again. Sweat streamed into her eyes, and her bulky sparring gloves could not wipe it away. The pungent mixture of sweat and the scent of Tiger Balm tingled her senses.

Five judges sat with stoic expressions at a table on the dais to her right. The senior judge, in a quiet voice, said, "*Sijak,*" Korean for "start," to begin the fifth round.

Jade's opponent launched a rear round kick. She expected the move. He had been using the same technique for most of the match, and had landed a few blows with it. At first.

But now she was on to him. She blocked his shin with her left forearm while jabbing a front kick to his stomach. It connected. He expelled a short breath, surprised, and hunched back to his sparring position.

They circled, breathing hard, eyes locked.

Jade had been training for this moment for three years, but after six matches and five rounds in this one, she was exhausted. She had to end this. Now.

He began to raise his back leg for another round kick. *Doesn't he know any other kicks?* Jade didn't wait. She jumped up, her lithe body coiling as she turned clockwise. At the apex of her twenty-inch vertical jump, her right leg straightened and whipped across her opponent's head, connecting at his temple. As he fell, Jade completed the 360-degree spinning hook kick, landing softly on the mat in her original stance, her gloves near her head in a protective position.

She held her stance, then relaxed. He was not getting up.

Jade removed her headgear and released her ponytail. Her light brown hair, wet and clumpy, fell to her shoulders. *Lovely*, she thought, sarcastically. The spectators had been holding a collective breath, but they began buzzing when they realized she was a woman. The *dobok* (uniform) was not the most flattering attire for the female anatomy. As a biracial woman—thanks to a Japanese mother and a black father—her looks often drew the appreciative stares of strangers. Or, maybe this crowd just appreciated a good kick.

She crouched over her fallen competitor, concerned that she had hurt him. She offered her hand to help him up.

"Are you all right?"

He nodded, not meeting her eyes. He waved away her hand and struggled to his feet. Jade knew he was disappointed.

This was his third time testing for this rank. *Whatever.* She had tried to be nice.

They both stood at attention, feet together, hands at their sides, facing the panel of judges.

"Mr. Randall," said the senior instructor, Master Won Ho. "I'm sorry. You didn't pass. Not because you lost, but because you forgot our core tenet of courtesy. I would like to have a word with you after this testing."

He turned to Jade.

"Ms. Harrington, by the power vested in me by the Tae Kwon Do Association, I now bestow upon you the rank of fourth-degree black belt. Congratulations."

Jade's chest swelled, but she didn't smile. The skin around Master Won Ho's eyes crinkled, and he nodded at her. She nodded in return, the beginning of a smile creeping onto her face.

The spectators clapped. Jade surveyed the crowd, not recognizing anyone except for a few classmates. But she didn't know them well enough to share in the glow of this accomplishment. Her past made it hard for her to make friends. Ever since she was a kid, after what happened, she found it hard to trust anyone. Still.

As she packed her gear, spectators came up to congratulate her and relive her spinning hook kick.

She thanked them and left the arena.

Alone.

CHAPTER TWO

Pittsburgh, Pennsylvania

I SAT IN A rental car across the street, watching.

They had already consumed several rounds of drinks at an Italian restaurant on the bottom floor of a downtown skyscraper that housed radio station KABC up on the top floor. The dinner rush was gone, except for seven station employees still going strong at a table near the front.

Most of the conversation was directed at a tall, broad-shouldered man. Whenever he spoke, his companions laughed as if he were a comedian. This funny man was named Randy Sells.

Sells stood and drained the rest of his beer before stumbling toward the back of the restaurant, bumping into chairs along the way. The restaurant didn't have its own restrooms, so patrons had to use the ones in the office building. I had scouted that out earlier.

I got out of my car, and sprinted across the street and through the lobby. I had to beat him to the restroom. I turned right and then left down a long hallway. I won. I heard his footsteps echoing behind me.

He stopped. I stopped, too. He may have heard me, but he could not see me.

Sells started walking again. His footsteps rounded the corner, toward me. I slipped out the back door next to the bathroom and into the alley behind the building. I left the outside door ajar.

The stench of rotten food and urine hit me. Nauseated me. I kept my composure and remained silent. And I waited.

Sells entered the restroom.

A few minutes later he came out, shaking his hands dry.

I eased the door open, took two quick steps, and put my arm around his neck. And squeezed.

He brought his arms up to free his throat and began to writhe away from me. He was bigger than I thought.

"What the hell do you—"

I re-established my grip, took the stun gun out of my pocket, placed it under his rib cage, and fired.

I held him tight and close as the electrical current pulsed through his body. After a time, he stopped struggling.

I whispered in his ear, as if to a lover, "There are consequences to what you say."

He sagged into me, and I dragged him outside and laid him on the pavement. I stared at the handsome face and reached for my trusted bat, where I'd hidden it earlier. Time for batting practice.

My swing was getting better.

CHAPTER THREE

Washington, DC

WHITNEY FAIRCHILD, JUNIOR Democratic senator from Missouri, strode down the steps of the Capitol. Landon Phillips, her legislative director, struggled to keep up despite his long legs.

Landon briefed her on her remaining schedule for the day, reading from his electronic tablet as they crossed Constitution Avenue toward the Russell Senate Office Building.

"You shouldn't read that while crossing the street," Whitney said.

"You're right, Senator. Bad habit." He stopped reading and carried the tablet like a book. "At three o'clock, you're scheduled for a photo op with kids from the elementary school with the highest points under the new Missouri scoring system. This will give you a chance to say a few words about education reform."

"Such as my plan to eliminate scoring systems?"

Landon ran his fingers through his long hair. "Uh . . . , that might not be appropriate for the occasion."

"How about my plan to let teachers teach children how to learn rather than how to take a test?"

"Not enough time."

"How about firing nonperforming teachers?"

"Ditto."

"You're no fun."

"You're having lunch today with Senator Sampson at the Four Seasons," Landon continued, "ostensibly to discuss Agricultural Committee work, but really his goal is to convince you not to separate farm subsidies from your welfare reform bill."

"He wants to break bread now after everything he's been saying about me?" Whitney said. Sampson was Whitney's rival for the Democratic nomination in the upcoming presidential primaries. Turning serious, she said, "Email his LD and work on a separate bill capping subsidies. The subsidies should be directed toward small- and mid-sized farmers only."

"Will do."

"Wait until after lunch."

A trim, fit man with black hair, a dark business suit and red tie, caught up to them.

"Senator Fairchild, may I speak with you?"

"Of course, Senator Hampton." To Landon: "Give us a moment."

Landon walked a few paces away, finding something, as always, to read on his electronic tablet.

She smiled at Hampton, his professorial glasses augmenting his self-proclaimed intellectual persona. "What can I do for you, Senator?"

"I can deliver the votes on welfare reform, if you back off supporting the anti-personhood legislation."

"You know I can't do that."

The Virginia Republican smiled as if it pained him. "But this is a state issue."

"No, this is a civil-rights issue."

"What about backing off the ERA? The deadline expired in 1982. It's dead already, for God's sake."

Whitney was shaking her head before he had finished speaking. "That's because most people think equal rights is already the law. Eric, you're wasting your breath. Give me something we can work together on. What about education? Immigration? The deficit?"

His lips parted to say something else, but he closed them.

"Maybe. I'll see what I can do. I'll be in touch. Good day, Senator."

He walked away. Landon rejoined her.

"What did he want?"

She filled him in.

"That's not going to happen."

"Not in my lifetime."

CHAPTER FOUR

Washington, DC

THE BIGGEST STUDIO at the Patriot News Network was painted orange and yellow. Loud colors for a loud man. Cole Brennan sat behind the microphone during his fourth commercial break of the hour, watching CNN, ABC, FOX, CBS, and NBC on the TV monitors on the wall opposite him. There was no breaking news.

Cole surveyed the guest list, waiting for his music intro to fade out. He put on his headphones. His producer said, "Our next caller is Frank from New York City."

"Frank from New York City. What's on your mind?" Cole asked.

"With all due respect, Cole, I disagree with what you just said. Income inequality isn't a recent phenomenon. The difference in wealth between the haves and have-nots widened over the last forty years. The rich continue to migrate to gated communities, cutting them off from the rest of us. If something isn't done, the divide will be permanent. The resentment between the rich and everyone else will only get worse. I believe . . ."

Cole, the number one-rated radio talk-show host in the

United States, sipped his ice-cold sweet tea while Frank jabbered on. He believed that when someone began a sentence with "With all due respect," he wasn't being respected at all.

"Well, Frank," he interrupted, "what you neglected to say is the so-called rich create the jobs and pay the most taxes in this country."

"But that's not true—"

He hung up on Frank and spoke into the microphone.

"He also neglected to say education makes a difference. Not for those people who graduate from college with philosophy or African-American studies degrees and wonder why they can't get a job, default on their student loans, and stick us with the bill. I paid off my student loans, and so did you. Our kids can do the same."

The next caller asked about welfare reform.

"Good question," Cole said. "I believe it's far more compassionate to help people become self-reliant rather than dependent on the government. Don't you agree? The Commiecrats' grand scheme is to expand the number of folks on welfare and working in Big Government, ensuring them two voting blocs for life."

His producer signaled him: five seconds left.

"Well, everyone, we've run out of time. This is Cole Brennan protecting your life, liberty, and pursuit of happiness. Join us again tomorrow for 'The Conservative Voice.'"

He stood.

"That's a wrap."

He left the studio. "Great show, Mr. Brennan," said several of his young employees. He ignored them as he sauntered down the hall to his spacious office.

Cole sunk into the leather executive chair behind his desk

and spun to remove a cigarette from the humidor on the credenza behind him. He didn't light it because of the stupid regulations that governed the workplace. How could the government tell him he couldn't smoke in his own office?

He scanned the walls lined with pictures of him with former Republican presidents, the current Senate minority leader and Speaker of the House, every important new person in the conservative establishment, and celebrities like Clint Eastwood and Arnold Schwarzenegger. Most celebrities were Socialists, but some, like Clint and Arnold, weren't afraid to come out of the closet and stand up for American conservative values.

His eyes rested on the photograph of his hero, former President Ronald Reagan. Well, he was trying to "win one for the Gipper," all right. Next, he settled on a picture he had taken with singer Gloria Estefan. Unlike some conservatives who preached family values, but lived quite the opposite, Cole believed in them and had never cheated on his wife. The singer was beautiful and charming, though. He smiled at the memory of meeting her.

Cole's eyes landed on a photograph of himself with President Richard Ellison. He scowled and shook his head. Ellison needed to get with the program. He hit the speed-dial button for the White House residence.

The president came on the line. "This better be good."

"We need to meet."

"Why?"

"I want to make sure we're on the same page."

"About what?"

"The game plan."

"This isn't a damn football game." Ellison exhaled. "Never mind. When?"

"Tomorrow. I'll leave instructions with your secretary."

Cole hung up, grabbed his jacket, and put it on over his pale green polo shirt. Ellison didn't like being told what to do, but so what. Ellison owed Cole. Cole was the kingmaker. With the support of his millions of listeners, and his influence on the financiers of Republican candidates, he put Ellison in office. And he could take him out. Ellison sometimes forgot that.

He should take the stairs from the third floor, but he had never met an elevator he didn't like. Yes, he needed to lose a few pounds—okay, maybe a hundred—but he was, as they say, fat and happy. Except when he thought about Ellison.

As the elevator car descended, Cole thought about ways to eradicate income inequality from the nation's political discourse. The country had more important issues to address.

Correction: more important conservative issues.

CHAPTER FIVE

Arlington, Virginia

"WHAT'S THAT NOISE?" Jade's boss, Supervisory Special Agent Ethan Lawson, said through the cell phone. "What are you doing?"

Jade glanced down at her gray Stanford basketball shorts and her black sports bra. The sweat glistened on her triceps and flat stomach. She stopped dancing.

"Nothing," she said, muting "Holiday" by Madonna.

He hesitated. "Okay . . . I hope you've been enjoying your vacation."

She looked around the living room of her two-story Arlington townhouse. Her collection of '70s and '80s albums were spread over the hardwood floor. A stack of books she planned to read this week towered high on the coffee table. She normally didn't have time for her favorite things.

"It's a staycation, and it hasn't started yet."

"It's already over, I'm afraid."

She sat on the sofa. "What happened?"

"The Pittsburgh Police Department needs a consult on the murder of a local radio personality. You are it. I've booked you and Merritt on a flight out of Dulles. You leave in three hours." He hung up.

She moved to the kitchen where Card, her cocoa-colored cat, squatted, attacking the Purina ONE in his bowl, as if he hadn't eaten in weeks. Card was short for Cardinal, the nickname of her alma mater.

Jade wasn't close to a lot of people, but she loved this cat.

She picked him up and stared into his eyes.

"Sorry to interrupt our vacation, but I need to go. I'll call your girlfriend to look after you while I'm gone."

She gave him a squeeze and a kiss and set him down. He rushed back to his bowl to resume eating, as if he had never been interrupted. Jade tried not to take it personally.

She called as she left the kitchen.

"You rang?" said a female voice, sleepy, playful.

"I need you to check on him."

"Card?" Zoe, her best friend, asked.

"Just for a few days."

"You owe me one."

The sudden silence indicated she had hung up.

CHAPTER SIX

Andrews Air Force Base, Maryland

PRESIDENT RICHARD ELLISON settled into his driving stance. Everyone around him remained library-quiet as he twisted his hips and raised his golf club high overhead. The whacking sound as the club met its target at the wrong angle was followed by the cracking sound of the ball slicing to the right and into the trees. A high-pitched squeal emitted from behind the president. The sound seemed incongruous with the big body from which it came.

Laughing, Cole Brennan said, "You can't drive worth a shit, Richard."

The rest of the foursome, Senator Eric Hampton and Representative Howard Bell, remained stoic as Ellison walked off the tee.

Cole swaggered up, placed the ball on the tee, and swung. The sound was true, and the ball sailed straight down the fairway.

Hampton and Bell took off in one cart. The president folded his tall, lanky frame into the passenger side, next to Cole. As he drove, Cole marveled at the championship golf course of Andrews Air Force base on this lovely spring day, basking in its military presence: the servicemen in uniform, the flags, order.

The Secret Service followed them in a cart at a discreet distance.

Ellison remained silent.

The president had the lean, sinewy build and handsome, rugged, weather-lined face of a cowboy. What one would expect of a man from Wyoming. Still sporting his tan, despite his many years in Washington, Ellison's lined forehead illustrated his troubles. With the country's deficit problems and the rising tensions with China, who could blame him?

Cole regarded the president. "Richard, I'm glad you sliced the ball again, because I needed a little word with you. One on one."

Ellison continued to stare through the cart's windshield.

Cole cleared his throat. "Even though this is an election year, I feel you're straying off the reservation."

"Get to the point." Ellison's Wyoming drawl was more pronounced when he was irritated.

"Okay, then. You need to stop talking about this left-wing income-inequality bullshit. Why do we always let the other side frame the political discussion? The rich get richer, because they work harder. They deserve to keep the spoils from their efforts. I never saw my dad growing up. He worked on Wall Street. He worked all the time to provide his family a better way of life. He doesn't owe anyone anything."

"Interesting word choice, Cole. 'Spoils' means plunder, taken from an enemy in a war or from a victim in a robbery. Don't say that in public or you'll give some activists the ammunition to resurrect the 'Occupy Wall Street' movement."

"Cut the shit, Richard. You know you're not my first

choice, but you were the only alternative at the time. None of the wingnuts could win the general election. But I put you in office, and I can take you out."

"Are you threatening the president of the United States?"

Cole realized he needed to tone it down. He stole a glance at the Secret Service men in their cart. One of them may have been a woman, but he wasn't sure. "I know you're tired of Washington and want to retire to your ranch, but we need you for four more years. This election is bigger than you and me. The future of our country depends on you."

"I'd stop pointing your finger at me if I were you."

Cole dropped his hand back on the steering wheel. "No more income-inequality BS. Your constituents don't care about it."

"They should."

"What're you going to do? Raise taxes on the rich? Increase the federal minimum wage? Switch parties?"

The president remained silent.

"Listen to me. I need you to be vocal in your support of pro-life issues. At least two justices will be named to the Court next term, and we'll finally be able to overturn *Roe v. Wade*. We're close on passing 'personhood amendments' in Mississippi, Louisiana, Arkansas, Montana, and Colorado. Why can't you be more like Hampton?" Cole smiled and waved at Senator Hampton standing near the green. The senator returned the wave. "Richard, if you don't get with the program, I swear I'll support someone else."

"Who? The uncontrollable billionaire businesswoman? The Libertarian wingnut? Or the governor who has destroyed his state, but has the saving grace of being a minority?"

He laughed. "Although he doesn't seem to remember he's a minority."

The knuckles on Cole's hand were white against the black steering wheel. He seethed inside, afraid to release his grip. He stopped the cart at the edge of the fairway.

Ellison was staring at him. "Face it, Cole, you're stuck with me."

Cole released his tight grip, glanced at Ellison, and then into the trees where the president's ball had disappeared. "This is your stop."

The president paused before alighting from the cart, turning to face Cole. "You're right. This election is bigger than you and I. Maybe we should cease pushing the social issues and focus on important things. Like the deficit and entitlements." Ellison's jaw clenched. "By the way, I'm a pretty good hunter. Next time, why don't we go hunting? I don't miss."

Ellison stepped out of the cart to hunt for his golf ball.

"Ellison," Cole said. He waited for the president to turn around. "Don't make me run."

CHAPTER SEVEN

Miami Gardens, Florida

"I AM COMMITTED TO helping the poor and the disenfranchised realize the American Dream. Yes, we will extend a hand in need, but the American ideal will not be handed to you on a silver platter. You must earn it."

Whitney scanned the huge crowd at Sun Life Stadium, home of the Miami Dolphins and the University of Miami Hurricanes football team.

"Welfare is not a permanent solution. All of us must take personal responsibility for our own lives. That's the best way to strengthen our families, our communities, and our nation. Under the Fairchild administration, workfare programs will be created to help welfare recipients receive the training they need to facilitate their return to the workforce.

"My administration will not forget that creating legislation is the fundamental job of Congress. It's appalling to me that every year this body is creating fewer and fewer laws. The role of lawmakers seems to have been forgotten among all the politics. Our major issues must be resolved, and the journey will not be easy. But as John F. Kennedy once said, 'Let us not seek the Republican answer or the Democratic answer, but the right answer. Let us not seek to fix the blame for the past. Let us accept our own responsibility for the future.'

"Ladies and gentlemen, as your president, I will accept the responsibility of restoring the United States of America to a country we can be proud of once again. A nation respected and admired by every other nation as the greatest and most powerful on earth."

The crowd stood and applauded. Whitney waved in its direction and left the podium. She shook hands with people lined up on either side of the red carpet laid down for the occasion. The hot Florida sun pressed down on her in her cream blouse and navy-blue suit. After posing for pictures, she walked into the coolness of the large, cavernous hallway of the stadium where her advance team waited. Sarah, her body woman, handed her a bottle of water.

Whitney gave her a grateful nod, took a long sip, and turned to her campaign manager, Ted Bowling.

"That seemed to go well."

Ted shook his head. "Well? Better than well . . . that was great! You were great!"

Ted had the remarkable ability to cough and talk at the same time. He lit a cigarette, and lifted his chin to exhale.

"They loved you! And your hair looked fabulous. The way the wind teased it, . . . it was majestic. Magnificent. We'll poll it, but I think you should wear your hair down from now on."

"And, perhaps, the speech resonated with them as well."

Ted missed the rebuke. He touched her elbow.

"We need to get going. Xavi is meeting us at the next stop." Xavier "Xavi" Fernandez was the Independent governor of Florida.

They walked past the player locker rooms and headed

outside to a Lincoln Town Car. Ted took a final puff on his cigarette and threw the butt on the ground, and began to grind it with the ball of his shoe.

Whitney stopped. "Pick that up."

Ted paused in mid-grind and bent to retrieve it.

Whitney turned and smiled and waved to the people seeking one last glimpse of her before ducking into the car. Ted climbed in the other side. She patted her forehead with a handkerchief and smoothed her hair before leaning her head back on the headrest and closing her eyes.

Her cell phone rang. She eyed the digital display before hitting the button. "Yes?"

"Senator? Landon. Senator Sampson called. He has a proposition for you."

"Did he tell you what it is?"

"No, but he wants to meet with you first thing when you get back from your trip."

"Anything else?"

"We're getting calls."

"About my speech?"

"A lot of people aren't too happy with the workfare program idea. Some are complaining you sound like a Republican."

"Hillary Clinton once said, 'I have a conservative mind and a liberal heart. I fight for change within the system.'"

"What do you want me to tell Sampson?"

"Tell Sean to set up a meeting." Sean was Whitney's receptionist and scheduler.

"Yes, Senator."

She hung up.

"What did Mr. Perfect want?" Ted asked.

"Not now, Ted."

"As you wish. Here are the talking points for your meeting with Xavi." He started to hand her a sheet of paper.

Whitney raised her hand to ward him off. "Give me a minute."

She turned from him and gazed out the window at the bleak landscape. Florida had broken a record for its number of days without rain. The land was dry, everything brittle. Scientists attributed the lack of rain to global warming. She needed to develop a centrist global warming message for her platform.

As she continued to gaze out the window, she wondered, *What was Senator Sampson up to now?*

CHAPTER EIGHT

Pittsburgh, Pennsylvania

PITTSBURGH POLICE LIEUTENANT John Cooper held the door for Jade and fellow special agent, Christian Merritt, as they entered Angelo's. It was an Italian restaurant in the Golden Triangle, Pittsburgh's downtown center.

Cooper, in his late forties, had an almost transparent complexion and a slight paunch. He nodded at the hostess.

"We're looking around."

She smiled and they headed toward a table close to the entrance.

"The group sat at this table. Sells sat here." He put his hands on the back of a chair facing the front of the restaurant.

Jade removed a red peanut M&M from the small bag she kept in her gray slacks and slipped it into her mouth. She glanced through the window.

"The UNSUB must have been watching him through the window." She scanned the restaurant, eying the waitstaff. "Did you check out all the employees, Lieutenant?"

Cooper stared at her longer than appropriate. Jade, accustomed to stares, ignored it.

He found his voice. "Uh . . . , call me Coop. My friends do."

Was he blushing?

"Yes, we did," Cooper continued. "They were either working or had an alibi."

"Were the alibis verified?" Jade asked. "Corroborated by others?"

"Of course," Cooper said, his words clipped.

Christian, his hair cut military-short, crossed his arms in front of his muscular chest. "What was the radio show about?"

"The rich getting richer and the poor getting poorer." Cooper shrugged. "I'm not sure why that's news to anyone."

"What about the callers that night?" Christian asked. "Any that caught your attention?"

"None, yet, but we're still checking. Most of them weren't too happy with the topic of the show. Heck, Sells didn't seem to want to talk about it, either. He was a pretty big deal around here. He was singlehandedly trying to revive conservative talk radio in Pittsburgh. Could've made some enemies along the way. After dinner, he told everyone he needed to use the john and to order another round of beers. He never returned." He cocked his head. "This way." He led them toward the back. "The restaurant doesn't have its own restrooms, so customers use the ones in the building."

He held the door open to a hallway and turned right. They arrived at the bathroom at the end of a long hall. Cooper knocked on the door and peeked in.

"Anyone here?" He motioned for Jade and Christian to follow. "We know Sells used the bathroom. We found a partial print on the inside door handle and a handprint on the wall over the urinal. His co-workers said he was drunk. We figured he needed the wall for support. No prints on the faucet; it's automatic."

A man, who appeared as if he had had several drinks himself, entered the restroom. He stared at Cooper, Jade, and Christian. Then he muttered, "Sorry, dudes," and stumbled out the door. Christian laughed. Cooper blushed again. Jade rolled her eyes. They went back out into the hallway.

"We think he was incapacitated in some way here—maybe tased—and dragged outside." He pushed the release bar on the back door, which opened into an alley. The narrow alley stunk of trash and urine. Farther down, a large dumpster took up most of the narrow lane. "When he didn't return, his co-workers went looking for him. One checked the bathroom and then out here, thinking Sells may have come out to talk on his cell phone or grab a smoke. He didn't see him. It gets pretty dark out here at night. Another co-worker checked the front of the building. After a while, they all figured he went home. You can leave the bathroom and go out the front of the building without going through the restaurant." He pointed to the pavement. "The victim was killed here."

Jade bent down a few yards from the door. Flecks of blood still dotted the pavement. "Cause of death?"

"Severe blows to the head. He lost a lot of blood."

"Spatter?"

"Cast-off pattern on the wall and the ground."

"So, you're thinking he was most likely hit with a blunt instrument."

Cooper nodded.

"Did you recover the murder weapon, Lieutenant Cooper?"

"Coop. And no."

"Any defensive wounds?"

"Nope. The victim's head looked like mush. He didn't put up much of a fight."

"Is this where you found him?"

"Not exactly." Cooper started walking down the alley. Jade and Christian glanced at each other and followed.

Cooper stopped at the dark green dumpster. "We found him in here. Someone threw him away with the restaurant's nightly trash. His tongue had been cut out."

❧

"Jesus," Christian breathed.

Jade stared down at the body on the stainless steel table at the Allegheny County Medical Examiner's office. Although it had been cleaned up, the face of Randy Sells had been beaten beyond recognition. *Was that the point?* Sells would have a closed casket at his funeral.

"No question as to the manner of death," Cooper said.

Jade scanned the length of the corpse and returned to his face. Almost all the damage had been inflicted to the right side of his face. "The UNSUB is left-handed."

Christian nodded. "And has anger management issues."

Jade's eyes didn't leave the victim. "Sells was a big boy. Our suspect must be strong."

"Or had help," Christian said. He turned to Cooper. "Who found him?"

"One of Angelo's busboys. He had started to swing the trash into the container when he noticed the vic. He dropped the bag, ran back into the restaurant, and told the manager, who called 911. The kid was shaking so hard during our interview, we had difficulty getting the story out of him."

"Time of death?"

"Between nine p.m. and midnight. Sells's friends were still drinking while he lay dying in the alley."

Jade continued to stare at Sells's face.

"Anything back on the tongue?"

"Sent to the lab. Results aren't back, yet."

"Cutting out someone's tongue is extreme," Jade said. "This seems personal."

"We agree," Cooper said. "We don't think the victim was chosen at random. Nothing was stolen as far as we could tell. He still had his wallet and cell phone on him."

Christian pointed at the corpse's bare neck. "According to the autopsy report you showed us, the victim wore a necklace with a crucifix. Maybe this is connected to his religion or church. A hate crime. Did you check it out?"

Cooper's cheeks reddened, a vein throbbed on the right side of his pale forehead.

"We're in the process of checking it out now. We've just started this investigation. We haven't even completed our interviews, yet. My boss called you in. Premature, if you ask me. He's nervous because Sells was a rising celebrity in this town, and Pittsburgh is ranked as one of the safest big cities in the country every year. There's a lot of pressure for us to solve this case quickly and protect our ranking. But this isn't some damn TV show. We need more than forty-eight hours to solve the crime."

Jade touched Christian's forearm before he reacted. She smiled at Cooper in apology.

"I think we've seen enough here, . . . Coop. We need to catch a flight. Is there anything else you want to tell us?"

Cooper broke his stare with Christian and turned to Jade. "Yeah, about the tongue. When we arrived on the scene, the vic was clasping it in his own hands. Like a rosary."

CHAPTER NINE

Athens, Georgia

"YOU SOUND TIRED," said Grayson, her husband.

"Sometimes I wake up with no idea which state I'm in, much less which city." Whitney lay back on the king-size bed in her hotel suite, cell phone pressed to her ear. "People seem to be receptive to our message," she said, "though some of my base may be disappointed."

"When are you coming home?"

"I thought we could meet in Ohio in a few days for dinner. A romantic dinner."

Grayson had always understood the demands of her career and never been resentful that she had to fit him into her schedule. As the CEO of Fairchild Industries, a St. Louis-based biotechnology and agricultural conglomerate, Grayson didn't enjoy much free time either.

"Sounds good to me," he said. "I need to see you. Hold you. What's wrong?" He knew her.

Grayson was normally too busy to miss her. "I could ask the same of you."

"I just miss you. That's all." He paused. "Is it Hampton? The women's rights bill?"

"Have you spoken to the children?" Whitney asked. She didn't want to talk about work.

"I spoke with Chandler today. He decided to intern with us this summer. I'm not sure why he wants to work for the family firm all of a sudden. I rarely talked to him last semester. He only calls when he needs—"

"—money," they said at the same time and laughed.

"And Emma," Grayson continued, "is freaking out about her final exams, and they're still three months away. Again, not sure why. She inherited her mother's brains."

Whitney scoffed. "Please . . . ." She thought of her son, Chandler, a junior at the University of Missouri, his hair falling on his forehead no matter how many times he pushed it back and her daughter, Emma, a freshman at Princeton, whose nose was the same as Grayson's. "I miss my babies."

"They aren't babies, anymore."

"I know. I talk to Emma every day about nothing at all, and those calls mean everything to me." She paused, sighed. "Dear, I need to run. My audience awaits. I'll call you tomorrow about dinner. I love you."

"I love you, too. I'm so proud of you."

She held the cell phone next to her heart.

At the discreet knock on her door, she placed the phone on the nightstand. "Coming."

Whitney rose, smoothed her shirt and skirt, and put her heels back on. She went out into the living room of the hotel suite. Ted Bowling and several others on her campaign staff sat on the beige sofas and chairs with laptops and papers spread out everywhere. Easels with white boards were placed throughout the room for a strategy session.

A presidential candidate was never alone, and the lack of

privacy would only become worse when she became president. Yes, she was able to grab a few minutes on occasion, such as just now with Grayson, but most of the time she was surrounded by the individuals in this room.

Whitney sat, crossed her legs, as she thought again of the unusual anxiousness in Grayson's voice. Scanning the faces of her team, she forced the thoughts of her husband from her mind. "What's the plan for tomorrow?"

CHAPTER TEN

Washington, DC

"HEY, COLE. THIS is Carl from Lubbock, Texas. Love your show. The reason for my call is I'm not too happy with Ellison. Why does he feel the need to compromise with the Socialist Democrats? Why isn't he doing more to protect and promote our conservative values?"

"Good questions, Carl. Sometimes, and I think you would agree, some of the folks in our party aren't 'right' enough for me. They don't stand up for our conservative heritage. They're either weak and willing to compromise with the Commies or they flip-flop as Romney did back in the day. Romney flipped more times than an Olympic high diver on steroids. I think President Richard Ellison sometimes forgets where he came from and who elected him to office. He may need help getting in touch with his 'inner conservative.' That's what I'm here for."

"Why don't you run, Cole? We need a man like you in the White House."

"Because my calling is to spread the word to you good folks. Thanks for the call, Carl. Next caller."

"Cole, this is Fred from Nebraska. Senator Sampson is

trying to keep the farm and welfare reform bills together. Do you support this?"

"Absolutely not. The federal government pays around thirty-two billion dollars per year to farmers, whether they grow crops or not. Our US Department of Agriculture—it's not a coincidence its acronym is DOA, dead on arrival—also provides subsidized crop insurance and marketing support for the farming industry at a cost to American taxpayers of five billion dollars a year. Crop insurance guarantees eighty percent of their revenue. Most other businesses must pay these expenses out of pocket without government help and with no revenue guarantees. Why should farmers be the exception?"

"Yeah, but Cole, I'm a farmer. I need that money—"

"Listen, Ted. You farmers resisted subsidy reductions for decades. Subsidies made sense when we were a country of farmers, but now you all represent a small percentage of the population. These subsidies are costly and transfer income from general taxpayers to farmers, who then overproduce, resulting in lower prices, and more subsidies. It's a vicious circle, Ted. Worse, these handouts hinder you guys from taking the actions needed to compete in the global economy. We want a free market, where those who invest and innovate reap the rewards. Prices should be set by supply and demand, not subsidies."

"But—"

"Did you know the average farmer makes more than the average US industrial worker?"

"Uh, no, I didn't, but—"

"Did you know millions of dollars in farm subsidies and crop insurance are paid to dead farmers? I'm talking fourteen million dollars per year of our money. Our government doesn't know whether you're dead or alive. It's not capable of managing this."

"But—"

"A fraud ring in North Carolina bilked the government for over one hundred million dollars. Listen here, Ted—"

"Fred."

"Senator Sampson is pushing this bill because his family owns farming corporations. He and his cronies in Congress are all farmers or ex-farmers, and they're trying to stuff their own pockets. Farmers need to be disciplined and self-reliant like the rest of us. Sorry, Fred, the subsidies must go. This is tough love, my friend. I'm not even going to answer your question about welfare reform. You all know how I feel about it. Next caller."

"Yo, Cole, this is Adam from St. Cloud, Minnesota. What do you think of Senator Fairchild as a candidate?"

"Well, Adam, from St. Cloud, Minnesoooooooooooooota. I think she is the chick version of Mitt Romney. She was a bleeding-heart liberal when she was in the House. Now, all of a sudden, she is talking about compromise and making lazy people work? I don't buy it, and the American people won't buy it. Liberals think the public is dumb. That we don't understand what's in our best interest, so they need to make decisions for us. The Commiecrats love her, because the women's libbers have been nagging them to death to nominate a female candidate. She doesn't stand a chance.

"Before we go, remember to pre-order my book coming out this summer, *Communism in Russia is Dead, but Alive and Well in the USA*. Ain't that the truth! You can also purchase my other books, newsletters, apparel, and DVDs on my website, www.theconservativevoiceonline.com.

"This is Cole Brennan protecting your life, liberty, and pursuit of happiness. Join us again tomorrow for 'The Conservative Voice.'"

ꝭ

The black limousine was at the curb in front of the studio, and the driver held the door open for him. Cole Brennan lifted his bulk and sat in the seat facing the front, a glass of cognac in the cup holder. On the short drive to his home in Bethesda, Maryland, he sipped the brandy as he made a quick call to his agent, who had been pestering him for the final manuscript of his new book. Cole had no problems pre-selling the book, but finding the time to write these days was proving problematic. He completed the call by assuring his agent it was almost finished—*Not!*—as the limo ascended the long driveway to his sprawling home. Before the car had stopped, five of his six children ran toward him. The oldest, Cole Jr., followed them, too cool to run.

Cole hugged each of his kids and held the hands of his youngest two as they strolled toward the front door. His wife, Ashley, still retaining the figure of the fashion model she once was, stood in the doorway, smiling, holding his second cognac of the evening.

He grinned and gave her a quick kiss, and stepped inside the massive foyer. They shuffled down the hallway and entered the large family room at the back of the house. Cole plopped on the overstuffed sofa. The kids gathered around him and all started to speak at once.

"Dad! I got an 'A' on my test."

"Dad! Don't forget my game this Saturday!"

"Dad! Boys are gross."

"Dad, watch this!" another of his sons said, and he tumbled into a forward roll.

Cole laughed. "Very good, Ronnie. One at a time. What was your test in, Madeline?"

"English."

"Who are you playing this weekend, Sport?"

"The Spartans!" Ryan, his seven-year-old, said.

Cole turned to his eight-year-old daughter. "Kaitlin, I'm a boy, and I'm not gross."

She continued to stare at him with an expression as if she'd eaten something distasteful.

"What is it, sweetheart?"

"Dad, some kids were talking about you at school today."

"Sweetheart, people are always talking about me. Go on. What did they say?"

Kaitlin hesitated, then said, "They said you only like rich people and people who look like you."

Cole was stunned. "What? That's not true. I-"

Ashley clapped her hands. "All right, kids. Dad just got home. Let him rest for a minute. Go wash your hands for dinner."

"Okay!" the four youngest said, as they raced out of the room. The two eldest children sauntered after them.

"No running!" Ashley called after them. She glanced at Cole, uncertain. She tried her best to eliminate conflict in their home, since his job was stressful enough. He smiled and moved his hand holding the drink to the side, providing room for her to climb into his lap. She gave him a kiss.

He squeezed her to him.

"Why do kids run everywhere? My last inclination is to

run anywhere. Unless someone's chasing me." He laughed, but it sounded forced even to him.

Kaitlin's words didn't bother him. He had heard worse many times before. Given his profession, he had grown immune to what people said about him.

No, it wasn't what she said that hurt him. It was the expression on her face that tore at his heart. He was rich and revered in this country because millions of Americans agreed with his values and where he stood on the issues, while here in his own household, he saw doubt about his character on his daughter's face for the first time.

CHAPTER ELEVEN

Washington, DC

THE HEADQUARTERS OF the Federal Bureau of Investigation took up the entire block between Ninth and Tenth Streets on Pennsylvania Avenue in Northwest Washington, DC. The J. Edgar Hoover Building's Brutalist architectural style, popular in the mid-twentieth century, was now listed by *Washingtonian* magazine as one of the "Buildings I'd Tear Down." A travel website proclaimed it "the ugliest building in the world." Although Jade Harrington agreed with the widespread assessment, her affinity was strong for the historical building and the twelve flags in front depicting the evolution of the United States flag since before it became a republic.

The first floor, built to accommodate commercial businesses that never materialized, remained empty—and now, for security reasons, always would. Two red barricades blocked the entry into the parking garage. Yellow chains and ten-foot high barricades cordoned off the stairs. Tours of HQ, once a popular DC tourist attraction, were canceled indefinitely for renovations. Those renovations would never be completed.

The building appeared to be a fortress. And it was.

The Monday after returning from Pittsburgh, Jade dropped her briefcase beside her desk in her fourth-floor office, grabbed her favorite FBI mug, and headed for the break room for coffee. On her way back, she stopped by Christian Merritt's cubicle, or rather his pictorial shrine to his wife, four kids, and golden retriever. "Hey. How was your weekend?"

Christian shifted his solid frame in his desk chair. "Good. You?"

"Watched the Wizards."

"Why do you think they're called the Wizards? I don't understand why they don't use their magic to win a game."

"There's always next season. What are you working on today?"

"The Morales case. You?"

"Doing some research on Sells. See if I can dig up anything to help Cooper."

"Don't you mean 'Coop?'" Christian batted his eyes like a coquettish female. "Uh . . . , 'Call me Coop. My friends do.'"

"Shut up," Jade said, giving Christian a playful push. His rock-solid body did not budge.

She returned to her office and straightened the files and other items on her desk, making sure the stacks aligned with the desk's edge.

An overpowering cologne announced the arrival of Special Agent Dante Carlucci. He leaned against her door frame, watching her.

"A tidy desk makes a tidy mind?"

Jade continued to straighten the items.

"Something like that," she said, not looking up.

Dante had curly brown hair, a long nose, and one ear higher than the other. All of his features were a little off, but in combination made him handsome. And he knew it. He wasn't her type, though. He knew that, too.

Dante had been a rising star at the Bureau. That is, until Jade arrived in the division. Since then, his star had fallen, while hers continued to rise. During her first week, he had also hit on her, as he did with every woman he met under fifty. He had not taken the rejection kindly.

"How come you never ask me what I did on the weekends?" he asked.

"Why should I? You always do the same thing."

"You're jealous 'cause I'm getting some."

She booted up her computer. "So you say."

"How's Zoe? Man, she's fine. I sure wish she didn't swing on the other side of the fence."

Jade ignored him and popped a red peanut M&M into her mouth. Dante couldn't stay quiet for long.

"Why do you eat one M&M at a time? Who does that?"

"Me." Jade began perusing her emails until Dante gave up and left. She typed "Randy Sells" in the search bar. Thousands of hits came up. She clicked on one.

Randy Sells, KABC Talk-Show Host, Murdered

Popular Pittsburgh talk-radio host Randy Sells was found dead Friday night behind a downtown restaurant in what police are calling a homicide.

The body of the 28-year-old Sells, a political conservative whose talk show aired the last three years on KABC-AM, was discovered in an alley behind Angelo's Restaurant at 600 Grant Street at about

10:30 p.m. The body was beaten almost beyond recognition, according to police sources.

Jade read several more news items on the Sells murder but didn't learn anything new.

She paused for a moment and then typed "conservative talk show host" into the Google search bar. Four million hits. Jade perused the first few pages, most of the links referring to Cole Brennan. She knew of Cole—everyone did, and everyone called him by his first name—but didn't listen to his program.

Jade took a break, refreshed her coffee, and wandered over to Pat's cubicle. Patricia "Pat" Turner, fiftyish and overweight, looked like someone's grandmother. Individuals who met her were fooled by her appearance. Jade was not. Pat had been with the FBI forever. She could run the place.

"What're you up to?" Jade asked.

Pat finished typing on her computer. "Nothing now. What do you need?"

Jade leaned against a filing cabinet. "Looking into this Sells murder." She brought Pat up to speed on what she had done so far. Pat tapped the keys on her keyboard as Jade talked.

Pat added "murder" to the search request. Randy Sells's murder topped the search results.

She clicked through the next several pages and the links changed to stories about conservative talk-show hosts in general. Nothing helpful.

"What about 'killed?'" Jade asked.

Pat clicked through a few pages of search results. She clicked to the next page. Jade leaned over her shoulder, expecting another dead end.

Halfway down the page, she pointed to a link for Pat to click on.

The story was dated ten years ago.

Chattenham College Radio Personality Killed

A Chattenham College talk-radio personality was found dead earlier today next to his car in the campus radio station's Main Street parking lot in what police are calling a homicide.

Kyle Williams, 22, a Chattenham student who hosted a controversial conservative talk-radio show at campus station WCCO-AM, was found on the ground beside his car. Police say Williams suffered at least one blow to the head with a blunt instrument.

The Chattenham County Police Department requests that anyone with any information about this crime call 215-555-5555. Grief counselors will be available to talk to students and staff. A candlelight vigil will be held on the campus's Quad on Friday.

There weren't any follow-up articles on progress or suspects or arrests.

Jade looked at Pat. "Are there others?"

They spent the next two hours searching the Internet and other databases without success. By this time, Jade had pulled up a chair and her coffee sat on Pat's desk, cold and half-full. Forgotten.

Jade stood and paced the corridor between Pat's cubicle

and the cubicles of other agents. *Were the two murders connected? Why ten years apart? Were there others?*

She popped her head back into Pat's cubicle. "I gotta run. I'm late. Keep working this."

❧

An hour later, Jade Harrington paced the sideline, glaring at LaKeisha, her point guard.

"LaKeisha, run the offense!"

LaKeisha smiled at her as she dribbled in place near the half-court line. She gave Jade a thumbs-up.

"You got it, Coach."

Jade tried hard to hold the glare and prevent the smile trying to form on her face. LaKeisha's smile never failed to produce one of her own.

Jade coached a girls' basketball team made up of preteens from Anacostia, a rough DC neighborhood. Some people called the players on her team "at risk" kids. Jade thought of them as kids who had gotten the short end of the stick in the universal draw of circumstances that dictated where one was born. They just needed a break.

The old high-school gym in Southeast DC sported sagging nets, crooked rims, and dead spots on the court floor, but these kids didn't care. They just wanted their own place to play.

LaKeisha passed the ball to her teammate on the wing, faked as if she were going to set a pick for the other wing, and then sprinted toward the basket for a give-and-go pass. After receiving the ball, she went up for a shot, but instead passed it behind her back with her left hand—LaKeisha was right-handed—to a forward cutting down the lane. The forward made the easy layup.

Jade shook her head and laughed. LaKeisha never did things the easy way. For her, the more difficult the shot or the pass, the better. Sounded like someone else Jade knew. Herself.

Jade, a former All-America basketball player at Stanford University, enjoyed her time with these kids. No matter how busy she was, she tried her best not to break her commitments with them—and to be present. For the next hour, she would not think of Sells, Kyle Williams, or the work piling up on her desk. In truth, she never felt as free as when she was on a basketball court. Whether the court was in Palo Alto, Madison Square Garden, Japan, or on the playground.

It was home.

The sight of the teams running up and down the court dredged up the memory of that day after elementary school. That day was never too far from her thoughts. The day she thought of as "before."

Three girls in her eighth-grade class had followed her home and beaten her up. They called her "Bink"—and worse—although Jade was black and Japanese, not Chinese. She didn't bother to correct them. After her attackers left, she stayed on the ground for a long time, bleeding and bruised and broken. Through her tears, she recognized another girl from school whom she did not know.

The girl reached down and helped her up.

Jade realized many things that day. Her parents couldn't protect her. Her teachers couldn't protect her. With no brothers or sisters, she had to learn how to protect herself. She also learned that kindness could come from strangers. The next day—"after"—she decided: never again. She hadn't cried since.

Jade convinced her parents to enroll her in Tae Kwon Do, and she learned to defend herself. She started practicing basketball. Every day. She slimmed down and her body became stronger. She got rid of her glasses, replacing them with contact lenses. After she'd been named an All-America her junior year in high school, with scholarship offers from every major college in the country, all the kids who had teased her wanted to be her friend.

No one ever messed with her again—or became her friend.

The whistle sounded, ending the game.

Most of her players left the gym as Jade stuffed basketballs into a bag. LaKeisha dawdled nearby before coming up to her.

"You know I like messing with you, Coach."

Jade straightened, holding a ball.

"I know you do, but would it hurt you to make the easy shot for once instead of the fancy pass?"

LaKeisha was a talented player—Jade's best—with an excellent chance of going far in the sport, if she didn't get pregnant, go to jail, or end up dead—the three fates all too common for female students at this school. The girl smiled, her mini-twist hairstyle springing from her head in every direction.

"Did you always take the easy shot, Coach?"

No. "Just do it, LaKeisha. Okay?"

"I'll try, but it's not in my nature." She grew serious, a foreign emotion for her. "You know what I like best about you, Coach?"

"What's that?"

"I can work on my skills, close to home, and I feel safe. And it's not because you're an FBI agent."

Jade froze, beating back the emotions from her childhood. LaKeisha broke into a big smile, serious time over, the moment broken. She grabbed the basketball from under Jade's arm and sprinted for the door under the Exit sign. Over her shoulder, she yelled, "You need to protect the ball better, Coach!"

Jade called out after her as the door slammed shut.

"You better bring it back to the next practice!"

Jade sat on the bench and laughed, stuffing the last ball into the bag. She sobered as her thoughts returned to work. To the two murders. *Why so long between them?*

She thought about what Lakeisha said. She liked working on her skills close to home.

Jade stopped closing the bag in mid-zip.

Maybe the killer was honing his mission close to home, with the Williams murder, and then decided to branch out.

She whipped the cell phone out of her pocket and texted Pat.

Try conservative television commentator, blogger, journalist, columnist.

Got it, came the response.

&

Jade, still in the black Adidas track suit she had worn to the game, was sprawled out on the wicker sofa in her best friend's apartment in Adams Morgan, a diverse neighborhood in Northwest DC.

Zoe, kicked back in an adjacent chair, had her feet up on the coffee table. The television was on, muted, and African music quietly played on the stereo. The apartment sported walls splashed with different hues—indigo, eggplant, and lime—and displayed art she purchased in Senegal and framed posters from various local and national political campaigns Zoe had worked on: marriage equality, the equal rights of women, Occupy DC, and the taxation without representation of DC citizens.

The bookshelves contained Nigerian statues, mementos from Zoe's time in Ghana with the Peace Corps, and Ivory Coast knickknacks, including swaths of Kente cloth, reflecting Zoe's fascination with all things African. The aroma of patchouli wafted throughout the living room.

Jade lay on her back, shooting a round pillow into the air like a basketball. "Who sings this?"

"Shantae Ndiaye. The hottest singer in Africa right now."

"Don't you own any Prince?"

"No. Unlike you, I live in the present decade. You need to expand your horizons, including your musical tastes. So, how was your vacation?"

Jade rolled her eyes. "One day a vacation does not make. I had started planning what I was going to do for the week when Ethan called and sent me to Pittsburgh for a consult." She caught Zoe staring at her. "What?"

"I wish I had your high cheekbones."

Jade eyed her former college roommate with the funky hair and the game-show-host smile, and threw the pillow at her.

"Shut up."

Zoe caught the pillow as the doorbell rang. She returned with two brown paper bags, a thin layer of grease on the bottom of each. She put the Chinese takeout on a pile of magazines on the coffee table, picked up their empty beer bottles, and went to the kitchen for replacements.

Jade grabbed the carton labeled Kung Pao Chicken and a pair of chopsticks and ate straight from the container. She chased the food with a sip of Zoe's ice-cold Tsingtao. They enjoyed the meal in comfortable silence.

"How's work?" Jade asked.

"Tough. Most of our candidates are in tight races with lots of money on the other side. We don't receive enough funds to support all of them. Of course, we're working on Senator Fairchild's presidential campaign." Zoe's nonprofit organization helped elect pro-choice, Democratic female politicians.

"She's still behind in the polls. Do you think she'll win the nomination?"

Zoe smiled. "You're such a jock. It's always about winning for you."

Jade gave a wry smile. "What else is there? Besides, you're a little competitive yourself."

"True. I wouldn't count out Senator Fairchild. She's smart, attractive, politically savvy, with a better chance against Ellison than Sampson. It's also about time the US had a woman president. We're one of the last developed countries who haven't." Zoe got up and moved toward the bathroom. "We share that dubious honor with Japan and Italy, by the way. Be right back."

Jade picked up their empties and headed to the kitchen. She must have bumped Zoe's desk as she passed it, because the sleeper screen disappeared and the laptop sprang to life. She started to pass by, but something made her stop. Jade placed the bottles on the desk and began to read.

AlextheGreat: *I've been searching for a job for two years. I have a college degree. Sent out thousands of resumes. I can't even get hired at McDonald's. I don't have enough money for food. I don't want to be on* *food stamps or collect unemployment. I want to work. What should I do?*

PittFan: *That sucks.*

JoanofArc: *What was your major?*

AlextheGreat: *History.*

PittFan: *Ouch.*

A chat room. Jade continued to read.

JoanofArc: *Have you tried temping? That could be a way for you to earn money and an assignment may turn into a full-time job.*

AlextheGreat: *Good idea.*

SusanB: *What about teaching?*

Oedipus: *Why would anyone enter the teaching profession today? Teachers are vilified as lazy, union employees who make the rest of us pay more in taxes. With cutbacks at the state level, it is difficult to land a teaching job much less keep one.*

PittFan: *Agreed. And teachers don't make shit. They're disrespected, glorified babysitters.*

SusanB: *I wouldn't go that far. Who taught you how to write and express yourself so eloquently?*

PittFan: *True. Hey, did you just slam me?*

Oedipus: *The fundamental issue is, because of the Great Recession, millions of our elderly are forced to work into their golden years, crowding out young* *workers like Alex. If things don't change, we will be the first generation worse off than the generation before us.*

SusanB: *During this downtime, Alex, why don't you become more involved with Senator Fairchild's campaign? Instead of sitting around feeling sorry for yourself, make yourself useful. Go out and do something.*

PittFan: *Ouch. How do you really feel, SusanB?*

Oedipus: *I think volunteering is a good idea. 'Letting the market work' is not working. The 1% keeps getting richer while the rest of us keep falling behind. People still can't find work, toil in jobs for which they are overqualified, or have given up. The key is removing Ellison from office.*

PittFan: *Right on, brother. Hey, did you all hear about the conservative talk-show host in Pittsburgh who got whacked the other day? I couldn't stand the guy, but . . . man!*

Jade froze.

SusanB: *One fewer preacher of hate.*

JoanofArc: *That's awful, SusanB.*

The chat continued, but Jade's eyes started to lose focus. The cursor on the monitor was next to SusanB, which, knowing Zoe, could only be short for Susan B. Anthony.

Who were these people? What was the point of this chat room?

Zoe came back into the living room and stood still.

Taking the offensive, Jade pointed to the screen. "What's this?"

Zoe waved her hand dismissively and sank deep into her chair. "It's a liberal chat group I belong to. Something I do for fun. Like minds and all that."

Jade's eyes scrolled down the text. "Seems pretty intense."

"It can be, yeah."

Jade grabbed the empties and headed to the kitchen. She returned, handing Zoe a fresh Tsingtao.

Jade settled on the sofa and took a long pull of her beer. "Was that the last chat conversation?"

"We were in the middle of a discussion when you got here."

"'One fewer preacher of hate?'"

Zoe gave her a small, shy smile. "Am I being interrogated for something?"

Jade carefully placed her beer on the coffee table. "I don't know. Should you be?"

"Why are you so interested in the murder of a radio talk-show host in—" Then, Zoe made the connection. "—Pittsburgh."

Jade leaned forward. "How involved are you with this chat group?" *Could Zoe be involved in this murder, even tangentially? She can't be. Right?*

"What do you mean, involved?" Zoe sat up. "I don't like where this conversation is going."

"Why aren't you answering the question?"

"Why are you snooping through my things?"

"Zoe . . . ."

Zoe stood. "I think you should leave."

Jade rose and stared at her best friend. Zoe's eyes were bright, her eyelids blinking rapidly.

"I'm just doing my job," Jade said.

"I'm not your job." Zoe pointed toward the front door. "Leave."

CHAPTER TWELVE

Columbus, Ohio

THE RESTAURANT'S OAK tables and dark decor complemented the enticing aroma of Tuscan cuisine. Whitney spotted Grayson at a table near the back of the restaurant, and her heart fluttered at the sight of him. Other patrons began the inevitable whispers and pointing as she glided toward his table. Whitney smiled and nodded at them, but did not stop. Grayson stood, smiling, as she came nearer. He gave her a quick hug, a chaste kiss, and pulled a chair out for her.

"Darling," Grayson said, grabbing her hand. "You look amazing."

She glanced down at her beige wool and cashmere coat and back at her husband. He was still handsome, with light brown hair, a slender face, and a straight-edged nose. If she didn't know how much he loved her, she would worry about him with other women.

"You're not so bad yourself, although you look tired. Are you getting enough sleep?"

He shrugged. "There's a lot going on . . . at work."

Grayson ordered wine.

"I'm so glad you could get away," Whitney said.

"Fairchild Industries can survive without its CEO for one day."

"How's business?"

"The lab developed a genetically engineered seed we think will do well in the marketplace. We think it'll be ready next quarter. Revenues for existing products are up. We froze hiring and wages so profits are up, and cash reserves are high. Business is good."

"So many companies are taking the same approach. Or they're outsourcing jobs overseas, two of the reasons why the real unemployment rate is not budging. Perhaps you can hire a lot of people once I become president. Help me drive down the unemployment rate."

The waiter offered them the bottle Grayson had selected. Grayson swirled, sniffed, and tasted the wine. "Excellent."

The waiter poured and left.

They raised their glasses. "To us!" Always the same toast.

"Darling," Grayson said, "the private sector's responsibility isn't to lower unemployment, but to provide the most value to its shareholders." He sipped his drink. "For me, that means our family."

"I know." She sighed. "Unemployment is a long-term problem with no easy answers. The infrastructure bill I co-wrote would repair decrepit roads and bridges and create thousands of jobs. It could solve so many ills. Instead, it's languishing in committee. You would think my colleagues would act after the number of collapsed bridges over the last few years."

"All I know is you're a fighter. Keep fighting." He frowned. "Are you okay?"

"I'm fine. Really." She paused. "It's Hampton. He's using the classic Overton Window, and I'm not sure how to fight him."

"What Window?"

"The Overton Window. A theory postulating a range of ideas considered viable politically and acceptable to the public. By proposing a radical idea, you either expand or move the window until it becomes acceptable public opinion."

Grayson was trying to catch up. "Okay . . . ."

"For example, a politician may try to expand the window of narrowing a woman's right to choose by banning abortions except in the cases of rape and incest. Another candidate comes along and advocates no abortions under any circumstances. This position will be dismissed as extreme under current public opinion, but makes a ban on abortions except in cases of rape and incest seem more reasonable and more acceptable. The window has been shifting and expanding for years. To change a political outcome, you must expand your constituents. That's Senator Hampton's game plan."

Grayson had caught up with her. "And, if Ellison is re-elected, he'll be able to appoint one or two justices to the Court and *Roe v. Wade* will be overturned."

"To paraphrase Bill Clinton, 'Abortions should be safe, legal, and rare.' If *Roe v. Wade* is overturned, abortion will be none of those things. The rights of women ebbed away over the last decade. But things won't change until some women are faced with hard, individual choices, and then realize they don't have a choice."

"Darling, this issue is so controversial. Do you think you should focus so much on it? You're not the only one responsible for solving it. Perhaps you're taking it too personally."

"I'm a woman. I must take it personally."

They remained quiet for a moment.

"So," Grayson said, "the primaries are down to the two of

you. Senator Paul Sampson doesn't seem like the kind of guy who'll give up, though."

"And I'm not that kind of woman."

He raised his glass to her. "This I know."

"I'll need you and the children to make some appearances with me. I don't want them to miss a lot of school, but Ted says it's important that people see us as a family. See me as a mother."

"You are a mother. A good one." He touched her hand. "We'll work it out."

A woman came up to them, blushing. "I'm sorry to interrupt. We admire you so much, and my daughter, Bella, here wants to be like you someday. Wants to be president. Can I please take a picture of you with her?"

Whitney leaned toward Grayson and away from the woman. "I did not think I would live to see the day when every child in the United States, regardless of race or gender, could grow up believing she or he could become president. Isn't it wonderful?"

To the woman, she said, "It would be my pleasure."

She rose and put her arm around the young girl. Her mother snapped their picture with her smartphone camera. Other diners moved toward their table. Another woman shoved a baby into Whitney's arms. Whitney never understood why parents would hand their baby over to a stranger, even a stranger running for the Democratic nomination for president of the United States. She pasted on a smile, turned toward the woman who had whipped out her smartphone, and kissed the baby.

Whitney scanned the people now waiting in the impromptu line and exchanged a glance with her husband.

So much for a quiet, romantic dinner alone.

CHAPTER THIRTEEN

Washington, DC

THE NEXT MORNING, she passed Pat's cubicle on the way to her office.

"It's in your inbox," Pat called after her.

Jade hurried to her office.

Jade,

I found these two articles. There were no follow-ups on the investigation or subsequent arrests.

Pat

Jade clicked on the first link.

Popular Columnist Taylor LeBlanc Found Dead

Advocate columnist Taylor LeBlanc was found dead today in his condo in Perkins Rowe. Baton Rouge Police confirmed that the case is being investigated as a suspected homicide.

LeBlanc, 30, who interned with The Advocate while a

student at Louisiana State University, worked for the newspaper his entire career.

The date line was two years ago. The next article was dated five years ago.

Pete Paxson Found Dead

Conservative blogger Pete Paxson of Houston had a date last night. He never made it. Paxson, 34, was found dead this morning in the parking garage of his apartment building. The Houston Police Department has ruled his death a homicide.

Paxson was an engineer for the Shell Oil Company by day and wrote his blog at night. Paxson, divorced, is survived by a daughter.

She looked up to find Pat standing in the doorway. Pat handed her a piece of paper. "Names and phone numbers of the lead detective for each case."

She turned and left.

Jade shook her head, smiling. Pat was a godsend.

Jade called the detectives on the list. No suspects, no arrests. It didn't appear robbery was the motive in any of the cases. In the Houston case, Paxson's Rolex watch was still on his wrist and the keys to his late-model BMW in his pocket when he was discovered.

She came across a gruesome discovery that connected all the cases.

All the victims' tongues had been cut out.

None of the police departments had disclosed this fact to

the media. Criminal investigators often kept a salient detail secret to screen out anyone making a false confession or providing deliberate, misleading information. A sensational detail like a missing tongue would have lit up the police tips' hotline numbers.

Jade skipped lunch and spent the rest of the afternoon building her case. Near the end of the day, she picked up a stack of printouts and headed down the hallway to her boss's office. Ethan Lawson was talking to Dante. She knocked on his door frame.

"I need to talk to you," Jade said to Lawson.

Lawson looked at Dante. "Give us a minute."

"I'd like to finish this conversation later," Dante said.

Lawson nodded.

Dante stood as she crossed to the other guest chair. With his back to Lawson, Dante bestowed on her a bright insincere smile.

"Always the teacher's pet, I see."

Jade gave him her winning smile. "Just trying to follow in your footsteps."

He frowned and hesitated before walking out.

She admired the large FBI emblem on the wall behind Lawson depicting the scales of justice and the words Fidelity, Bravery, Integrity. On either side hung his diplomas: a bachelor's degree from the University of Florida and a Juris Doctor from George Washington University.

"J. Edgar Hoover went to GWU Law School, you know," Ethan said.

"I know. You tell me every time I come into your office." She handed him a summary she had written with a few of the articles she had printed out. "The Sells case. I think there are others."

Lawson began reading. He took his time.

Jade waited.

He finished the last page, leaned back in his chair, and considered her. He twirled the wedding ring around his finger.

"What do you need?"

"Not what," Jade said. "Who."

Lawson nodded. He knew whom she meant and picked up the phone.

He stared at Jade while he spoke. "Max, we have something. It's right up your alley." He listened. "Agent Harrington's on her way."

❧

An hour later, Jade drove past the replica of the US Marine Corps War Memorial at the entrance to the FBI training academy at Quantico, Virginia, thirty-six miles south of Washington, DC.

She entered Max Stover's small, cramped office without knocking. Max was a special agent for the Behavioral Analysis Unit 4 of the National Center for the Analysis of Violent Crime, which provided behavioral-based support to the FBI and other federal, state, local, and international agencies in the investigation of unusual or repetitive violent crimes against adults. The public would call him a profiler, although the FBI didn't list an official position by that name.

Max looked up from reading the report Lawson had emailed to him. Pale, slender, with short, fair hair balding on top, Max was newly single after his wife left him six months ago following thirty years of marriage. He had thought they had come to an agreement of civil co-existence. His job came first; she came second. He provided a good home for her with everything she needed. Except him. She decided she wanted more. He had heard that her new boyfriend wasn't making the same mistake.

Jade moved some papers and files from a chair and sat down across from him. "Thanks for seeing me right away."

"Of course," Max said.

"I discovered four cases that may be related," Jade said.

She described her trip to Pittsburgh, her conversation with Lieutenant John Cooper of the Pittsburgh PD, and the preliminary information she and Pat had found through the Internet and the FBI databases on the murders of the other three conservative media personalities.

"The time between the murders is shortening," Max said.

"I realized that, too."

Max pushed up his glasses. "Who would have the motive to kill conservative commentators?"

"A liberal or someone who disagrees with conservative ideology?"

"Perhaps. Or another conservative who may be envious. Or for some larger agenda we may be unaware of. It's too soon to tell. We need more."

"The removal of the tongues is significant."

Max nodded, as if she were a student answering a question in class. He leaned back in his chair, thoughtful. "He silences them. Forever. Because of their profession? Did they know something the perp wanted to remain a secret? Or something else?"

Basketball players have those nights when every shot goes in. It's called being in the zone. Max, too, tended to get into a zone when he analyzed motives. Jade could have walked out the door now, and he wouldn't have realized it.

"All the tongues were left at the scene. He doesn't keep them as trophies unlike some serial killers," Max continued. "If we're dealing with a serial killer. It's possible anything associated with the victims would make him angry or uncomfortable."

"Or be a painful reminder of something," Jade said. "What about the UNSUB putting the tongue in Sells's hands like a rosary?"

"He was unconcerned the body would be found and took the time to stage the victim's presentation. The staging was important to him. He's trying to communicate a message to someone. The police? The media? The public? The victim's family? Someone else? All the above?"

"What about the removal of the crucifix?"

"A lot of religious possibilities with both the tongue and the crucifix. The tongue symbolizing a rosary is conjecture. It may mean something entirely different. The stolen crucifix may not have anything to do with the victim's or the perpetrator's religion."

"Or lack of religion," Jade pointed out.

"Was the necklace valuable?"

"A couple hundred dollars."

"Conceivably, it was a shiny object that caught his attention. Like impulse shopping. Impulse stealing. But according to your information, the UNSUB didn't steal anything from the other victims. Why did he deviate from the pattern?"

"You're raising more questions than answers."

"That's my job." Max smiled, which always appeared more like a grimace to Jade. "The UNSUB is a planner. He studies his victims' daily patterns and knows when they'll be alone. He possesses some degree of superior intelligence." Max snapped out of it. His tone changed. "How are you, by the way?"

"I'm fine."

"As one of my best students ever at the academy, I doubt you're just fine."

"You're only saying that because I'm your goddaughter." It wasn't true. Max was harder on her because he was her godfather. And more like a father to her, since her parents had been killed by a drunk driver when she was in college.

She couldn't think about them now.

They sat in silence for a few moments.

"My gut tells me these crimes were committed by the same person," Jade said. When Max didn't respond, she continued. "And he's still out there." Jade waited. "He can't get away with this."

"I know," he said.

"I need to go after him."

"I know that, too," he said.

CHAPTER FOURTEEN

Washington, DC

SENATOR WHITNEY FAIRCHILD arrived at the door of the United States Senate chamber at the same time as Senator Eric Hampton. He paused, and with a quick hand gesture, indicated for her to proceed first.

"How are you this fine morning, Senator Fairchild?"

The man was charming.

"Never better, Senator Hampton." They walked down the aisle together. Whitney asked, "Are we in agreement?"

Hampton, his hair parted on the side and slicked into place, pushed his glasses up on his nose with his index finger. He clutched a black leather folio in his other arm. "Yes, we are."

They parted midway, and Whitney squeezed her way through to her assigned desk. She greeted the senators on either side of her as a new legislative day began. After an hour of bill introductions, joint resolutions, and committee reports, she listened as the education bill was called to the floor for consideration and to the opening statement by the chairman of the committee that introduced the bill. Another senator from the same committee offered an amendment.

Pleased that Hampton promised to deliver sufficient votes from his side on her welfare reform bill, Whitney was happy to cast her vote for education reform, which she supported. It was better for her that the bill was proposed by the Republicans; her support demonstrated to the American people her willingness to reach across the aisle. Everything was proceeding as they had agreed. As planned.

Senator Hampton rose and addressed the presiding officer, who granted him permission to speak.

"Thank you, Senator. I'm happy to support the education reform bill put forth," he paused, "and I'd also like to propose an amendment, if I may, entitled The Protection of Rights for All Citizens. Over the last two hundred years, our nation made extraordinary strides in providing equal rights for all citizens. Now, is the time for us to extend this legacy of fairness to a group that cannot speak for itself, but who is crucial to the future of this nation. The unborn."

The lull of the proceedings had relaxed Whitney, but she jolted to full alert at Hampton's last statements. His amendment was not unusual; senators introduced nongermane amendments to bills all the time. This was not why she sat up in her seat and stared at him in shock and surprise.

He had lied to her.

He continued to address the presiding officer: "My amendment will extend equal rights to all persons at the moment of conception in every state of the land."

He went on to explain that his proposed legislation would defund Planned Parenthood and eliminate all its facilities in the United States.

When he finished, Whitney stood. She forced herself to appear calm to everyone else, but she placed her hand on the desk for support to stop it from trembling. Even though Hampton had given his word, she should not have been surprised. She should have known better.

Whitney allowed a brief thought on how the course of her own life would have been different, if she had had access to Planned Parenthood as a teen.

After the presiding officer recognized her, Whitney took a deep breath. "With all due respect to the senator from Virginia, the rights of one group are being ignored by his amendment, the group who makes up the majority in this country. I am speaking of the rights of women and their right to make decisions about what happens to their own bodies."

Whitney spoke for over an hour. She spoke of the Equal Rights Amendment, which fell three states short of ratification in 1982. She proposed repealing the deadline and attaining the ratification of the remaining three states. She spoke of pay equity; today, women were still paid, on average, seventy-seven percent of what men were paid for the same job.

As she took a sip of water, her phone vibrated on the desk. It was a text from her daughter, Emma.

Thinking of U. I luv U, Momma.

Whitney willed her eyes from tearing. Emma's words could not have come at a better time. This was why she kept fighting. For her daughter and all the daughters in this country.

Whitney remained standing and spoke in the Senate chamber for the rest of the afternoon.

CHAPTER FIFTEEN

Washington, DC

"MY LONG-TIME LISTENERS know I don't invite guests onto the show often, because you all tune in to listen to me. But today, we have a very special guest. The president of the United States of America, Richard Ellison. Mr. President, welcome." Cole Brennan glanced at Ellison sitting in the swivel chair across from him in the studio.

"Thank you, Cole. It's a pleasure to be here today."

"Now, Mr. President. You're up fifteen points on whoever the Commiecrats nominate, and one may think you can put the campaign on cruise control and win this thing. But what are you doing, sir, to ensure victory?"

"Well, Cole, I'm not taking anything for granted. In my travels all over America, I have listened to people and heard their problems. Financially, people are still hurting, and we're doing everything we can to help ease their anxieties about the economy. Our economic plan is a good one and we believe we're on the right path to restore this country to economic prosperity."

"One way I think we can help ease their anxieties, Mr. President, is to eliminate regulations on our wealth creators.

Think of all the jobs that'll be created when business owners can spend more time growing their businesses and less time filling out forms."

"That's right, Cole. My administration tried to repeal Dodd-Frank, Sarbanes-Oxley, and all the financial regulations enacted during the Great Recession. We've not been successful yet, but when I'm re-elected, and our party controls Congress, we will be. We'll eliminate environmental regulations that hinder development and hamper job growth. A free-market economy produces greater economic growth in the long run, more jobs, and greater prosperity for all."

"I couldn't agree more. President Ellison, how can we assure my listeners and good conservative folk everywhere that you are the man to lead the conservative movement for the next four years?"

"Examine my record. I believe our party is best suited to reduce the budget deficit. During my first term, wasteful spending has been reduced and the government shrunk by fifteen percent. In my second term, I hope to eliminate the progressive income tax structure, which punishes the American Dream, and enact my flat-tax proposal."

"What about passing the second Defense of Marriage Act?"

The president hesitated. "That may be difficult in the current environment. As I said, my administration is focused on the economic prosperity of our citizens, and—"

"—which starts with the nuclear family," Cole said. "One man, one woman in a union recognized by God. Switching gears, Whitney Fairchild seems to be moving up in the polls and gaining with independent and women voters. She's taken a centrist approach and abandoned the Socialist policies she is known for. If she becomes the other party's nominee, what's your strategy, Mr. President, for putting this woman in her place?"

"Senator Fairchild is a well-meaning, and, I believe, good person, but she doesn't possess the experience, character, or the fortitude to be president. She has flip-flopped on many issues. I've been consistent in my views since I was the governor of Wyoming, then as a US senator, and now as president. The American people want someone who will stand by his principles. I am that man."

"A 'personhood' amendment has been proposed in the United States Senate. The federal government is finally realizing that the unborn are entitled to the same rights and freedoms we enjoy. Do you support this amendment?"

Ellison hesitated again. "I believe this issue is best decided by the states."

"But you do believe life begins at conception?"

Ellison glared at him. Cole stared back, glad this interview was being conducted on the radio rather than television. He motioned with his hand for Ellison to answer.

Ellison pursed his lips and spat out, "Yes."

"I want to thank you, Mr. President, for coming on our show today. Godspeed."

The president didn't respond.

"We're going to a commercial break and will be back in a minute. Don't go anywhere. This is 'The Conservative Voice' with Cole Brennan."

The ON AIR light went dark. They stared at each other for several moments. President Richard Ellison bowed his head, stood, and left the studio without another word.

CHAPTER SIXTEEN

Crystal City, Virginia

THE VODKA SLID through the blocks of ice as I poured the liquid into a glass and took the drink over to one of the floor-to-ceiling windows. My penthouse condo afforded a stunning, panoramic view of the Potomac River, the Kennedy Center, and the Washington Monument. On a clear day, the US Capitol was visible in the distance. Traffic, still snarled at this time of the evening, snaked up the GW Parkway. I soaked in the beauty of my city—our city—as I sipped my drink.

Cole Brennan's broadcast just ended. Why do I continue to listen to him? Why do I torture myself? Because I must. It is my duty. That is the curse of every great person throughout history, is it not? To suffer? Joan of Arc suffered. As did Martin Luther King Jr., Gandhi, and John F. Kennedy. Perhaps they were great because they suffered. Why should I be any different?

I thought back to Brennan's broadcast. President Ellison was not a bad man, but his moderate views didn't stand a chance against Brennan and people of his ilk. I didn't like how he put words into the president's mouth. I did not like it at all. I needed to do something about it.

Like Kyle. Kyle had been a good start. A success. It was good training. Then, I extended my reach. I was disappointed with the lack of media attention after LeBlanc and Paxson. The journalist and the blogger. Now Sells. Doesn't anyone care?

I shook my head, turned from the window, and wandered to the space I used as an office, next to the dining room. I sat in my gray Herman Miller Mirra chair and tapped the touchpad. The three computer monitors on my desk sprang to life.

Good. My friends were here.

Some might think you cannot call people you have never met your "friends." I could make friends in the physical world. I choose not to. I much prefer the characters I meet in books. They are more interesting and more genuine than the people I meet in real life. But I had something in common with my online friends. The issues. Only the issues. The issues that mattered.

The cursor was next to my name. I typed: *Sorry, I'm late. What are we discussing tonight?*

SusanB: *Women's rights.*

PART II

CHAPTER SEVENTEEN

Washington, DC

ETHAN LAWSON, IN a pressed white shirt and dark gray tie, leaned back in his office chair.

Jade sat across from him.

"What's the latest?" Lawson asked.

Jade recited without notes, "I followed up again with the detectives assigned to each case. Kyle Williams, from Chattenham, Pennsylvania was killed ten years ago with a blunt instrument. Pete Paxson of Houston, Texas, was also killed with a blunt instrument five years ago. Carpet fibers were found at the scene. Taylor LeBlanc was murdered in Baton Rouge two years ago with a blunt instrument. A hair and carpet fibers were found at the scene."

Unlike hair, trace evidence such as carpet fibers might not lead them to the suspect, but would help convict a suspect once he was identified.

"Did they match the Paxson fibers?"

"No," Jade said. "Randy Sells, the latest victim, was also killed with a blunt instrument. No carpet fibers, but a hair was found in the blood at the scene. Test results aren't back yet."

"Not much to go on."

Jade leaned forward. "Ethan, all of them had their tongues cut out."

"Yes, there's that."

"And all the victims were conservative media commentators."

"Yeah, there's that, too. Okay. What do you propose we do?"

"I need a task force. We need to go after this person."

"Jade, you have a pretty full caseload as it is. At this point, these killings may be tragic coincidences."

Her back straightened and she gave Lawson a look. Her look. "You're kidding, right?"

"I know. It's not funny."

"No, it's not," Jade said. "I have a feeling about this. I'm going to investigate it with or without your support. On my own time, if I have to."

Ethan twirled his wedding ring and sighed. "I'm sure you will. Who do you need?"

"Christian, Max, Pat, and Austin."

"I see you haven't thought about this."

Ethan came from around his desk and sat in the guest chair next to her. His brown shoes glistened. Jade bet she would see her reflection in them if she bent for a closer inspection. The faint whiff of shoe polish brought back memories of her father, an Army colonel, sitting on a small, wooden stool in the kitchen of their split-level home, surrounded by rags, brushes, shoes, and tins of black and brown Kiwi polish. She loved watching the care he demonstrated with every brush.

Ethan said, "I'll authorize the task force . . ."

"Thank you." She started to get up.

". . . as long as Dante is included."

Ethan knew how she felt about Dante. "I know what

you're thinking," he said, "but that's nonnegotiable. Dante possesses useful qualities you don't appreciate. You'll see."

She didn't bother to argue. She had what she wanted.

CHAPTER EIGHTEEN

Washington, DC

SENATOR WHITNEY FAIRCHILD rose from the chair in her office and walked around the large mahogany desk. She gave Senator Paul Sampson, her opponent in the Democratic primary campaign, a wide smile, took his right hand in both of hers, and squeezed. She had read once that Bill Clinton had shaken hands this way with those individuals who meant something to him. She was sure Sampson knew that as well. Although her gesture was disingenuous, she hoped he would be flattered by it.

She motioned for him to sit as she returned to the high-backed brown leather chair behind her desk.

Sampson arranged his massive frame in the guest chair. "Quite a speech the other day."

"Thank you for the filibuster threat. It shut Hampton down." *And is the reason for your visit today.* "I owe you one."

"Yes, you do." He stared at an oil painting of Susan B. Anthony high on the wall behind her.

Whitney glanced over her shoulder. "Before Susan B. Anthony retired, she said, 'Failure is impossible,' encouraging her fellow suffragettes to keep up the good fight. She believed one half of the American people should not be kept in bondage." She turned back to Sampson. "We need her now."

Sampson appraised her. "Maybe she's here."

Whitney was surprised by the compliment.

"I'll support your welfare reform bill," Sampson continued, "even with its silly little workfare program, but I need you to combine the bills. Those farm subsidies are essential to the people of the great state of Nebraska."

Whitney rose and moved to a cabinet built into the wall. She opened its doors to a stocked bar and turned to him. "The usual?"

He nodded. She picked up a bottle of whiskey she reserved for guests and filled a glass a quarter full. She poured a glass of red wine for herself. She handed him his drink. Instead of returning to her desk chair, Whitney sat next to him and crossed her legs. Sampson gave them a quick, appreciative glance as Whitney sipped her wine. "A combined bill will die in the House," Whitney said, "and you know it."

His eyes were like pinpoints over his ruddy cheeks, his love of drink an open secret on the Hill.

"The bill can pass with full Democratic support. Otherwise, farmers will suffer. What's the alternative? What are all those people going to *do*? Do we plan to retrain them? To do what? Think of the national security risk and economic threat of becoming dependent on foreign sources for our food." His voice softened. "My people need those subsidies. If you do this for me," he paused, peering into his glass, "I'll drop out of the race."

This caught Whitney off guard. She and Sampson were separated by a few points in the polls, less than the margin of error. He was handing her the nomination.

"That's a heavy price to pay."

"But I want to be considered for VP."

Of course. Sampson was a seasoned pro and would never give without taking. Whitney calculated the costs versus benefits of his proposal. His request went against the platform on which she was campaigning, and everything she believed in.

She shifted her drink to her right hand and extended her left to him. "You have a deal."

CHAPTER NINETEEN

Baton Rouge, Louisiana

A MAN WITH A complexion of dark, roasted coffee stood outside the security station, holding a sign with the word Harrington written in block letters. His eyes never strayed from hers as she walked toward him.

Jade stopped in front of him, peering down slightly. "Detective Miles Thomas?"

The man offered his hand. "That's me. Agent Harrington?" He tilted his head and glanced down and back up at her. "No heels."

"Nope."

"Huh. Welcome to Baton Rouge." He extended his arm toward the exit. "This way."

They were traveling down I-110 South in his unmarked Chevrolet Caprice within minutes. The early-model vehicle was well kept; Detective Thomas took pride in his car.

"Good flight?"

"Not too bad. As usual, I was stuck fighting for space on the armrest with the guy next to me. I'm not sure why guys think the armrest is theirs. Do you?"

Thomas kept his eyes forward, moving his muscular

forearm from the armrest between them. "No idea. I know you're in a big hurry, so let's get to it. Where to?"

"I'd like to see the crime scene."

"The condo was empty for a long time, but someone lives there now. Let me make a call."

After he hung up, Thomas said, "This case received a lot of local media attention at the time. Taylor LeBlanc was *the* torchbearer for conservative politics in Baton Rouge."

"Who called it in?"

"We received an anonymous tip."

"How?"

"Text."

"Did you trace it?"

Thomas shook his head. "The texting program allows the public to send in anonymous tips."

After merging onto I-10 East toward New Orleans, he took the second exit, Bluebonnet Boulevard. They passed a six-story building on the left, and Thomas waved his hand. "LeBlanc worked there."

A mile later, he turned into Perkins Rowe, an upscale commercial and residential development. He parked in front of the Barnes & Noble. They walked through the bookstore, its back entrance opening to the rest of the shopping complex and residences.

Jade stared at the numbers above the door as the elevator ascended. "Any luck with the neighbors?"

"We interviewed all of them living on his floor. No one saw anything on the night in question. Although they live close together, these neighbors don't socialize with each other much. A few would run into LeBlanc every once in a while in the neighborhood. The consensus was he was a nice enough guy, kept to himself, but had many female visitors."

A representative of the leasing company, a skinny woman with hair over-processed and dyed blonde, waited at the end of the hall.

"Hello! Hello!"

"Hello, again." Thomas whipped the gold badge from his belt. The rep waved it off and smiled at both of them without bothering to look at it. She turned and opened the front door.

"The occupants are at work, so you shouldn't be disturbed. The place appears a lot different from the last time you were here, Detective. Thank God! Please lock up when you leave."

He nodded. "Thank you."

Jade took in the condo's lofty ceilings, hardwood floors, and open floor plan.

Thomas scanned the room.

"She's right. LeBlanc had a gigantic flat-screen television on that wall. Black furniture: leather sofa, coffee table ottoman, TV console, bookcases. Not a flower, throw pillow, or family photograph in sight. He did, however, own an extensive game collection with every iteration of Madden Football, NBA, and FIFA soccer. Oh, yeah, and lots of action movies." To her expected question, "Never married. No girlfriend at the time, although he had an on-again, off-again relationship with a young female co-worker at the paper."

"Fingerprints?"

"About forty sets. We processed all of them through IAFIS"—the Integrated Automated Fingerprint Identification System, an FBI database containing thousands of fingerprints. "Nothing." Meaning none of the owners of the fingerprints had ever been arrested for a crime or worked for the government.

"After ruling out the cleaning lady, we determined the thirty-nine remaining prints belonged to Caucasian women."

"Using the latest fingerprint technology, I see. What else?"

"No sign of forced entry. No sign of a struggle. We found the victim fully clothed, bound by rope. He was lying in front of the stereo system, arms crossed over his chest."

"In what condition was the body?"

"A complete mess. Head battered. Only the right side, though. There were blood and brains everywhere."

"Tongue?"

"I'll show you the photos when we get back to my office," Thomas said.

"Who found him?"

"A few of the neighbors called the leasing company complaining about the loud noise coming from the condo."

"What was it? Music? An argument?"

Thomas grunted. "A recording of a speech he gave. Burned to CD. It was set to replay over and over again."

Jade paused to absorb that. "Tell me about his column."

"Published weekly. Dedicated to conservative issues. Readers could write in and comment."

She nodded toward the CD player. "What was the speech about?"

"I don't recall. I'll check on that for you."

"Any of his readers ever disagree with or become angry at LeBlanc?"

"LeBlanc could be obnoxious. He'd write articles some people found politically incorrect—sexist or racist—but his friends and co-workers said he was neither of those things."

"What about the women he dated? Did any of them feel betrayed or angry?"

"As far as we can tell, not enough to kill him. His co-workers said he was okay to work with and he got along with everyone. He received the occasional hate mail. We checked out the senders, but came up with nothing. He wasn't depressed or anxious about anything. He had a core following, active in local charity work. He had everything going for him."

"Where did he hang out?"

❧

They strode toward The Wine Shoppe two blocks away.

Jade downshifted her gait to allow Thomas to keep pace. Despite the short walk, her silk shirt stuck to her back from the humidity. "What do we know about his movements that night?"

"His editor said LeBlanc left sometime after eight. We believe he parked his car in the residence lot over there"—he waved to his right—"and walked to The Wine Shoppe and had several glasses of wine and some bar food."

"Time of death?"

"The coroner estimated between midnight and three a.m."

"You told me on the phone a witness—the ex-girlfriend—saw him leave with another man. No one else saw him?"

"We couldn't find a corroborating witness. The manager said LeBlanc was a frequent customer, but the place is usually packed and he couldn't swear LeBlanc came in the night of the murder."

They entered the bar and walked around so Jade could get a sense of the place. She shielded her eyes when they came out, the sun brighter after the bar's dark interior.

Thomas gestured at the retail establishments around them. "LeBlanc's co-workers said he loved Perkins Rowe because it had everything: restaurants, a grocery store, clothing stores, a gym, and a movie theater. He used to always tell them he never had to 'stray too far from the reservation.'"

Thomas stopped and faced Jade. "Murders like this don't happen in this part of Baton Rouge. He probably felt safe here."

Jade shrugged. "He was wrong." They resumed walking toward the car. "I'm hungry," she said. "Do you mind?"

ꟼ

Detective Miles Thomas stopped at a squat building, the paint long since peeled away, squeezed between two modern office buildings. Jade tried to hide her surprise as she emerged cautiously from the car.

Thomas shut the car door. "Don't let the decor fool you."

A small sign, the same color as the faded paint, hung on a nail at a crooked angle next to the door: Momma's. The hole-in-the-wall exterior opened up to a cozy interior of ten small wooden tables. The cheap wood-paneled walls were filled with pictures of different individuals with Momma, the thin, light-skinned woman behind the counter at the rear of the restaurant. Jade recognized some of the individuals in the photographs: Former Senator Mary Landrieu and her brother, New Orleans Mayor Mitch Landrieu, former Governor Bobby Jindal, New Orleans Saints quarterback Drew Brees, NBA greats Shaquille O'Neal and Pete Maravich, and WNBA all-star Seimone Augustus.

Thomas pointed. "Our mayor, Kip Holden, former Governor Kathleen Blanco, and, of course, you know, Lolo Jones and Glen 'Big Baby' Davis."

"Instead of who has eaten here," Jade said, "the better question is who hasn't?"

Thomas ordered a Coke. She asked for a Pepsi. Thomas shook his head, disappointed.

She eyed him and then the waitress. "What?"

Thomas tried to stifle a grin. "You're in Coke country."

The waitress nodded a slow, all-knowing confirmation.

Jade conceded. "I'll have a Coke then."

After the server brought their drinks, Thomas raised an eyebrow at Jade.

She was about to take a drink. "What?"

He inclined his head at her extended pinkie as she held her soda.

She smiled. "Don't let the pinkie fool you." She sipped the drink, trying not to grimace at the sharp flavor.

He laughed.

Since this was Jade's first time in Baton Rouge, Thomas ordered a sampling of everything: gumbo for an appetizer, jambalaya, red beans and rice, and crawfish étouffée. She put her foot down when he attempted to order alligator. She developed an instant philosophy of not eating anything that could eat her.

The waitress placed their meal on the table. The aroma of the dishes made Jade's mouth moist.

Thomas glanced at her plate. "Do you always separate your food like that?"

Jade shrugged. "I don't like different foods touching each other."

Thomas shook his head, and, as if to prove a point, mixed all his food together. He popped a forkful into his mouth.

Jade shook her head. "That's disgusting."

Thomas smiled. "You look like you can still play ball." He had done his homework.

"A little."

He laughed. "Yeah, right. I'll let it go or next thing I know you'll be challenging me to a game."

Jade took a sip of her Coke. "What about your name? Miles Davis?"

"My mother, a jazz fan, wanted me to be a musician. I always wanted to be a cop. When I was growing up, playing 'cops and robbers' with toy guns was still okay. I was always on the side of the good guys." The light in his eye dimmed. "When I became a teenager, some of my friends started playing with guns for real."

"How'd you get out?"

"My mother enrolled me in a Big Brother program. Someone took an interest in me and saved me from the fate of most of my friends who are either in jail, on drugs, or dead. This city earned the distinction as one of the top US cities for murders per capita. Mostly black-on-black homicides." His shoulders inched down, as if he alone bore the burden to save his black brethren.

Thomas, though a big man, had a certain gentleness. They discussed their careers and his eyes lit up when he talked about his wife, Tracy. His wife was a lucky woman. During the conversation, he remarked she was light-skinned, which still seemed to matter in the Deep South.

Later, at the police station, Thomas signed Jade in as a guest. The atmosphere buzzed as they weaved their way between the desks of the other officers.

In his office, he pointed at the conference table in front of his desk. "I pulled the case files. Let me grab them."

She peered around him at the mess on his desk, the top covered with stacks of paper, towering in some cases a foot high. Coffee cups of various life spans acted as a buffer between the stacks. *How could anyone work like that?*

She dropped her briefcase on a chair and stretched her arms and rotated her neck. The big Creole lunch had started taking its toll. She wanted to take a nap. Thomas returned with the files and a laptop.

He sat next to her and tapped on the keyboard.

He brought up an autopsy picture of LeBlanc. "Not the easiest thing to look at after lunch."

"Occupational hazard," she said.

She examined the photograph. The right side of LeBlanc's head, matted with blood and brains, was unrecognizable but similar to the damage inflicted upon Randy Sells, the Pittsburgh victim. Thomas pulled a manila folder out of the stack, in an expert motion like the one Jade used to use in the game KerPlunk as a kid. He handed the folder to her.

"The autopsy report confirms he was killed by blunt-force trauma to the head."

Jade began clicking through the crime-scene photographs on the computer. Thomas moved to the window, and closed the blinds halfway to block out the afternoon Louisiana sun. His action also removed the glare from the screen. Thoughtful.

"What do you think about the tongue?"

Thomas sat down in a chair and parked a foot on the table, his shoes scuffed and worn. "It's significant. To silence him forever? Retribution? It was cut after he died."

"Did you find it?"

"Keep clicking."

Jade scooted back in her chair when she came to the

photo. "Wow." A vinyl album sat in a new turntable record player, ready to play. In place of the tonearm rested LeBlanc's tongue. "Is he playing with us or is this a clue?" She squinted at the photograph. "What was the vinyl?"

"*Tragic Kingdom.*"

"No Doubt? Really?"

"You've heard of them?"

"Of course." She clicked to another page. "What about the arms crossed over his chest?"

Thomas dropped his foot from the table. "Prepping him for his funeral? Some religious significance? How could there be an open casket with that much damage? Who knows? I still have more questions than answers about this case."

"I know the feeling."

Jade thought of the Pittsburgh commentator holding his tongue in his hands like a rosary.

Do the victims' religious beliefs have something to do with this? Or the killer's? Or possibly his lack of religion?

She finished perusing the photos and opened the folder with the autopsy report. She started to read. "Anything come up on the rope?"

"Made out of nylon and polyester. Manufactured by Everbilt. This particular rope can be found in any Home Depot store in the country."

"That narrows it down." She continued reading. "Not much food in his stomach and his blood-alcohol content was point-one-six."

"Twice the legal limit here."

She flipped another page, and eyed him, eyebrow raised. "Rohypnol?"

He nodded.

"Could he have ingested it unintentionally?" she asked.

"According to the lab, yes. In pill form, it's tasteless and dissolves in liquid. If the liquid is clear, the drug turns bright blue. But in dark liquids, such as the red wine the victim drank, it becomes cloudy. In a dark room, like The Wine Shoppe bar, he wouldn't have noticed."

"How long would it have taken for him to feel the effects?"

"Within thirty minutes up to several hours."

"So your witness may not have seen someone helping a drunk friend home, but rather a killer who had drugged his victim."

"And before you ask, we were too late to obtain fingerprints at the restaurant. They'd sanitized the glasses before we got there the next day."

Jade examined a close-up photo of a strand of hair. Light brown, Caucasian, human.

"Where was the hair found?"

"On the victim's shirt. No match came up in CODIS." CODIS was the Combined DNA Index System database managed by the FBI.

She closed the file. "What about his finances?"

Thomas grabbed another file midway down the stack. Jade was glad she would never play him in KerPlunk.

"Nothing jumped out at me. He earned a pretty decent salary and lived within his means. Owned the condo and made his mortgage payments on time. He had one credit card he rarely used and paid off his balance every month. His credit report, unenlightening. He paid all his bills on time, but only had an average credit score. He probably didn't have *enough* credit. Only in America. He didn't owe anyone any money as far as we can tell, and he didn't gamble."

"Do you think someone killed him for his political views?"

"Possibly. During my research I also discovered"—he got up, searched through a stack, and handed her a file—"this. In 1984, members of a white nationalist group killed a Jewish, liberal radio talk-show host in Denver, Colorado. So, yes, it's possible."

Jade read the article and the police report. "Anything on LeBlanc's computer? Phone records?"

"Nothing on the hard drive. Checked out his Twitter and Facebook accounts. Some followers disagreed with his viewpoint, but most comments were benign. He didn't use his home phone much. We found the ex-girlfriend through his cell. A graduate of LSU, she'd been with the paper only a few months before she and LeBlanc started dating."

"But she was at The Wine Shoppe that night."

"Yes, but they weren't together. She saw LeBlanc talking to some guy at the bar. Didn't introduce her. She said LeBlanc and the guy were in a heated discussion."

"An argument?"

"No. More like a debate. She thought it had something to do with LeBlanc's work."

"Did she give a description?"

"She believed he had brown hair, but the bar was dark. And, oh, he was kind of cute."

Jade rolled her eyes. "Any way she could've been involved?"

"We didn't think so. We checked her out. She was pretty shaken up by his death."

"What time did LeBlanc and this guy leave the bar?"

"Eleven thirty."

"Consistent with the time of death."

"I tried everything. Even asked for the public's help

through pleas on television, radio, and billboards throughout Baton Rouge and New Orleans. Nothing."

It looked to Jade like the case still ate away at him.

They spent the rest of the afternoon reviewing every file and photo in detail and brainstorming ideas. Later, he leaned back in his chair and gave her a tired smile. "I'd better be getting you to the airport. Oh, before you go, let me check on that speech for you. The one playing in his condo when we found him."

She gathered her things while he rummaged through his files.

"Here it is," he said.

She stopped and eyed him, expectant.

He returned her stare and shrugged. "Income inequality."

CHAPTER TWENTY

Bethesda, Maryland

THE DC AREA doesn't enjoy many perfect-weather days, with winter sometimes switching to summer with only a brief touch of spring. Today, however, was one of them. The sound of what seemed like hundreds of happy, laughing kids running around filled the air. A soccer ball was kicked down the field, chased by twelve kids, six from each team. The coaches on both sides yelled "Spacing!" to no avail.

Cole Brennan loved the crisp scent of recently mown grass. He stood on the sidelines with his wife, Ashley, and a few of their children watching their son, Ryan, play. Blond hair flying, Ryan sported a huge smile on his face. Cole's heart filled with love and pride as he gazed upon his son. Cole envied him. To be innocent and carefree. When the worst thing in the world that could happen to you was that no one passed you the ball or you didn't score a goal. Much preferable to having the fate of your country's future weighing on your mind. He glanced at his wife, reached for her hand, and turned back to the game.

Hannah, the best player on the team, sent a perfect pass down the left side of the field. Ryan sprinted his little heart out to arrive first, slowing as he approached the ball. He dribbled it toward the opponent's goal.

Cole dropped Ashley's hand and cupped his hands around his mouth.

"Go, Ryan! Go! Go! Go!"

Cole wanted to run down the sidelines along with his son as other fathers did.

Ryan shifted the ball to his strong foot. He was now one-on-one with the goalie. He reared back his right foot and shot the ball with all the power he had, almost falling down in the process. The ball veered to the right, missing the goal by ten yards.

Cole's heart fell as Ryan shuffled back up the field, his head down.

"That's all right, Ryan! You'll score next time! Keep your head up!"

The game ended a few minutes later. Cole was grateful these games were short. Ryan wouldn't miss another shot and Cole would be able to sit down soon. He was not accustomed to standing for long periods of time.

"Dad?"

Cole tore his gaze away from his son to find his daughter, Kaitlin, staring at him with the look she had been giving him on a regular basis as of late.

"Yes?"

"Some kids at school were talking about you again today."

"Don't they have anything better to do?"

"They said you don't have a heart."

"They're wrong, sweetheart. I do have a heart. It's just not a bleeding heart."

Cole's high-pitched giggle faded away when Kaitlin's

expression didn't change. He stole a quick glance at Ashley, but before he could say anything else, Ryan ran to where they stood.

Cole mussed Ryan's hair.

"Good game, Champ."

Ryan beamed, remnants from the post-game strawberry juice box forming a red circle around his lips.

"Thanks, Dad. I almost scored!"

"Yes, you almost did, son."

Cole and Ashley sauntered toward the parking lot, Ryan between them, and the other children a few steps behind. None of the other players' parents had said "hello" when they arrived or spoke to them during the game. He had picked up on the furtive glances. Maybe even dirty looks, he couldn't be sure.

That is what I get for living in a liberal city. Now, these people are poisoning my daughter with their liberal way of thinking. We need to move.

CHAPTER TWENTY-ONE

Washington, DC

WHITNEY SPENT THE afternoon in her office reviewing briefing books and pending legislation. A little after seven p.m., Landon knocked on her open door and stood in the doorway.

She affixed her signature to the document she had just read and looked up him. "How is the reading going?"

He sighed. "Not well."

Whitney extended her arm to place the pen in its gold-plated holder in the center of her desk. "Why not?"

"Because every time I make a dent in my stack of books," he said, "you give me more work to do. It isn't fair."

She leaned back in her chair and smiled at him. "When I proposed this reading contest, I wanted it to be predicated on the number of books read." Whitney and Landon shared a love of reading, particularly books on history, politics, and current events. "You should have made it easy on yourself and read all the short books on your Kindle. But instead, you had the idea to change the contest to number of pages. Bragging rights are at stake. Are you raising the white flag?"

Landon was never one to back down from a challenge. "Do you need anything else, Senator?"

"What are you doing this evening?"

"Reading."

She rose. "Join me for dinner and then a meeting with Ted later."

"Yes, Senator," he said. "Is this invitation another ploy to prevent me from winning the contest?"

ණ

Whitney and Landon sat at a table in the back of the American cuisine restaurant enjoying an after-dinner coffee. An older establishment, the restaurant had not changed with the times and, in consequence, was nearly empty. The social climbers and power players in DC did not dine here, which was okay with Whitney.

Landon took a sip from his cup. "How does it feel being the de facto nominee?"

"As if the fight has just begun."

"The campaign will start to get ugly. Their PACs are flush. Expect an avalanche of negative ads."

"Could be worse. We could still be resolving our differences by dueling."

"Can you imagine the Capitol surrounded by a mass of duelists?"

"The American people would need to elect a new Congress." She paused. "Perhaps that's not such a bad idea."

They shared a laugh. Landon's smile no doubt drove the young women crazy. He would go far in politics.

"You haven't mentioned how you feel about my compromise with Sampson," Whitney said.

"Not my place, Senator. You did what you felt like you had to do."

"I wanted to talk to you about the campaign. I need something substantial to make a move."

"I thought you were focused on women's rights."

"I am, but I need something else. Something with a broader appeal."

"Health care reform's been taken. Education reform appropriated by the other party. Campaign finance?"

"People don't care about campaign finance reform, and politicians have no incentive to change the status quo."

"The deficit? It's a financial reality. We must reduce spending, and you would be perceived as doing what is best for the country rather than for your party."

"After the election."

"Social Security?"

"Can't win."

"Income inequality."

"The country's not ready."

"Climate change?"

Whitney sighed. "I know firsthand the impact of climate change on my state. The increased ice storms, droughts, and extreme hot and cold temperatures have hurt Missouri's agricultural production. We need to reduce greenhouse-gas emissions, but the regulatory impact may hurt middle-class families."

"And ship jobs overseas."

"Climate change is important to me, but not the issue I want to bet my campaign on. The sad part is, Al Gore will end up having the last laugh, but our grandchildren won't find the joke funny."

Landon shook his head. "Combating the untruths. Used

to be facts were facts. Now, facts are relative to which party you belong to. What did Senator Moynihan always say?"

"'Everyone is entitled to his own opinion, but not to his own facts.' Some politicians and organizations, like Patriot News, realized their agenda could be propagated by what Lenin once said: 'A lie told often enough becomes the truth.'" Whitney sipped her coffee. "I also believe it comes down to the 'Genius of the And.' People are oppressed by the 'Tyranny of the Or'; that you must believe in one idea or the other but not both. F. Scott Fitzgerald said, 'The test of a first-rate intelligence is the ability to hold two opposed ideas in the mind at the same time, and still retain the ability to function.'"

Landon nodded. "The conservatives have mastered the formula of a simple message repeated over and over again: pro-life, pro-family, pro-guns, pro-smaller government. If only our party would craft a consistent, coherent, and simple message that could compete. The problem is trying to distill complex issues down to simple-minded sound bites."

Whitney set her cup in the saucer. "Corralling individual Democrats to stay on message is harder than herding cats."

She glimpsed the pink wristband underneath his shirt cuff as he also replaced his cup. Someone in his immediate family was a breast-cancer survivor. Mother? Sister? She needed to be better about remembering these things.

Landon hesitated. "I've been working on something." When she remained silent, he hurried on. "A transaction tax on hedge-fund managers." He described how his proposal would work and how much tax revenue would be generated.

Whitney was skeptical, but listened in silence. When he finished, she gave him her most serious expression. Or at least, she tried. "We would never want to put forth a proposal for political reasons."

He didn't try to conceal his smile. "Of course, we wouldn't."

❧

Her driver dropped them off at her national campaign headquarters, in an office building on K Street in Northwest Washington, DC. The outer area, where the phone bank was located, had been bursting with activity an hour ago. The volunteers—calling citizens at home and interrupting their dinners, TV watching, video-game playing, or tweeting—had left. The walls displayed several oversized pictures of her. Whitney still found gigantic close-ups of her face disconcerting.

They entered the conference room. On one wall, a large sign read, Senator Whitney Fairchild for President - Our America, Our Future. Ted Bowling glanced up from his laptop, an almost imperceptible shadow darkening his face when he saw her companion.

Whitney waved her hand in front of her nose. "This room smells like an ashtray, Ted. You know you're not supposed to smoke in here."

"Sorry, Senator, stressful day."

She sat and crossed her legs, as Landon sat next to her, removing the electronic tablet from his briefcase.

Ted began speaking.

"I just emailed the numbers to you. We're down twenty points against Ellison. Your approval rating with women is trending higher—I think the ERA is helping—but the numbers are still soft in other categories: young voters, Latinos, middle-class white men. We need to do something big."

"I agree. Go on."

Ted coughed. "Income inequality. Talked about in the media for years. Over the last forty years, the top one percent of the US population is seven hundred and fifty percent better off, while the middle- and the lower-income classes' wealth—"

"I know the numbers, Ted."

"There are a lot of voters in that ninety-nine percent." He rapped the table with his knuckles on each word. "The 'wealth creators create jobs' line is a lie, which is becoming more apparent every year. The only thing wealth creators create is more wealth for themselves. We must develop a policy that won't be considered a 'wealth distribution' tactic or 'class warfare,' terms that turn off independents, moderates, blue-collar workers, and all those afraid of anything reeking of Socialism."

"Be that as it may, what do you suggest?"

"Poll after poll shows the majority of Americans are not opposed to tax increases on the rich. We've enacted increases before; we can do it again. This would result in a small increase in taxes for the rich, relative to their incomes, but billions of dollars in additional revenue."

Whitney brought her right index finger to her lips with her thumb under her chin, her thinking position. "Hmm . . . ."

Ted continued in earnest. "The strategists and I also think we should propose increasing estate taxes to pre-George W. levels."

She remained silent.

Landon cleared his throat. "May I make a suggestion?" He waited until he had their attention. "There are a lot of ways to increase revenues. One idea I had was to impose a tax on the financial markets. The original purpose of financial firms was to raise capital for the private sector. Instead, they focused on making as much money as they could trading for themselves;

helping businesses find capital became an afterthought. To generate higher returns, these firms took on increased risks. Our lost decade showed the awful, sometimes irreparable consequences of speculation on our markets and our economy."

"What do you propose?" she asked, although he had told her at dinner earlier.

"Levying a transaction tax on hedge-fund managers and other large, complicated financial transactions. This would decrease speculation and create an incentive for long-term investment. In the short term, tax revenues will rise."

"Why do you think your plan will work?" Ted asked, in a tone indicating he believed quite the opposite.

"The European Union implemented a similar tax several years ago. Yes, the financial markets took a hit at first, but, as their economies recovered, investors began to consider the tax as another cost of doing business."

Whitney shifted in her chair. "Why hedge-fund managers?"

"I don't believe we should tax every transaction, which would hurt individual investors. To Ted's point, the Republicans oppose any increase in taxes or regulations on the 'wealth creators.' Most hedge-fund companies employ five employees or fewer. Sometimes, it's one person, a computer, and an algorithm that buys and sells based on discrepancies of supply and demand in the market. These firms generate billions of dollars a year. One firm during the Aughts generated a billion dollars in one day."

"The Aughts?" Ted asked.

Landon ignored the sarcasm. "The last decade."

Whitney nodded. "So you're saying these fund managers don't create jobs or *make* anything."

"Well, not exactly. But they don't create the jobs ascribed

to them by the other party. And, to top it all off, they're taxed at the capital-gains rate, which is a third of the ordinary rate, or what a normal business person pays." Landon pulled an accordion folder from his briefcase and handed it to her. "I took the liberty of running some numbers under various scenarios."

Ted still did not try to hide the sarcasm in his voice. "Of course you did."

Landon ignored him. "I also propose a change in tax policy to discourage short-term investment. Capital gains on stocks sold within one year would be taxed at seventy-five percent; one to three years, fifty percent; twenty percent after five years; and zero percent beyond that. We should also eliminate capital-gains taxes for those Americans making less than, say, one hundred thousand. This will bring in new investment and allow investors' wealth to grow tax-free. It's all in my analysis."

Ted stared at Whitney, his face flushed. "We should poll this first."

"Who in the ninety-nine percent would be against this proposal?" she asked.

Ted and Landon did not answer her rhetorical question while she perused the proposal she had read in the restaurant earlier. Landon had written a one-page summary with supporting analysis, data, and charts. She closed the report cover.

"No one." She answered her own question. "I like it." Whitney gave Ted a sweet smile. "Polls be damned."

CHAPTER TWENTY-TWO

Chattenham, Pennsylvania

JADE HARRINGTON LISTENED to the computerized female voice guide her as she drove down the Delaware Expressway, thinking about the Baton Rouge, Pittsburgh, Houston, and Chattenham cases. No explicit evidence tied the cases together so far, besides all four victims' involvement in conservative media.

Oh . . . and they all had their heads bashed in and their tongues cut out.

Jade turned onto Interstate 476 and headed north. Her cell phone rang.

"Hey, you." Zoe.

"How's my kitty?" Jade asked.

"Card's fine. Lonely. Meowed he wanted to come home and live with me, but I told him you needed him."

"He'd come back once he found out you'd try to turn him into a vegan."

"He'd live longer. And I'm not a vegan."

"Thanks again for taking care of him. After what happened at your apartment . . ."

Silence, then, Zoe said, "We're best friends. It's going to

take a lot more than you being a knucklehead to drive me away. Where are you?"

"On a case."

"I know, silly."

Jade did not respond for a moment. "I may need your help with something."

"Really?"

"Don't sound so happy. Talk to me about income inequality."

"What about it?"

"It was a major issue during the Occupy Movement, but you don't hear about it as much now. Why not?"

"Depends on where you live. The problem's still there. Simmering. And one day it will boil over."

"Why?"

"The issue hasn't gone away. When the poor and the middle class realize the American Dream is just that—a dream—they'll revolt."

"What's the solution?"

"How much time do you have?"

Jade glanced at the navigation system display. "Not much."

"When are you coming home? We can discuss it then."

"Not sure," Jade said, "but I'll let you know. I'm flying into Reagan."

"National."

"Sorry, I forgot." Zoe refused to call the former National airport by its proper name. Jade passed the sign indicating her exit was one mile away. "Listen, I need to go."

Driving through a quaint town of pizza joints, cafés, a Dunkin' Donuts, bars, restaurants, and a dry cleaner's—everything a college student could ever need or want—she turned right a half mile later at the small wooden sign: Chattenham College, Home of the Eagles. Founded 1863.

Jade drove down a long, paved drive with oak trees on both sides interspersed with tall, black, old-fashioned street lights. She veered right, around an administration building made of fieldstone and meandered through the heart of the campus: rolling lawns, a plethora of trees and shrubs, wooded hills, classrooms, and dormitories. Students sporting back-packs ambled along the sidewalks in ones, twos, and threes. A peaceful campus.

She located the college radio station in one of the older buildings and parked behind a campus police car. A uniformed black gentleman with short gray hair waited for her in the cramped, barren lobby, reading a copy of *Sports Illustrated.*

The officer eyed her and nodded with approval. "You must be Agent Harrington."

Jade, not sure what test she had passed, said, "Yes."

"Nice to meet you. I'm Nate." He stuck out his hand. "I'll be honest with you. I was surprised to learn of the FBI's interest in this old case. Come on. I'll take you up to the studio." Nate headed down a hallway and led her up a narrow flight of stairs.

"The campus is about four hundred acres with two thousand students," Nate said over his shoulder. "Founded in 1863 by Quakers. The station has been around since 1939, six years after the invention of FM radio. It's one of the oldest college radio stations in the country."

"Who manages it?"

"It's always been run by the students."

On the second floor, Nate opened a door to a modest room. The term "studio" was generous. The room consisted of a small area with engineering equipment and a space for the DJ. Vinyl albums and CDs packed the scuffed white shelves.

She examined a mural on the wall displaying an impressive pictorial history of the school. She peered closer. In the corner of the drawing, a woman held a basketball with laces, wearing an early twentieth-century uniform, skirt and all. Jade was thankful she never had to play ball in a skirt. Her penchant for diving after loose balls could have been problematic.

"This mural is amazing," she said. "It's a shame it's tucked away in here. It should be in a museum."

After a moment, she straightened and turned to Nate.

"What can you tell me about the victim, Kyle Williams?"

"I remember Kyle. A loner. Although the school's mission is to be fiercely independent, it's still pretty liberal. He never fit in. Kyle was the only person who ever had a conservative program at the station. He often got into heated discussions with his co-workers."

"Anyone in particular?"

"We interviewed all of them at the time. They didn't care much for his politics, but they liked him well enough. None of them seemed to have a motive for murder and their alibis checked out."

Nate started toward another staircase.

"Kyle had just completed his show and went down these stairs and out the back door. That's the last time anyone saw him." Nate paused. "Except for his killer, of course." He exited the building and Jade followed him toward the corner of the parking lot. He stopped at the farthest space under a huge American elm tree in full bloom. "His car was parked here. His body was a couple of feet from the driver's side door. His car keys were found next to him and he still had his wallet on him."

"On the phone, you said the weapon was a blunt instrument."

"According to the medical examiner and my personal observations."

"Any evidence?"

"No murder weapon. No fingerprints. No evidence. The victim was a good kid. I knew him and liked him. He didn't deserve this."

"Do you have much crime here?"

"No, except for the typical college stuff: underage drinking, public intoxication, disorderly conduct. We had a huge problem with date rape many years ago. More so than now, anyway. Around the time Kyle was killed, now that I think about it." He shook his head. "I've worked here for almost twenty years." He stared down at the asphalt. "Never saw anything like what happened here. Before or since."

Jade glanced back toward the building and scanned the grounds. Her eyes settled on Nate. "I'm going to spend some time out here, if you don't mind."

"Take all the time you want. Call me if you need anything else."

Nate ambled away, rounding the building to his car parked out front.

Jade stood for a long time on the spot where Kyle Williams had died. When working a case, she always tried to use the name of the person as much as possible rather than "the victim." Sometimes, the essence of a murdered person was lost during an investigation.

Jade never wanted to forget who she was working for.

ൿ

The foundation of the house was built with the same fieldstone as the buildings at the college, the siding of the house once white. Green shutters hung next to the windows, paint chipped, one crooked, as if it didn't want to be like the others. The yard boasted more brown patches than green.

Jade knocked at the wooden, weathered door. And waited. No footsteps approached, although someone was at home. She was expected. She knocked again.

The door opened with effort, partially concealing a woman who appeared close to seventy but, according to her file, was in her mid-fifties.

"Mrs. Williams?"

The woman nodded.

Jade held up her badge. "I'm Special Agent Jade Harrington. We talked on the phone." No response. "May I come in?"

The woman half nodded, stepped back, and swung the door open the rest of the way. Jade entered a darkened foyer and followed Mrs. Williams as she shuffled a few steps into the sitting room. A large bay window faced the front yard. The woman sat on a sofa with her back to the window. She clasped her hands on her lap. She didn't offer refreshments.

"Mrs. Williams, as I told you on the phone, we're investigating the death of your son."

"Why?"

Not the question Jade had expected. *Didn't she want her son's killer found? No matter how long it took to solve the case?* "There's evidence that his death may be related to others."

She continued to gaze at Jade, but didn't ask the obvious

question. After a moment, she broke eye contact with Jade and stared at her hands.

"He was such a good boy. Had such a bright future. He could've been anything he wanted to be. I died, too, the day my son was taken from me."

Jade waited a beat. "Mrs. Williams, can you tell me anything about what happened that day?"

"He still lived at home. Before school, he ate breakfast, kissed me on the cheek, and told me to have a good day. I never saw him again." She looked at Jade, her eyes pleading for forgiveness. "I should have told him I loved him."

"Did he write, make notes, keep a journal? Anything like that?"

The older woman glanced to the left before shaking her head.

She was lying.

Jade pressed. "Are you sure?"

The woman's lips formed a hard line, another quick shake of the head.

Jade let it go and asked her many questions, but didn't learn much more than what she had learned from Nate. After a half hour, Jade realized the trip to this house was a waste of time. She started to get up. "Thank you, Mrs. Williams, for your time. I won't keep you any longer. I can show myself out."

She was still examining her hands. "I didn't tell . . . He did. He did keep a journal."

Jade sat back down. "Do you still have it?"

Mrs. Williams nodded. "I found it in his room."

Jade remained cool. "May I see it?"

~

Kyle's room appeared unchanged since his death. A poster

of Kid Rock pointing an index finger straight ahead hovered above the headboard of the neat, twin-size bed. Other than the poster and a small desk, the room was bereft of trophies or personal items. A thin book lay on the nightstand. His mother picked it up and handed it to Jade.

"I found it a few months after his death under the mattress." She shrugged her shoulders and gave Jade a weak smile. "I finally got around to washing his sheets."

"Did you read it?"

With a slight shake of her head, no, Mrs. Williams looked away.

Jade didn't think she was telling the truth again. It didn't matter. She held the journal, and then opened it, flipping through the pages until she came to the last entry, written the night before Kyle died.

I don't know for sure, but I think someone's been following me. It's creeping me out. For some reason, I think it's C. But why? I should tell someone, but who? What would I say? Everyone would think I was paranoid. That I'm the creep.

Jade sat on Kyle's bed, ignoring Mrs. Williams' quick intake of breath. She scanned several entries. More of the same. "Mrs. Williams, why didn't you take this to the police?"

The woman was back to staring at her hands again. The silence dragged on for so long, Jade thought she hadn't heard the question. Jade was about to repeat it.

"I couldn't," Mrs. Williams said, her eyes filled with anguish. "It's the only part of my son I have left."

Jade nodded and closed the journal. She moved toward the desk. Textbooks were intermingled with books on Ronald Reagan, Barry Goldwater, and other conservative thinkers. Towering above them all was a Chattenham College yearbook.

Jade's pulse quickened. She opened the yearbook to the index and scrolled down until she located the radio station. She turned to the appropriate page. In a corner, among the text and the large motto of the station, was a photograph of the radio station crew. She found Kyle Williams: short, slight build, blond hair, smiling. She read the names under the picture. The crew had a couple of "Cs."

Jade glanced up at the older woman, trying to appear nonchalant. "May I borrow these?"

Mrs. Williams shifted, uncomfortable.

"I'll bring them back." Jade stared into her eyes. "I promise."

CHAPTER TWENTY-THREE

Columbus, Ohio

WHITNEY ROLLED OVER, knowing she should be getting ready for another day of campaigning. She was exhausted, even though presidential candidates were not allowed to get tired. If that leaked out, she could imagine Ellison's camp airing an ad of her sleeping, with the sonorous voiceover: "*What will happen when Senator Whitney Fairchild receives the call at three a.m.? Will she hit the snooze button, roll over, and go back to sleep?*"

She heard an insistent knock on the door of the hotel suite. A few minutes later, Sarah, her body woman, knocked on her bedroom door. "Senator, Ted's here. He says it's urgent."

Isn't it always? "I'll be right there."

Whitney sighed and went to the bathroom to freshen up. Still in her pajamas, she threw on the cream-colored, hotel-provided robe and slippers. In the living room, Ted sat on a sofa, his suit rumpled, his tie skewed, and his hair uncombed. *Was that the same shirt he wore yesterday?*

"Good morning, Ted."

"Good morning, Senator."

She turned to Sarah. "Please order breakfast. The usual.

Thank you." Sarah nodded and left. Whitney turned to Ted. "What is it?"

"You need to start going to church."

"Why?"

"Americans expect their president to go to church."

"Why does the faith of the president matter? I thought this country was founded on the principle of freedom of religion, which denotes a freedom *from* religion."

"Optics, Senator."

"Ted, did you really wake me up for this?"

"And this." He flung the *Columbus Dispatch* down on the coffee table, a large photograph of Grayson and her smiling above the newspaper's fold. The photo was taken at an event earlier this year, a rare occasion when her husband had joined her on the campaign trail. The headline screamed Personal Bailout? Below, in a smaller font, read Graysongate: Husband of Presidential Candidate Benefited from Federal Funds.

She picked up the paper. The news item explained in detail how Grayson's company avoided paying millions of dollars in taxes as a result of a bill she had sponsored as a member of the powerful Appropriations Committee. In the article, Senator Eric Hampton accused Whitney of nepotism and implored her to withdraw from the presidential campaign. The bill in question was passed years ago, which Hampton knew. The article insinuated she proposed and pushed this bill through for her husband's benefit. Of course, she knew Fairchild Industries would be a beneficiary of the bill. But that was not her intent, only a consequence. A lot of American businesses benefited. That was the point.

She dropped the paper back down on the coffee table. "Hmm . . . , I wonder why this is coming out now."

Ted eyed her. "Is that it? Will anything else come out?"

Sarah had let in the room service server who placed the breakfast items on the table and left as quietly as he had arrived.

Whitney poured herself a cup of coffee, grateful for the interruption. "No."

"Obviously, this is from Ellison's camp," Ted said. "It's already on *Drudge*."

She reached for a croissant. "Ah . . . then it must be true."

Ted overlooked her sarcasm. "We must issue a strong denial and nip this in the bud. We can say when you introduced this bill, you were trying to help companies keep jobs in the United States. You had no way of knowing your husband's company would benefit. Yada, yada, yada. I've scheduled a press conference for you this morning."

She nodded, wondering how long she would need to ride the elliptical to work off the croissant. She had to find more time to work out. Constituents did not like overweight female politicians. "Okay. I will do one press conference on this subject. With the twenty-four-hour news cycle, this story will be forgotten with the next 'Breaking News' headline."

She finished the croissant.

"So, our president wants to play hardball," Whitney continued. She disliked negative politics. But she disliked losing more. Whitney had learned her profession in the rough-and-tough arena of Chicago politics. She didn't back down from anyone. She smiled at Ted, the smile that had helped her to become the most powerful woman in DC.

"I read somewhere that when you are a female US senator, people tend to underestimate and trivialize you." Her smile evaporated. "But I can play hardball, too. What do we have on him?"

Ted didn't hesitate. "When Ellison was in high school, he and a bunch of his popular friends got drunk and went from ranch to ranch punching and kicking pigs. I think one was set on fire. Many of the pigs died."

Whitney took a sip of her coffee. "Was he arrested?"

Ted shook his head. "The farmers were paid off by the boys' rich daddies. 'Boys will be boys' and all that. The kids left for different colleges the next year, everyone sworn to secrecy. The incident forgotten."

"What an awful story." She replaced her cup on the table. "I never liked that saying. 'Boys will be boys.' As if they possess a license to do whatever they want."

"Unfortunately, we didn't have cell phones back then to capture it on video, but the public still doesn't like cruelty inflicted on animals. This would hurt Ellison. Bad."

Whitney did not hesitate. "Use it."

CHAPTER TWENTY-FOUR

Washington, DC

IN A WINDOWLESS conference room at the Bureau, Jade popped an M&M into her mouth and scanned the faces around the table: her task force, code named CONFAB. Jade came up with the name herself: to honor the victims' profession.

CONFAB consisted of Christian Merritt, Dante Carlucci, Max Stover, Pat Turner, and a hungry, freckle-faced rookie agent named Austin Miller.

Jade brought everyone up to speed on the case. "We can presume our victims were killed because they were conservative media personalities. Who would have a reason to kill them?"

"Every liberal in this country," Pat said, typing notes into her computer as she talked.

"We may need to narrow it down," Jade deadpanned.

"Someone who was offended by something each of the victims had said?" This from Christian.

Dante, his chair leaning against the wall at a precarious forty-five-degree angle, said, "A rival who wants to be the top dog?"

Jade nodded. "Possibly." She turned to Max. "Talk to me."

"The UNSUB has complete disdain for his victims. He makes no attempt to hide the bodies and leaves them in disrespectful states. The multiple blows with a blunt instrument are overkill, demonstrating his rage. Something is causing him to accelerate the murders. The time between them is getting shorter. He will strike again."

Max had the team's full attention. Jade motioned with her hand for him to continue.

"He cuts out the victims' tongues, but doesn't keep them as trophies. Why?"

"He's in a hurry?" Christian asked.

"No room in his refrigerator?" Pat asked.

Jade frowned at Pat. "He doesn't want them."

"Perhaps," Max said.

"Why wouldn't he want them?" Austin asked.

Max shrugged. "He doesn't want anything to do with the victims after the act."

"Or maybe he doesn't like trophies," Jade said.

Christian crossed his arms in front of his chest. "Where was the tongue of the Houston victim found?"

Jade responded without glancing at her notes. "In a trash can by the elevator in the parking garage."

"Complete disdain is right." Christian eyed Max. "Best guess of what kind of person we're searching for?"

"A highly organized individual with advanced social and planning skills. I believe he possesses above-average intelligence and comes from an upper middle- to high-income family."

Dante leaned forward, allowing his chair to drop to the floor without softening the landing, startling Austin. "Is he also a loner who wet the bed and picked the wings off insects as a kid?"

"I bet the UNSUB felt unloved growing up," Max continued, ignoring Dante. "May be an only child. He suffers from depression and feelings of despair."

"I'm curious, Max," Dante said. "What do you do away from work? What're your hobbies?"

"I don't have any hobbies."

"Everyone has a hobby."

Pat said, as she continued to type, "Dressing up like the characters on *Miami Vice* on the weekend and asking out as many women as you can is not a hobby."

Dante's face reddened. He leaned his chair back.

"What's *Miami Vice*?" Austin asked.

Christian laughed.

"Let's get to work," Jade said, turning to Christian. "I want you to focus on the three latest killings: Pittsburgh, Baton Rouge, and Houston. Let's see if we can track the UNSUB by where he's been. Check out the manifests for flights, hotels, and rental-car agencies in those cities around the dates of the murders. Maybe we'll get lucky and he used the same name."

Christian nodded. "Got it."

"Pat, you research the lives of the four victims and create a dossier on each of them. Besides their occupation, were they connected in some other way? Were they ever in the same place, such as a conference? Did they belong to the same professional organizations? Where did they go to school? Where did they work before? Subpoena email, cell phone, computer records, anything you need."

Pat started typing at a different pace, already working on the assignment.

"Dante, I want you to check out the college yearbook. Interview everyone who worked at the Chattenham station at the time, all Kyle Williams's friends, and cross-reference your lists with Christian's."

Dante's eyes bored into hers. "I know how to do my job."

"Then, you also know why your job is the most important."

Austin glanced at Dante and back at Jade. "I'll bite. Why?"

Jade answered him, without breaking eye contact with Dante. "Serial killers often end up living near their first victim."

Dante looked away first.

"How do we know he was the first victim?" Christian said.

"We don't," Jade said, "but we must start somewhere. I think Chattenham may be the key."

Jade turned to Austin. "I want you to listen to every broadcast of the victims for the last few years of their lives. Did the same person call more than one of them or become mad or upset? The college station may not have kept its recordings but find out. Same with the blogs and columns for Paxson and LeBlanc. Read them and readers' comments."

Austin threw up his hands. "That'll take months!"

"Then you better get started," she said.

Dante smirked at Austin.

"Dante can help you, if you need it," Jade said.

Dante's smirk disappeared. "What are you going to do, Chiefette?"

She tensed and willed herself not to punch him in the face. Her voice softened to a low, dangerous level.

"Don't call me that, Dante. Belittling me is unacceptable. And I won't stand for it."

He mumbled a response.

"What was that?" she asked. *One word. Just say one word.*

His eyes tried to hold hers and failed. He stared at the table. She addressed the rest of the group.

"I'm going to get in touch with the MEs and ask them to review their cases again in light of the new evidence. Inform them that their cases may be connected to others."

"We need to make sure all the evidence gets entered into the database," Christian said.

"Good point," she said. "Everything should be entered into the database before you leave for the day. Any leads, evidence, suppositions, wild theories, anything, needs to be entered, even if the info doesn't seem important. Got it?"

Everyone nodded, except for Dante.

She stood and started gathering her materials. "Okay. This is our room for the duration. When in town, I want us to meet here twice a day: nine a.m. and five p.m. Be prepared to debrief me on anything since the prior meeting. If you discover anything important between meetings, don't wait. Tell me immediately. Any questions?"

"Are we keeping our base here or moving to Pittsburgh?" Christian asked.

"Here for now until we determine how big this thing is and depending on what we find. You and I may head to Pittsburgh again to lend support to the local police force." She stared briefly at each of them in turn, ending with Dante, whose gaze she held. "I shouldn't need to say this, but I will. This case is highly sensitive. Do not discuss it with anyone outside of law enforcement, especially the media."

CHAPTER TWENTY-FIVE

Washington, DC

HER DRIVER BACKED out the Lincoln Town Car in a cautious crawl. Whitney glanced over her shoulder at the reporters in front of the gate to her driveway. Most of them hesitated before moving aside grudgingly. One brave soul stood behind the car until the last second, unaware of how her driver felt about reporters.

Whitney couldn't hear what they were saying, but she could read their lips.

"Senator! Did you realize the bill would benefit your husband?"

"How much money did you and your husband personally make from the bill?"

"Are you going to drop out of the race?"

She almost laughed at the silent movie playing out around her. The intense faces, the animated mouths.

A man pounded his fist on the glass. She recoiled, despite the unlikelihood of his breaking through. Her driver put the car in drive. She caught his eye in the rearview mirror and nodded her thanks.

He gave her a reassuring nod.

Whitney disliked Washington's love for "-gate" scandals. FOX News had been covering Graysongate nonstop since the story broke. The network demanded she quit the campaign. CNN was neutral. MSNBC supported her. Most of its commentators maintained that with all the legislation she considered, she had no way of knowing which particular bill would benefit her husband. A congressional ethics investigation was underway, and she wondered how long it would be until she received a subpoena.

Any momentum she had been building in the polls had stopped.

Her cell phone rang. She checked the screen. Her son.

"Mom!"

"Chandler, this is a nice surprise."

"I'm checking to make sure you're all right."

"I am. Why?"

"Because we're getting harassed, Mom. Emma's being followed around campus. The press is following me here like I'm on *The Voice*. And I saw on the news a crowd protesting in front of Dad's company."

Whitney's heart dropped. "Is Emma okay? Are you okay?"

"She's dealing with it like the rest of us. We're tough. Like you. Why do they call it Graysongate? Can't they be more original?"

"The media are often as original as Hollywood."

"Like *Fast & Furious*? How many sequels can you make? Well, I wanted to call and tell you that I love you."

"Thanks. I appreciate that. I love you too, son."

"Mom? Guess what?"

"What?"

"You've arrived in Washington."

"How so?"

"You've got your own scandal! Maybe you need to hire Olivia Pope."

He laughed and hung up.

Whitney gazed out the window, smiling. No, she did not need a fixer like Olivia Pope, but, like Olivia, she would indulge in a generous pour of wine later at home. She replayed the conversation with Chandler in her mind and realized something. Her son had not asked whether the allegations were true.

CHAPTER TWENTY-SIX

Washington, DC

COLE BRENNAN SETTLED into his studio chair. He was in a good mood. The ratings for Cole's show were higher than ever, and Ellison's poll numbers had ticked up during Graysongate. Then, the unfortunate Piggygate surfaced. Cole shook his head with regret.

Graysongate could have been Whitney's Whitewater. What a missed opportunity. He never understood why the media made such a big deal out of boys being boys. Why did they care so much about a few pigs? People ate pigs, didn't they? The incident happened so long ago. The media wouldn't be satisfied until they turned all men into—*what do they call them?*—metrosexuals. In other words, girls.

He received the "Go" signal from his producer.

"Good evening, everyone. I'm Cole Brennan and next I want to talk to you about the good ol' Post Office.

"Liberals have said for years we must keep the United States Postal Service open. Our country was brought together by those carriers who delivered your mail and neither snow, or rain, or heat could stop them. The liberal elite's main argument is that those people living in remote areas need the post office to pay their bills, send letters, and to receive prescriptions. For some of these small towns, the liberals moan, an inverse relationship exists between the size of the post office and its importance to the community. If we eliminate their post offices, these towns will die.

"Well, here's my suggestion for people living in those remote communities. Move!"

Cole laughed.

"The Postal Service was formed to run like a business, but it's a money-losing business. Lots of money. When a company brings in less money than it spends, its management—or the bank, or its creditors—eventually shuts the operation down.

"Like everything else in Washington, the Postal Service is broken. The use of email and private carriers resulted in declining volume, which is never coming back, folks. People only go to the post office when it's absolutely necessary or during Christmastime. Furthermore, its costly, inflexible unionized workforce doesn't give a crap about the institution it represents and continues to receive lucrative compensation packages despite the service's horrific financial condition. Remember the good ol' days, when President Reagan fired the air traffic controllers? That's the kind of courage we need now.

"To top it all off, the unions and Congress joined together in their resistance to consolidating or closing facilities or decreasing delivery from six to five days a week. A lot of this resistance from Congress, the Super Committee, and the Super Super Committee comes from those weak legislators afraid of receiving a call from Ethel Humperdinck from Podunk, Oklahoma who is upset because her post office, which services five people in a hundred-mile radius, might have to cut back its services.

"The liberals are always saying we should be more like Europe. Europe is perfect and sophisticated and humane. Well, for once, they're right. Let's be more like Europe. Many countries in Europe privatized or partially privatized their mail service using good, effective management and common-sense labor practices. Privatization and competition increased productivity, decreased costs, improved on-time delivery, and provided better service to everyone.

"The Democrats want to form a committee to figure out what to do about the Postal Service. I'll save them the time and the taxpayers' their money. Privatize it! And do it now!

"I only have time for one caller today. Go!"

Cole listened to a question about Whitney's financial tax proposal.

"Well, I think the idea is idiotic. One, if you assess a tax on financial transactions in the US, global investors will invest elsewhere, so our stock market will shrink. Two, hedge-fund managers will trade less. Therefore, revenue will decrease, shrinking our overall economy at a time when we can least afford it. Hedge-fund managers create wealth for this country, which creates jobs. It's a myth they're all rich billionaires. Most of them are everyday Joes, like you and me, trying to make a living.

"This financial transactions tax is a bad idea. Next! And I don't mean next caller, I mean next election. You must help me defeat Whitney Fairchild at all costs."

CHAPTER TWENTY-SEVEN

Fairfax, Virginia

WHITNEY SURVEYED THE crowd in the massive high school gym in Fairfax County, Virginia, the first in the United States to surpass six figures in median household income. Large blue and gold banners hung from the ceiling displaying years of district, regional, and state championships in a wide variety of sports. The students were engaged this morning, although she suspected their enthusiasm was more from getting out of class rather than hearing her speak. No matter. Her audience was not only them, but their parents and the numerous cameras representing all the major cable news networks and local television stations.

She gripped the podium. "Some of you will be old enough to vote in this election, which is a good thing because this election is about you and your future. Why?" She paused. "There's a lot at stake, such as the future of our country's educational system and how we make higher education affordable. Whether you'll be able to find a decent, well-paying job when you graduate from college. Whether you will be able to afford to buy a home. You don't want to live with your parents forever, do you?"

"No!" every student yelled, as if they had rehearsed together.

Whitney staggered back as if the volume of their voices had pushed her. She waited for the laughter to die down before returning to the podium. She smiled.

"I didn't think so. Just checking to see if you were paying attention." She paused again for the appreciative laughter to subside. Her expression turned serious. "For our country, the status quo is no longer an option and no longer acceptable. We need broad, sweeping reforms in education, in how we manage the economy, in how we create a comprehensive domestic clean energy program, which will eliminate the national security risk of relying on foreign oil. We need to invest in our infrastructure, science, technology, and the middle class. We need to make sure you and your children and your grandchildren live in an environment with clean water and without pollution. At the rate we are polluting this country, it won't be long before a medical face mask will be required to venture outside. With your help and your parents' help, we can make the needed changes to prevent that from happening.

"I want all of you to do something for me now. Take out your cell phone." She paused. "I want you to post to Instagram or Snapchat your story, telling your friends to vote. If they're not registered, tell them to register. Let's see how many people we can reach!"

The students cheered.

"When you're finished," Whitney continued, "hold your phone in the air."

Whitney waited.

A few minutes later, a sea of arms was raised, cell phones held high. The sight was overwhelming. She was glad the moment was captured on camera. "Amazing. Look around you," she said. "You just made a difference in this election. Thank you."

Whitney scanned the room and leaned forward into the microphone as if she were sharing a secret with them. She softened her voice.

"My husband and I have two children. As their mother, I am concerned about their future. 'Our America, Our Future' is not merely a campaign slogan to me. It's my promise to you and to my children." She spoke louder. "America has always been the beacon of hope. The land of opportunity where everyone through hard work and education can be whatever he or she wants to be. You can be whatever you want to be. This is your future and what I promise to give you when I am elected president of the United States of America."

Throughout the auditorium, students stood and gave her a standing ovation. Most were shouting, "Whitney! Whitney! Whitney!"

She smiled and waved for a long time, before allowing Ted and her recently assigned Secret Service agents to escort her off the stage. The special agent in charge, Josh McPherson, closed in next to her. His conservative dark suit could not minimize his bulk or the gun concealed underneath his arm. Upon meeting him last month, she had developed an immediate rapport with this man and trusted his warm, confident manner.

Outside of the high school, reporters asked if she would take a few questions. She shielded her eyes from the early June afternoon sun and nodded.

"Senator Fairchild, what do you think of the rumor Ellison is considering privatizing the US Postal Service?"

She gave the reporter her characteristic wry smile. "I

normally don't comment on rumors, but I find it interesting Ellison is taking policy advice from Cole Brennan."

The reporters chuckled. Behind her, some of the camera operators had followed her outside.

"The history of the United States Postal Service is inseparable from the history of our country," she continued. "I believe a role for the Postal Service in America still exists. I do not believe privatization is the answer. Small, rural towns and island communities would suffer irreparable harm. Private companies will find these areas unprofitable to do business, so they won't deliver to those locations."

"If you were president, what would you do?" shouted a reporter in the back.

"*When* I am president," she said, "I would consider partial privatization as a possibility, but only in combination with compensation reforms and a reduction in overhead costs. Consolidating post offices, reducing hours, and approving select retailers to offer mail services will save taxpayers five hundred million dollars per year. We must end prefunding requirements for retirees and allow the Postal Service to manage its own health-care costs, instead of Congress. My team is evaluating all of our options and putting together a plan to save the Postal Service while making the agency more efficient and cost-effective."

"Senator Fairchild," said an older, female reporter named Judy, "how come your family is never on the campaign trail with you?"

"Well, as you know, both of my children are away at college, receiving an education and having a great time. The last thing they want to do is hang out with Mom on the campaign trail. Campaigning may be fun for us, but not so much for them."

The reporters laughed.

Whitney smiled and continued. "As for my husband, he has a pretty important job himself and employees who depend on him. Well, thank you all, I must be—"

Judy persisted. "Senator, I have one more question."

"Okay, one more, but then I must be going."

"Senator, speaking of your husband, is there any truth to the rumor he is having an affair?"

Whitney hesitated for a moment—only a moment—and recovered. She turned to face Judy, who had been covering her campaign for the last nineteen months.

"I haven't heard that one, but no, none whatsoever. Whoever planted that lie does not know my husband. Or me. You surprise me, Judy. I would think for as long as you've been in this business, your sources would be better."

Judy stood her ground, but with compassion in her eyes. "With all due respect, Senator, why don't you ask your neighbor in Missouri about it?"

For the first time, Whitney's voice faltered. "My neighbor?"

CHAPTER TWENTY-EIGHT

Washington, DC

JADE EXAMINED HER own notes before glancing at her team seated around the conference-room table.

"I called all the medical examiners and didn't find out anything new," Jade reported. "Williams, Sells, LeBlanc, and Paxson were killed as a result of blows to the head by a blunt instrument. Strands of hair were found at the LeBlanc and Sells scenes. The hairs found at the LeBlanc scene were Caucasian. No results back, yet, from the Sells case. And we know all the victims' tongues had been cut out."

"Since there's been no evidence of resistance, could the killer have known all his victims?" Christian asked.

Max nodded, thoughtful. "It's possible. Or he—or she—could be one of those trustworthy or charming, Ted Bundy-looking types."

Jade turned to Christian. "What do you have?"

"So far, not much. We scoured thousands of reservations at airports, hotels, and rental car agencies in both Baton Rouge and Houston. Nothing. The perp could've used assumed names." He threw his pen on his notebook. "If only we had a photo."

"Agreed," Jade said. "Get a list of the students who attended the school at the time of the murder. Maybe a name will jump out at us or we can cross-reference it later."

She glanced at Pat.

Pat shook her head. "None of them went to the same school, lived in the same location, or worked together previously. None belonged to the same associations or attended the same conferences, as far as I can determine."

"Austin?"

"I've listened to hours of tapes and haven't found any instances where the same person called both victims, yet."

"What about the college radio station?"

"The good news is the station did keep its recordings. I talked to the current manager and he said its audience back then was limited, mostly students at Chattenham and residents who lived in the town. The audience for the Pittsburgh radio station is also local."

Christian leaned in, peering over at Austin. "Any calls stand out to you?"

"The majority of the callers agreed with the radio talk-show hosts. It's almost cult-like; it's scary. Sometimes callers disagreed with the host and were shouted down by other callers. Few disagreed. I am trying to follow up on them as best I can, but these callers only give a first name. Bottom line, nothing."

"What about the blogs and newspaper articles?" Jade asked.

Austin shook his head and sat back.

The theme song from *Miami Vice* trilled from a cell phone. Everyone glanced at each other and then at Dante, who seemed more surprised than anyone. He fished the phone out of his pocket and pressed the ignore button. He glared at Pat.

Pat was typing on her computer. "Don't look at me."

Dante glowered at Jade.

Jade cracked a smile. "Don't look at me, either."

Austin joined in the laughter, holding up his arms as if surrendering. "I don't even know what that is."

Christian stared at something interesting in the file on the table in front of him.

Dante scowled. "Very funny, Merritt."

Christian winked at Jade.

Jade never allowed herself to depend on anyone, but Christian always seemed to know the right thing to do or say at the right time. Zoe was her only friend, but at work, Christian was her rock. She turned to Dante. "Talk to me."

Dante glared at Christian one more time before flipping through the pages of his notebook. He leaned back in his chair and began to read. "As you recall, the victim—"

"Kyle Williams," Jade interjected.

Dante continued, as if he hadn't been interrupted, "—wrote in his diary he thought a 'C' was following him. I found two 'Cs' in the yearbook picture: a Carly Simms and a Christie Yardley."

Christian murmured, "I don't believe a woman is behind this."

"I don't either," Jade said.

Max took off his glasses and used a handkerchief to polish them. "It would be unlikely this is the work of a woman, but I wouldn't rule it out."

"Can I finish?" Dante asked.

Jade nodded.

"I was able to get in touch with the ten students in the photograph," Dante said, "including Carly and Christie. None of them could imagine who would do such a thing. One of the students died in a car crash three years ago, which would rule him out for the LeBlanc and the latest killing."

Pat, typing, said, "Alibis?"

"All of them had alibis, but . . ."

"What?" Jade said.

"There's a problem."

Jade tried not to roll her eyes in frustration. Working with Dante sometimes was like pulling teeth. "What is it?"

"Ten students posed for the picture. But in order to staff a twenty-four-hours-a-day radio station, the school accepts applications from any student who wants to be a DJ. Students are selected based on their competency, style of music or talk-show format, and maintaining a certain GPA."

Jade motioned her hand for him to hurry up.

"How many students were on the staff at the time of the Chattenham killing?"

Dante closed his notebook, an incongruous grin on his face. "Over one hundred."

CHAPTER TWENTY-NINE

Washington, DC

"SO, WHITNEY SAYS this election is about their future? The way things are going, these students won't have a future. Student debt, not to mention the national debt, will be a yoke around their necks for the rest of their lives. Our educational system is broken. We are in the middle of the pack among developed countries. Our students couldn't do a math or science problem if we wrote the answers on the back of their hands. Where's her plan?

"And, yes, our kids want to live with their parents forever. We allow them to stay on their parents' health insurance policies until they're twenty-six. Twenty-six! At twenty-six, you're no longer a child! You should be having children of your own. Health insurance is a privilege, not a right. The Socialists are always talking about rights. A right to health insurance, a right to marry whoever we want, a right to clean air, a right to a first-class education, while I don't have the right to smoke in my own freakin' office?

"And concerning President Richard Ellison taking his policy advice from me, well . . . it's about damn time!" Cole laughed into the microphone.

"The United States Postal Service, as we know it, is dead. We can't bring back those nostalgic times of the men and women—I know I mustn't forget about the women—mail carriers in their blue sweaters, blue shirts, blue shorts, and blue socks bringing us our mail in a blue bag rain or shine. But listen: email is not going away, folks. The volume the Postal Service enjoyed back in the day is never coming back. Never. As a country, we must accept this and move on. A piecemeal approach won't work. Partial privatization isn't the answer. We must privatize the whole thing. The Postal Service is like a cancer. You can't remove a little bit of the cancer or the disease will continue to spread. You must remove all of it.

"I need you to do something for me. Make sure you call or write President Ellison about this issue. I know for a fact he enjoys hearing from you."

CHAPTER THIRTY

Washington, DC

WHITNEY SETTLED INTO the back seat of the Lincoln Town Car. She should be making phone calls to donors, but she didn't feel like it. Instead she leaned her head back against the headrest, leaving her cell phone in her purse. Her driver had taken a circuitous route from the Capitol to avoid the press, this time because of the allegations of Grayson having had an affair. Sensing her mood, the driver remained silent for the duration of their drive home. She gazed out the window at a city even more stunning at night, thanks to The Height of Buildings Act of 1899, which allowed for the unobstructed view of the city's many historical buildings. She didn't notice them tonight.

Before she left the office, Landon told her the campaign event at Randolph High school broke the Internet, her Twitter account adding one million followers in less than three hours. The kids talked about how cool she was, although they probably used a different adjective. Overall, an overwhelming success. For once, she didn't care.

The rumors had turned out to be true.

Grayson admitted to her on the phone that he had slept

with the woman next door, whose husband died young of a heart attack five years ago. She hadn't been a friend of Whitney's, but was a good neighbor who had done a lot for their family over the years. Someone she had trusted.

Her thoughts, though, were mostly of Grayson. She now wondered when he had asked her when she was coming home in that conversation long ago, whether it was eagerness or something else. Maybe, he didn't want to be surprised.

This was not the first time her faith had been shattered by someone she loved. Someone she trusted. She had been raped as a teenager by a boyfriend who was "tired of waiting." She had become pregnant. With the boyfriend long gone, Whitney wanted an abortion. Her liberal parents wouldn't give their legal consent, surprising her. Instead, they sent her to live with an aunt outside of Chicago for the nine-month duration. The aunt died a year before Whitney was elected to Congress.

She gave the baby up for adoption and returned to her life in Missouri, telling her classmates she had spent a year at boarding school. Whitney decided then to never put herself in another situation where her choices in life were not hers to make. And she became a lifelong pro-choice advocate. She never tried to find her rapist's offspring.

After high school, Whitney attended Northwestern University on an academic scholarship and during the summers interned for local Chicago politicians. There, she caught the political bug, and after graduation, enrolled in Harvard Law School. Whitney ruminated now on how many individuals ran for Congress today without a legal background and no knowledge of the Constitution. She believed this was part of the problem in Washington.

After Harvard, she returned to Chicago and volunteered

for Brad Davis's mayoral campaign. She served on Davis's staff after the election, which was how she met Grayson Fairchild. Whitney walked into a meeting between the mayor and Grayson regarding tax incentives to move a large subsidiary of his father's company to the city. She gazed into Grayson's blue eyes; he stared at her, and it was all over for both of them. They had a long-distance relationship for a year before he proposed. After a beautiful wedding for a match that pleased both sets of parents, the newlyweds settled in St. Louis, the headquarters of Fairchild Industries.

Whitney had Chandler about a year after the wedding and Emma two years later. Although she enjoyed being a mother, the political bug never left her. Grayson understood when she explained she wanted to help people. Whitney entered and won her first political race for a seat on the county council. A couple of years later, she campaigned and narrowly won a state representative seat. When the US House representative for her district died in a car accident, Whitney ran in the special election to replace him. Her opponent painted her as an inexperienced legislator and a housewife, but the voters in her district responded to her honesty, her sincere willingness to help people, and her intelligence. Her attractiveness didn't hurt either. The women turned out to vote for her in droves, and so did the men. She won by a landslide.

Four terms later, she ran for the US Senate when one of the senators retired. The people of Missouri loved her. She was one of their own. She won again by a wide margin.

Whitney decided to run for president to stop the erosion of women's rights and to express her frustration with the country's direction. She believed she could bring a divided country back together. People trusted her. She did not offer pie-in-the-sky rhetoric, but practical solutions and results, as evidenced by her many accomplishments in the House and Senate.

Now, her campaign was no longer about proving a point.

It was about winning.

Their neighbor had always been there for Whitney. When Whitney was away on state business and then in DC, the woman had checked on her family, brought them warm meals, shuttled Chandler to lacrosse practice in a pinch, helped Emma get ready for a homecoming dance.

When Judy, the reporter, had first asked Whitney about the affair, she couldn't conceive that it might be true. Now, she had a decision to make. Divorcing Grayson in the middle of a presidential run was out of the question, wasn't it? She fell back on the question that guided her political life. WWHD? *What would Hillary do?* She knew exactly what HRC would do.

Landon had informed her about the chatter on Twitter and other online sites, the additional rumors spawned, the vicious talk, and the few-and-far-between calls for the couple's privacy.

The most remarkable development was that although the affair was killing her on the inside, it was helping her poll numbers. The American public loved a scorned woman.

The vehicle stopped, jolting her from her thoughts. The driver came around and opened the door, extending a hand to help her out. She took it and thanked him as she stepped by him. He hustled to the other side to retrieve her bulging briefcase and followed her into her Georgetown home. He placed the briefcase on a stand for that purpose in the elegant foyer, tipped his hat, nodded, and left without a word.

The house was quiet. Unlike most of her colleagues, she

lived primarily in DC, refusing to be in perpetual campaign mode. She was sent to DC to do a job, and to do it she needed to be here. At first, living apart from Grayson was hard, but over the years she welcomed the solitude after days spent with ever-demanding constituents, colleagues, the media, and lobbyists.

Leaving the lights off, she kicked off her shoes and padded to the library off the foyer. The curtains remained open and the moonlight provided sufficient visibility to navigate the furniture. She walked around the rolling ladder for the books on the highest shelves and past the large, unlit stone fireplace. She went to her music collection in a section of one of the bookcases. Selecting a CD at random, she slipped it into the player. Skipping the bottles of wine, she selected the bottle of Yamazaki Single Malt Sherry Cask 2013 and a tulip glass and moved to the sofa. She poured several ounces into the glass, then sat back and drew her legs up under her. She swirled and sniffed the whiskey, took a sip, and cradled the glass in her hands.

She had to use two hands to keep the glass from shaking.

This was her favorite room in the house, the shelves filled with first editions whose titles she couldn't read in the dark.

Despite Chopin's "Nocturnes, Op. 9, No. 2" and the liquor, she couldn't relax.

She started to reach for the humidor on the coffee table; indulging in a Cohiba cigar seemed appropriate for the occasion.

"Hello, darling."

A lamp clicked on next to a chair, revealing her husband, Grayson, sitting there in his suit and overcoat, a bittersweet smile on his face.

Whitney rose without speaking. She grasped a highball glass from the cabinet above the bar and filled it with ice cubes, pouring an even dose of gin and tonic water.

She glided to Grayson's chair and dangled the drink before his face.

"Sorry, I'm out of fresh lime. I wasn't expecting you." She resumed her position on the sofa and brought her glass to her lips. She peered at her husband over the rim and sipped while he swallowed most of his drink.

He placed the glass on the cherry end table next to his chair. His hair was uncombed, spiking on top. He had been crying.

"It wasn't an *affair*. It was just one night."

"So what would you call it?"

"A mistake."

She bent forward, placing her own glass on the coffee table in front of her. "I see," she said. "How did it happen?"

He sighed. "Do you really want to know?"

"I need to know what I'm up against. How did this *mistake* occur?"

He was silent for a long time. "With you gone, with the kids gone, she still brings dinner over." A quick, reassuring gesture with his hands. "Brought. Brought dinner over. Especially when I worked late. We'd talk. When you're the boss, you have few people you can talk to about what's going on at work. She was so far removed from what was going on there. Easy to talk to . . . One night, we had a bottle of wine, and then another . . ." He shrugged, knowing nothing more needed to be said.

Whitney took in the pain of each word and swallowed her grief. "Have you spoken to the children?"

Grayson grabbed his drink and drained it. "Chandler's angry. And Emma is not speaking to me. Always protective of her mother. The press had left them alone for the last week, but now they're back in full force."

"They've been through enough," she said, her words harsh. "They don't deserve this, Grayson. Affairs are harder on the children than the couple."

"Mistake."

"I wish they had Secret Service protection."

He stared into his empty glass. "I know. Me, too. This is my fault. What can I do to make this right?"

She said nothing.

After a while, he indicated with his chin. "What're you reading?"

Whitney glanced at the book on the coffee table, for once, not interested in books. "Another Abraham Lincoln biography. I don't know how much more can be written about the man, but writers always find something."

Lincoln was her favorite president, leading the country during its deadliest war and through its greatest moral and constitutional challenges. She loved reading biographies: Churchill, Thatcher, the Roosevelts, Gandhi, Martin Luther King Jr., Hitler, Gorbachev. She never understood those people who did not like to read; she pitied them for what they were missing. Whitney learned from the mistakes and successes of others. A lifetime wasn't long enough to make all the mistakes yourself.

Grayson placed his highball glass on the end table and stood. "I need to get to the airport. Board meeting tomorrow.

But I needed to see you in person. To talk about this face to face."

Whitney didn't bother to get up. "Lock the front door on your way out."

He hesitated, continuing to search her face, and then left the room. She heard the front door close.

Whitney reached for the bottle and poured a refill.

She grabbed a cigar, cut the cap, and struck a wooden match. Opening one of the large windows facing the street, she sat on the cushioned window seat. She puffed as she stared out into the cool night thinking about how to use Grayson's "mistake" to her political advantage, ignoring the tears streaming down her face.

CHAPTER THIRTY-ONE

Crystal City, Virginia

MY PLACE WAS dark, except for the light emanating from the three computer monitors on my desk. A news report video played on the monitor to my right, reporters shouting questions as the senator left her office building.

"Senator Fairchild, why aren't you speaking out against the person or persons who leaked to the media about your husband's affair?"

"Are you getting a divorce, Senator?"

"Senator, how do you feel?"

"Senator, if you were in a room alone with the other woman, what would you say to her?"

I frowned. Reporters were not my favorite people.

Senator Whitney Fairchild, her posture perfect, stopped. She faced the reporters and the cameras.

"This is a very difficult time for my family and me. We are dealing with a personal situation and would be grateful if you would honor our privacy." She glanced down briefly, before scanning the faces of those around her. "We are all human. We all make mistakes. That's all I'm going to say about this matter."

The senator started to walk away, before turning back.

"Oh, one more thing." Her voice hardened. "Leave my children alone."

She walked to the waiting black car at a brisk pace. She shook her head and waved to the press, her expression unreadable.

God, she's beautiful.

I laughed when I realized what I had just thought. How can you talk to someone in whom you do not believe?

I paused the video, her face turned toward the camera, as she was about to duck into the car. I traced my finger down her forehead, her nose, her lips, and brought it to my lips. I yanked my finger away, surprised.

Her husband was a fool.

After I wiped my finger with the handkerchief I kept on my desk, I pressed play and ignored the rest of the news program. I turned to the center monitor.

My friends had arrived. I found it curious, yes, and a little sad, that conversing with them was the best part of my home life. I felt closer to my online friends, whom I had never met, than to anyone else. But I did not have time to think about that now. I caught up on the conversation. Pittfan, of course, was leading the discussion topic about the affair.

I lurked as the chat continued, waiting a few minutes before typing.

Good evening. I waited for everyone to return the greeting and typed, Entertainment Tonight *is over. We have more important things to discuss. We need to take it up a notch.*

CHAPTER THIRTY-TWO

Washington, DC

WHITNEY BREEZED THROUGH the anteroom of her office suite in the Russell Senate Office Building. Sean, her receptionist and scheduler, stopped typing and grinned.

"Welcome back, Senator."

"Thank you, Sean." She kept walking. "Give me five minutes and then send Landon in, please. Afterward, you and I can go over my schedule."

"Yes, Senator."

She put her purse in the lower right-hand drawer and scanned the top of her desk. She never checked her email first thing. She liked to find her equilibrium before dealing with all the messages that needed an immediate reply and the overwhelming majority that did not. She eyed the briefing books stacked on the right top corner of the desk, in order of priority. Sean had printed out her messages, also in the priority of whom she needed to call back first. She nodded her approval. She had a good team.

She did not think about Grayson.

At the knock on the door, she looked up. Landon stood in the doorway, a smile on his face.

"Come in."

He sat across from her.

She stared at his hair. Someone had taken an ax to it.

He rubbed his buzzed head. "My barber got a little carried away."

She squinted. "It'll grow out. Someday." She picked up some papers and started skimming through them. "Bring me up to speed."

Whitney had been out of the office for a few days on a road show through Michigan, Indiana, and, of course, Ohio. She had told Ted before the campaign began she was not going to stop doing her job even though she was running for president of the United States. During the previous election primary, a congresswoman from the other party missed almost half of the votes that came to the floor and had a two-month stretch when she didn't vote at all. Although Whitney suffered from perpetual jet lag, she flew back to the Hill for every vote. Representing her constituents was important to her. And why she was here.

Landon finished his briefing and left. She thought about the last couple of months and how the media had jumped all over the Graysongate story, the bill that benefited Grayson's business, and the negative impact on her polling numbers. Then, the president's animal cruelty scandal broke—Piggygate—and her poll numbers started to rise again. Finally, her husband's affair had catapulted her numbers through the roof. *What a crazy profession I have chosen.*

She returned to the memorandum in front of her. Another rap on her door.

"Senator," Landon said, a strange expression on his face. "I think you'd better come see this."

She held his gaze and frowned, but followed him into the anteroom. He stopped a few feet from the television where Sean and other members of her staff stood. She refused to have a TV in her office. Sometimes she needed a break from the noise.

The Breaking News flash was crawling across the bottom of the screen. An impressive graphic with the words Talk Show Killer at the upper right hovered next to the commentator's head.

"In an exclusive breaking news story, a person claiming to be the Talk Show Killer sent an email message to this network. Our investigative reporters now believe the murders of conservative blogger Pete Paxson of Houston five years ago, conservative newspaper columnist Taylor LeBlanc of Baton Rouge two years ago, and Pittsburgh conservative radio personality Randy Sells this past January are all related.

"The killer claims to have murdered Randy Sells because conservative talk radio dominates the airwaves and the time has come for moderates and the left to be heard." The pretty anchorwoman, whose hair seemed incapable of moving, glanced down at a sheet of paper and back up to the camera. "This person goes on to state that the public is being brainwashed and likens right-wing radio programs to the Nazi propaganda machine. Until the Federal Communications Commission brings back the Fairness Doctrine or news networks take it upon themselves to present both sides of significant issues, the murders will continue, according to this self-proclaimed killer. We will be reading the full email on the air at the top of the hour. We will also post it on our website, www.msnbc.com. MSNBC will keep you updated on this important story.

"After the break, we'll talk to a panel of experts about how MSNBC is the leader in providing fair and balanced reporting."

The group stood in silence for a few moments. Landon muted the television. Whitney's employees turned to her, studying her reaction. She shook her head.

"This is terrible news." She took in each of her staff members, her eyes resting on Landon.

"My office."

"Yes, Senator."

Sean went back to his desk and resumed working. The other staffers drifted back to their offices.

Landon put the television remote down on a *Roll Call* newspaper on the coffee table and followed Whitney into her office. He closed the door behind him. She sat behind her desk. He remained standing.

She stared at him. "Find out anything you can about the killings and whether they're related."

"Yes, Senator."

"And get a copy of the email."

"Yes, Senator." He stopped at the door and turned. "Do you want this closed?"

"Yes."

She leaned back in her chair and crossed her legs. She abhorred violence. The next thought—she could not help herself; she was a politician after all—was about the impact this news would have on her campaign. Would it help or hurt?

One thing she knew for sure: her husband's affair had become yesterday's news.

CHAPTER THIRTY-THREE

Washington, DC

COLE BRENNAN ENTERED the small, quaint church near the White House. The nave was quiet and empty, except for the lone man sitting in the front row. Cole ignored the beautiful, stained-glass windows he had admired on a previous visit and sauntered down the center aisle. He sat down, a little too close to the man. The man scooted away from him.

"Funny you asked to meet me in a church," the president of the United States said. "When was the last time you were inside one without the cameras present?"

"Ha, ha. Your sense of humor has always been underrated."

"What do you want, Cole?"

"Why didn't you tell me about your animal troubles? Why did I hear about it for the first time on the news?"

President Richard Ellison examined his hands. "I barely remember the incident. It was a long time ago. I was young. Sixteen. The court records were supposed to have been sealed."

"You didn't think it was going to come out? In this day and age? Everything you did from elementary school on is fair game."

"My daddy paid off a lot of people. Most people thought it was my brother, anyway. He was the one always in trouble." Ellison sighed. "There's nothing I can do about it now. If I could go back and change it, I would. It happened. My friends and I were drunk. Out-of-our-minds drunk. I made a stupid, youthful mistake, which I now deeply regret."

Cole laughed. "Save the speech for the cameras. I'm not saying it was a mistake, only you should've told me about it." He leaned back and crossed one ankle over the other and interlocked his hands over his belly. "In high school, my buddies and I talked this crane operator into putting an old Volkswagen Beetle on the roof of the school. The principal freaked out, not knowing how the car got there or how he was going to get it down. I was one of the ones he questioned, of course—I was always up to something—but talked my way out of trouble. I learned from that situation that I can convince anyone of anything, which is why I'm in the profession I am today."

"Fascinating," Ellison snapped. "Shit,"—the word coming out in two syllables—"Cole, I don't have time for—or care about—your glory days. Get to the point of why I'm here."

"You must get out ahead of this Postal Service issue. I set everything up for you. All you need to do is take the ball and cross the goal line."

"You're always telling me what I *must* do. Right now, I have other pressing matters."

"You always have other pressing matters."

The president's voice softened. "This time may be different."

"How so?"

"We've intercepted a threat."

"What kind of threat?"

"Terrorist."

"Where?"

Ellison shrugged, distracted. "That's all I can tell you."

"Have you seen the latest numbers? Your approval rating is down to forty-three percent. The race shouldn't be this close. She's inexperienced and a woman, for God's sake."

"I've seen the numbers. We're fine. Just a blip."

"I can't believe her husband's affair is helping her."

"Did you have something to do with that? The affair?"

Cole sat back, smug. "Like I said, everything from elementary school on is fair game. He should've known we're always watching."

Ellison shook his head in disgust.

"She's showing she's not tough enough to be president," Cole said. "'No comment. No comment.'" He mimicked Whitney. "Anyway, she'll be out of the office for a week once a month."

The president gave him a quizzical expression.

Cole shook his head, as if the president were an idiot. "Her period."

Ellison turned from Cole and said nothing.

The two men remained silent for a long time, lost in their own thoughts. The president stared up at the intricate sculpture of Jesus nailed to the cross. Cole, at the floor.

Cole lifted his head, a slow thoughtful movement. He looked into Ellison's eyes. "Maybe a terrorist attack wouldn't be such a bad thing."

"You're not joking," Ellison said.

"Presidents win elections because of wars and conflicts all

the time. You can demonstrate your leadership skills in our time of need."

"Then I would rather lose this election than hope for an attack that could kill thousands of our people," Ellison said. "What do you know about this serial killer going after conservative talk-show hosts?"

"Nothing much. Why?"

"Because the right-wing extremism of you and your brethren has something to do with it. That's why. The rhetoric has gotten out of hand, and I believe it hurts the party and galvanizes their base."

"Bullshit. Without me, you wouldn't have been nominated, and you wouldn't be where you are today. And don't you forget it."

Ellison gave Cole a sideways glance. "What if there is a serial killer out there? How would your show go on without you?"

The sarcasm wasn't lost on Cole. "There's that sense of humor again."

Ellison leaned forward, about to rise. "Do you remember how we met?"

"No, I don't."

"It was at a fundraiser. You sidled up next to me at a urinal in the restroom. That's when you made your first demand." He laughed without mirth. "Thinking back on it now, what an appropriate place." The president stood. "I'm done taking orders from you, Cole. Go ahead and run."

He walked toward the empty choir chairs and the side door, where his Secret Service detail was waiting.

For once, Cole Brennan had no response.

CHAPTER THIRTY-FOUR

Washington, DC

JADE SAT AT her desk, Christian and Dante hovering behind her. After being alerted by another agent, they watched the MSNBC broadcast on the Internet. Within minutes, the president of the network, at Jade's request, had forwarded her the email in its entirety. CART—the FBI's Computer Analysis and Response Team—was tracing its origins.

The three of them read in silence.

To Whom It May Concern,

Several years ago, a movement swept across this country called "Occupy Wall Street." The people participating in these protests did so for many reasons, but the main reason was to protest the unfairness of America's wealth belonging to the top one percent of the population while the other ninety-nine percent struggled during the Great Recession. The movement was not against capitalism per se, but against a system that was rigged to favor the few. The same could be said for talk radio.

Conservative talk radio controls 76% of the market,

which means a majority of US citizens are hearing one side of the argument on our myriad of complex issues. How is this different from the propaganda machine propagated by Goebbels under Hitler? Our citizens, some of them uneducated, functionally illiterate, or lazy, listen to this propaganda as if it were news. It is not.

There is a lot of big money behind conservative talk radio. The government must regain some control and make sure the media are serving the informational needs of all Americans. Our citizens deserve the right to hear both sides of an argument so they can engage in intelligent discussions and make informed decisions. Some would argue that citizens can just "Change the channel," but since a significant number of talk-radio stations are conservative, finding a liberal talk-radio station is difficult and a moderate one impossible. In addition, what if one does not want to change the channel? What if one wants to receive fair and equitable reporting like the good old days?

The party in power wants to turn back the clock. I agree. Let us do so in the following ways:

1) Restore requirements that broadcasting ownership must include local owners. Talk radio has been ambushed by large group owners holding multiple licenses in different markets. These owners are more likely to air conservative programming;

2) Provide incentives to women and minorities to own broadcasting licenses. Minorities and women are more likely to air liberal or moderate programming; and

3) Bring back the Fairness Doctrine requiring broadcasters to present both sides of controversial issues and give fair and balanced reporting.

If the above suggestions, or something similar, are not implemented immediately, then more conservative talk-show hosts are going to die. And there is nothing the FBI can do to stop me.

Sincerely,

TSK

Jade didn't take her eyes off the screen. "TSK?"

"His initials?" Christian said.

"Or a message like 'tsk, tsk,' as if he were scolding the reader," Dante said. He straightened. "All I know is this is a bunch of liberal B.S."

"What else?" she asked, ignoring Dante.

"Max said the killer has above-average intelligence. That jibes with whoever wrote this email," Christian said. "Check out the style, word choice, and sentence structure."

"I'm not sure how intelligent he is," Jade said, "if he thinks killing radio personalities is the best way to attain what he wants. I need to get this to Max."

She leaned back in her chair. "Let's look at this from a broader perspective. What is he trying to tell us?"

Dante circled around her desk and moved into her field of vision. "More people are going to die."

CHAPTER THIRTY-FIVE

Arlington, Virginia

THAT EVENING, JADE sat on the couch in her living room surrounded by files and papers, her cat, Card, on her lap.

An Earth, Wind & Fire album played on the turntable, the volume low. She paused to listen to the much-needed rain falling outside. This was her favorite room in the house, its hardwood floors in need of polish, the sparse but comfortable espresso-colored furniture, her shelves crammed with books and her precious album collection. She came out of her reverie when a key was inserted into the lock of the front door.

A moment later, Zoe poked her head around the wall that separated the foyer from the living room. "Hey, you. Hard at work, I presume?"

Jade gave her a tired smile. "Of course."

Zoe shook off her raincoat.

Jade did a double take at the clothes Zoe wore on her short, thin body. Skin-tight green leggings, a bright colorful African shirt, and some of the largest earrings Jade had ever seen. "Does that outfit even go together?"

Zoe laughed and held up a bag. "Food!"

"What is it?"

"Healthy takeout. Imagine!"

Jade pretended to whine. "Do we have to?" Zoe was always bugging Jade to improve her eating habits.

"Just because you look healthy doesn't mean you are healthy."

Zoe moved toward the kitchen at the back of the house, and Jade turned her attention back to the file she had been reading. Zoe came out with a tray holding a paper plate with two chicken wraps, a side salad, and a glass of water for Jade. Zoe left and returned with the same meal and a Hoegaarden beer for herself.

"How did you know?" Jade said, setting the file down beside her on one side and the cat on the other.

Zoe scrunched up her face and rolled her eyes. "I know how you are when you're on a case. You forget to eat, call your friends, and do all the other things us mere mortals do."

Jade stood. "Be right back."

She went to the half bathroom in the foyer, washed her hands, and double-checked that Zoe had locked the front door behind her. Jade returned, placing the tray in her lap, and took a bite of the chicken wrap. It was delicious. She realized she had forgotten to eat breakfast. And lunch.

"This is right on time. Thank you. How're things with you?"

"Fine. Busy. The possibility of being a part of helping to elect the first woman president and passage of the ERA has everyone at the office fired up and motivated."

"How's your friend?"

"She's fine. I haven't seen her much, because of work, but we're okay." Zoe paused. "I think." She laughed.

Jade had long ago stopped calling Zoe's partners "girlfriends." Her relationships didn't last long enough. Zoe went through girlfriends like Imelda Marcos went through shoes. Jade, of course, heard the rumors about Zoe and her in college, the conventional wisdom that if you were a woman basketball player, you must be gay. She didn't care about the rumors or what other people said about her. Her business was her own. Jade's only significant relationships in college had been with a basketball, her coach, and her teammates. Zoe was the one person she allowed to get close to her—sort of—and she wasn't going to change that to please others.

"What do you expect?" Zoe continued. "I grew up in a free love, peace, and happiness household with a father named Harry and a mother named Moon. Let's say I didn't have great role models for committed relationships. Anyway, enough about me. I know I can't ask what you're working on, but how's it going?"

"Actually, you may be able to help me with this case."

"Moi?"

"Yes, you. What are the chances of Congress bringing back the Fairness Doctrine?"

"Ah . . . so, that's your case." Zoe put down her wrap and thought for a moment. "Slim. Conservatives and libertarians don't want it back. They say it violates First Amendment rights and that it's an attack on conservative radio."

"Why do we label everyone?"

"Because that's what Americans do. Otherwise, we'd have to listen to each other."

"What about public opinion?"

"According to the latest polls, forty-seven percent of Americans want the Doctrine reinstated, thirty-nine percent don't. Regardless, the public doesn't care enough about the issue. The economy, immigration, health care, and national security are in the forefront of people's minds. Maybe with these killings and the issue getting more exposure, there could be some movement, but I doubt it."

"Did you read the TSK email?"

"Sure, and I can't say I disagree with any of it. You and I talked about this before. The gap between the haves and the have-nots will only get worse, and social unrest will increase as a result. I believe the Great Recession is payback for unbridled greed and capitalism."

"But how do you really feel?" Jade said. They shared a laugh at this.

Zoe finished the rest of her wrap. "You know I belong to this online chat room and we were discussing the email last night."

Jade remembered the chat room Zoe frequented and had a vague recollection of the discussion on the Pittsburgh killing right after she had started her investigation. She did remember their argument; one of the few they had had over the last decade. Jade realized Zoe was still talking.

"—can be intense, but the conversations are exhilarating. I love having discussions with like-minded, intelligent individuals."

Jade smiled at her friend. "I'm sorry. What can be intense?"

"Not what. Who. One of the chat members. Never mind, it's not important. You have more important things on your mind than my online discussions." Zoe got up with her beer and strolled over to the shelves displaying Jade's extensive album collection. "The Bee Gees, Janet Jackson, MJ, George Michael, Lionel Richie . . . I used to make fun of you for buying these old albums and now vinyls are back in. This collection is probably worth a fortune." Zoe shook her head in admiration. She turned to Jade dazzling her with a toothbrush-commercial smile and game-show host voice: "And the most amazing thing of all, they're all in alphabetical order!"

Jade laughed. She was inured to Zoe's teasing about her OCD tendencies.

Zoe reached for a brown journal. "What's this?" Her forefinger tipped the top of the book downward to a thirty-degree angle.

"Don't," Jade said. She hadn't told her best friend about her latest hobby, writing haiku poetry in this Japanese-style journal. The poetry was awful, but writing it brought her peace.

Zoe froze.

They knew each other well. By the tone of Jade's voice, Zoe knew not to disobey her. Jade knew Zoe had to exercise all of her willpower not to open it. Finally, Zoe slid the journal back in its place, turned to pick up their trays, and walked to the kitchen as if their last exchange hadn't happened. When she returned, she said, "I have an idea."

"What?"

"Why don't you meet with Senator Fairchild or at the very least someone from her office? She'd welcome a visit from one of the investigators on the case and may give you more insight into the political angle. I consider her legislative director, Landon Phillips, a friend. Back in the day, we worked together on some campaigns. I can call him with an introduction, if you'd like."

Jade thought about it for less than a second. She didn't need a friend of Zoe's to introduce her; her credentials ensured immediate attention from any senator. But letting Zoe introduce her to Senator Fairchild's legislative director might be a better, less official approach.

"I'd like."

CHAPTER THIRTY-SIX

Washington, DC

THE YOUNG MAN, who had introduced himself as Sean, stepped aside and indicated for Jade to enter.

Senator Whitney Fairchild rose from her chair and walked around her large mahogany desk. Jade's first thought was the camera did not do this woman justice. Despite the touch of sadness in her eyes, she was more beautiful in person than on television and carried herself like royalty. This initial impression was enhanced by the sound of classical music.

Senator Fairchild extended her hand. "Agent Harrington."

"Thank you for seeing me, Senator." Jade paused and listened. "Liszt?"

The senator studied her, surprised. "You're familiar with Franz Liszt?"

"Of course. This must be one of his symphonic poems, *From . . .*"

"*Von der Wiege bis zum Grabe.*"

"Right," Jade said. "*From the Cradle to the Grave.*"

The senator's smile broadened as she guided Jade to one of the guest chairs. "Please have a seat. Would you like anything to drink?"

"No, thank you, Senator. I'm fine." Jade retrieved a notepad and pen, putting her briefcase down on the floor next to her seat.

Seated, the Senator looked into her eyes. "Being an African-American female FBI agent cannot be easy."

Jade tensed, but did not react. How to answer. Somehow Jade knew this wasn't a woman who would accept the company line. That the Bureau was one big, happy family, where everyone was treated fairly regardless of the color of her skin. Yes, there was discrimination within the Bureau. She had to be twice as good as a white man to succeed. Jade held her gaze.

"Some days are more challenging than others."

Senator Whitney Fairchild crossed her legs. "I see. I am impressed by those who make things seem easy. I suspect you are one of those individuals, but believe me, I know what it feels like to be marginalized. Only twenty out of one hundred senators are women, while we make up more than fifty percent of the populace. 'We've come a long way, baby,' but we still need to fight the battle every day."

"Yes, we do."

"And, sometimes," the senator continued, "it is not the men who give us the most trouble, but other women. We always seem to be tearing each other down when we should be building each other up."

Jade liked this woman.

"Besides classical music, what are your other interests?"

"I read. Play basketball. I'm a fourth-degree black belt in Tae Kwon Do and speak fluent Japanese, a language much more helpful in the eighties than it is now. I should have studied Chinese or Arabic." She didn't tell Senator Fairchild about the haiku; her poetry hobby was hers and hers alone.

"You never know. Japan may make a comeback, yet. Nevertheless, I've done my research. Your background is impressive. Perhaps, you'll come work for me someday." At the knock, the senator glanced toward the door. "Ah, there you are. Come in."

Jade turned. A tall, slender, handsome man strode over to her. He extended his hand and smiled. "Hi. I'm Landon Phillips, the Senator's legislative director."

"Special Agent Jade Harrington." She rose; his handshake was warm, firm. Her eyes traveled from his green eyes to his straight white teeth. She remembered her mother's long-ago advice to always date a boy with perfect teeth. "If he takes care of his teeth, he'll take care of you," she would say.

Jade brushed away the thoughts of her mother's romantic guidance and sat down. The senator's eyes shifted from Landon to Jade, a mischievous grin starting to form. Jade needed to start this meeting before the junior senator from Missouri started playing matchmaker. Landon sat in the adjoining guest chair and crossed his long legs in front of him. An electronic tablet rested on his lap.

Jade glanced down at her well-used spiral notepad, the perforations beginning to shoot up through the wire. She had no qualms about doing things old school.

"Landon is being modest," the senator said. "He is my acting chief of staff and will be my liaison with your office. He speaks for me. What can you tell me about the investigation so far?"

Not much. Jade hesitated. She shifted in her chair. "We have composed a pretty good profile of the killer. We believe he is responsible for at least four murders. All the victims have been killed in a similar manner."

"Which was?" Landon asked.

"Some kind of blunt instrument. There is circumstantial evidence linking the cases." The severed tongues were more than circumstantial evidence, but no need to go into that now.

"What kind of circumstantial evidence?" Landon asked.

"I'm not at liberty to say at this time. Senator, what do you think would motivate a person to kill conservative media personalities?"

The senator brought a finger to her lips and removed it.

"As Albert Camus once said, 'There are causes worth dying for, but none worth killing for.' I don't understand why anyone would take the life of someone else for any reason, especially political ideology." The senator glanced down at her watch and back up at Jade. "I'm sorry. I have another appointment. Perhaps, the two of you can continue this conversation. I am sure Landon can give you a lot of good ideas. Excuse me."

The senator grabbed her purse, came around her desk, and shook Jade's hand. "It was a pleasure meeting you. Please keep me posted on your progress." She gave Jade's hand a brief squeeze and smiled. "And keep up the fight."

She left.

Stunned, Jade glanced toward the door and back at Landon. *What was that all about?*

The silence grew between them.

"Perhaps, we can—" Landon's hopeful expression changed when he noticed the look on Jade's face.

CHAPTER THIRTY-SEVEN

Palo Alto, California

WHITNEY SCANNED THE faces of her audience in the elegant ballroom of the Four Seasons in Palo Alto, California. Fifteen hundred people had paid thirty-five thousand dollars each to meet her and listen to her speak. Fifty-two million, five hundred thousand dollars; not bad for a few hours' work. The audience—made up of Silicon Valley billionaires and their families—was still in a frenzy after Beyoncé had finished singing her latest number-one song.

Whitney grinned as she waited for the buzz to die down.

"I should have delivered my speech first."

The crowd laughed.

"Thank you for coming. I know all of you have busy lives and I appreciate your taking the time to join me tonight." She segued into her speech, targeted to this group of technology and social-media entrepreneurs.

Thirty minutes later, she began to wind up her speech. Smiling, she said, "Reducing regulation is not something you typically hear from a Democrat." Her voice softened. "But I believe a president should not be a Democratic president or a

Republican president"—her voice rose—"but the president of the United States of America!"

Someone yelled from the audience. "Preach, Whitney!"

She chuckled and raised her arms to quiet the crowd. The applause was not quite as deafening as for the pop star, but close enough. She'd take it.

"I believe we need a candidate who appeals to the best in us, not the basest in us, if we are to return to our rightful place as the most powerful country in the world that every other country aspires to be."

Whitney glanced down at her notes and back up. She took a sip of water. The smile was gone.

"I would be remiss if I did not address something tonight. A sick individual declared that he or she will kill conservative radio talk-show hosts unless we enact certain legislation." She paused again, thoughtful. "This is not how we resolve differences in our country."

She surveyed the room.

"This nation was founded on the basis that all of us enjoy the right of freedom of speech, a right protected by the First Amendment of the United States Constitution. Even if the speech is racist, sexist, or hateful—distasteful as it may be—it's still protected by this wonderful document.

"As you know, Cole Brennan doesn't say many positive things about me." She smiled and paused. "But he has the *right* not to say positive things about me, and I will defend his right to do so. Evelyn Beatrice Hall once said, 'I disapprove of what you say, but I will defend to the death your right to say it.' As will I.

"Be that as it may, violence never solves anything. If you are displeased with what politicians are doing in Washington, use your voice." Whitney's voice rose as the applause increased in volume. "Use your feet! Use your vote!

"I want to thank you again for joining me tonight. God bless you, and God bless the United States of America."

Every person in the room stood in a rousing standing ovation. Whitney smiled and waved to every area of the room.

She walked across the stage and down the steps for a long night of smiling, shaking hands, small talk, and encouraging these donors to part with even more of their money for her campaign. She happened to glance up. Halfway down the crowded, massive ballroom, a young man in a dark suit and tie leaned against the wall, staring at her. He appeared familiar, but she couldn't recall where she had seen him before. The intensity of his gaze made her uneasy.

She shook the hand of the CEO of a social media company that recently went public, listening to his complaints about the long, arduous initial-public-offering process. While he was speaking, her eyes drifted back to where the young man had been standing.

He was gone.

CHAPTER THIRTY-EIGHT

Washington, DC

"BILL FROM PITTSBURGH is on the line. Go!"

"Hi, Cole. A few months ago, one of the up-and-coming stars of conservative radio was murdered here. Now, I hear there may be other victims, that other conservative commentators have been murdered. How do you feel about that? Are you afraid?"

"First of all, I'm not afraid. You can come after me like a modern-day Braveheart, with an army of dyke Femi-Commies behind you, and you won't shut me up. You can't shut up common sense. You will not shut up conservative talk radio. The movement is bigger than me or any of us good conservatives who spend our time on the radio.

"This is America. Hasn't this TSK ever heard of a thing called freedom of speech? What is he, a Communist? He can't silence everyone. People throughout this country are waking up to how the Socialists have taken over our schools, our government, and our country. We need to be able to speak our minds without watching what we say or worrying that the government is spying on us. Political correctness is polite crap to our political discourse. A person shouldn't be killed because he doesn't buy into the elitist, Orwellian school of thought. I'll bet you ten-to-one the killer is a graduate of one of our esteemed, liberal institutions in which all its students are taught the elitist code of what we should think and when we should think it. So, to answer your question, Bill from Pittsburgh, I'm not afraid of this liberal pansy hiding behind his email. He can only stop me from talking over my dead body."

His high-pitched giggle filled the air.

"Oops, I guess I shouldn't say that anymore, huh?"

❧

Cole Brennan surveyed the dining room and his six children sitting at the oblong table: Cole Jr., Colleen, Madeline, Ryan, Kaitlin, and Ronnie, named after the greatest American president. He smiled to himself at their constant bickering, one-upmanship, and teasing. He had come from a family of six brothers and sisters as well. This was what it meant to be a family. Big families were the backbone of America and the only hope for its future. *We need more of them*, he thought. He should consider doing a show called *Making Babies.* The Femi-Nazis would come out of the woodwork. Cole laughed out loud.

Kaitlin, his eight-going-on-thirty daughter, shot him a stern look. "What's so funny, Dad?"

"Nothing, sweetheart. Thinking about work."

"It's family time, Dad," she said. "No more working."

He turned toward her. "Oops, you're right. How was your day? Let's go around the table."

As each of the kids gave detailed reports of their day of swimming at the pool and playing with their friends, he couldn't help noticing Kaitlin's eyes never left his face. Her expression of disappointment—or distrust?—was palpable.

His gaze moved to his namesake. "Cole Jr.?" Cole never addressed his eldest son as "CJ," the nickname Cole Jr.'s friends had given him.

"Hangin' out," he said, sliding a forkful of green beans into his mouth.

"Football season is almost here," Cole said. "Preseason will be starting soon. Are you ready?"

Cole Jr. put down his fork with too much grace and stole a glance at his mother before staring at the food on his plate.

Cole glanced at Ashley and then back at him. "What is it, son?"

"I don't think I'm going to play football this year."

"Why not?"

His son glanced toward his mother again. He hesitated. A calm expression came over him. He had come to a decision.

"I'm just not into it."

"Not into football?" Cole paused. "Well . . . , okay. You can try out for something else . . . like golf or tennis or lacrosse. I wouldn't even mind if you played soccer." Cole speared a forkful of steak and shoved the morsel into his mouth, proud of his restraint. The old Cole would have forced Junior to play football, a man's sport. An American sport.

"I've been thinking the same thing. Going out for something else, I mean," Cole Jr. said, finally looking at his father. "I want to try out for the glee club."

Cole spit his chewed steak back onto his plate. "What?"

"I can sing, Dad. I can really sing."

Cole glanced at his wife, Ashley. Her serene smile never changed. Cole forced himself to stay calm. *This is a disaster.*

"Say, why don't we go out for a spin in the 'Vette? We can talk about this." Cole collected classic American cars, but his white, 1953 Chevrolet Corvette was his pride and joy.

"I can't, Dad. I'm going to the mall to hang out with my friends and maybe go see a movie."

Something told Cole even if Junior had no plans, he wouldn't want to go.

Cole realized something else. He pushed his plate away. He was no longer hungry. He looked at Ashley.

"Sweetheart, how about another drink?"

ꟹ

Later in bed, Cole lay on his back with his hands under his head staring at the ceiling, thinking. Ashley sat up next to him, leaning back against her pillows, reading the latest Harlan Coben mystery novel. He couldn't remember the last time he read a book for pleasure. He couldn't remember the last time he had read a book, period.

"How's your book?"

"Hard to put down." She laid it on her nightstand, and rolled over and snuggled up close to him, her hand on his chest.

He was grateful to be lying down; it was the only time he didn't need to suck in his stomach. They lay in silence for a few minutes.

"What's wrong?"

He didn't answer.

She raised her head, lines creasing her forehead. "I know you. I know when something's bothering you."

He glanced at her and back up at the ceiling.

"When I was a kid, my mother sang 'I Fall to Pieces' to us

when she was making dinner or trying to get us to fall asleep. She had a beautiful voice. Like an angel. Sounded like Patsy Cline. If I close my eyes and concentrate, I can still hear her." Cole paused. "Can he sing?"

"Like an angel," she answered. When he didn't respond, she continued, "Is it something else? Are you worried about this Talk Show Killer?"

"I thought about running."

"Oh?"

"I've been testing the waters. As a Republican and as a third-party candidate. My advisors say my fans are rabid, but my base is too narrow. I can't win. All I would be is a nuisance to Ellison and distract the party from keeping the White House."

"What else?"

Cole remained silent for a moment. He turned his head to her, his eyes moist.

"I don't want to lose what we have," he said, his voice quiet. "I'm afraid I'm losing my daughter. And my son."

CHAPTER THIRTY-NINE

Washington, DC

FOUR MONTHS AND no progress. Jade stood behind the guest chairs in Ethan Lawson's office, sweating through her white dress shirt because of the heat but trying not to show it. July in Washington, DC, could be brutal. The sweat began emanating from her pores as soon as she walked out of her front door this morning and hadn't stopped.

She wasn't surprised that Ethan asked her to his office first thing. The CART team got back to her with an initial analysis of TSK's email. They believed the sender used a type of software, called Tor, that routes internet traffic over a network of six thousand relays. The routing information for the email and its content were encrypted, preventing the linkage of the origin of the email to its final destination. It also made it difficult to trace a user's location. As a result, CART hadn't been able to tell her much. The FBI analyst promised he would keep trying. The killer's silence did not deceive Jade. He was out there. Plotting.

"What is it, Ethan?" she asked. "I'm late for my own briefing."

Ethan reclined in his chair. "This will only take a minute."

"I need more time."

"You don't even know why I called you in here."

"I know we haven't made a lot of progress, but—" She stopped to hear him out. "What?"

He leaned forward, twirling his wedding ring. His starched, white shirt unwrinkled. His eyes searched hers. "I wanted to tell you that I believe in you."

She had braced herself for a tirade, a rant, something else. When he did not continue, she squelched the gratitude threatening to overcome her. His attitude almost made the situation worse. Now, she couldn't fail.

A "thanks" was all she could manage as she strode out of the room.

❧

The other agents were seated around the table when she arrived for the morning briefing. She didn't apologize for being late; she wasn't much of an apologizer.

"Updates?"

No one spoke.

"Anyone?" she asked. "Christian?"

Her "rock" shook his head and crossed his arms over his chest. "Nothing."

"Pat?"

The older woman shook her head as well. "Still trying on the email. We're coming up empty."

Dante just stared at her.

"I'm sick of this case!" Austin said.

Everyone turned to the rookie agent.

"I've sat at my desk. Day after day. Listening to these stupid radio broadcasts, reading these stupid articles, and they say the same thing over and over again about the same topics. It's enough to drive me crazy."

"Look on the bright side," Dante said. "You might learn something while on the job."

Pat addressed Dante, still staring at her computer. "Oh, is that your secret? Education through talk radio?"

"You'll find something," Jade said to Austin. "You have to find something. All of us, we've got to work harder." An unintentional rise in her voice. "We're not working hard enough. We're not putting enough time in. While we're sitting around failing, he is out there plotting, planning to outsmart us."

Austin sank back in his chair, crossing his arms like Christian, his face flushed. Jade started to continue her pep talk when Max Stover interrupted her.

"Let's take a break, everyone. Except Jade. You stay here."

The rest of the agents shuffled out of the room. Christian, the last to leave, glanced back at her with a concerned expression before closing the door.

Jade stared at her mentor. "He's going to strike again. I can feel it."

Max nodded. "This guy is a bright one. He will kill again unless we stop him. But blaming your staff for the lull in progress isn't going to solve this case."

"I'm not blaming my staff. I was just giving them a pep talk."

Max eyed her. "Then sign me up for a different team."

"Okay . . . , I shouldn't have taken it out on them," she said. She stood and paced. "I've gone over all the evidence. Hundreds of times. We've followed up on every lead. But I'm missing something." She stopped and turned to him. "What am I missing?"

"Patience."

CHAPTER FORTY

Washington, DC

LEAVING THE ANTEROOM for a vote on the Hill, Whitney and Landon stopped in front of the television, which was tuned to MSNBC. The midday host's guests were a woman and a man. The man, Blake Haynes, was a young political analyst at a Rosslyn, Virginia-based progressive think tank and a frequent guest star on the network. The think tank, The American Progressive Council (APC), was a staunch supporter of Whitney's and a major contributor to her campaign and the political action committees that supported her.

Whitney had never met Haynes, but liked the young man's intelligence and prodigious memory, his short gelled hair, and the way he carried himself. She was reminded of the young man who stared at her at the Palo Alto fundraiser. She never found out who he was.

"Wait a minute," she said to Landon. "I want to hear this."

Landon turned up the volume.

"Why are the so-called patriots always the first ones who want to secede from the union?" Haynes asked, in response to the midday host's question. "They're like children who, when they don't get their way, end the game by taking their ball and going home."

Whitney laughed and clapped her hands. "He speaks his mind."

Haynes listened to the next question and glanced up before he spoke.

"As you know and I know, almost all scientists believe in climate change. The only people who refuse to believe it are the intellectual descendants of those who believed the world was flat."

Landon muted the television, as Whitney headed for the door to the hallway. She was still laughing.

⁂

Later that evening, Ted Bowling sat across from Whitney in a conference room at her campaign headquarters.

The door to the outer office opened and closed. Landon entered, coatless, shirt unwrinkled, and still wearing his tie, appearing as if he had arrived for work in the morning rather than a late-night strategy meeting. He always wore blue ties, Bill Clinton's favorite color.

"Hello, Senator," he said. He nodded at Ted. "Ted."

Whitney had recognized Landon's gifts when, as a legislative assistant, he helped her finish a floor speech at the last minute. The speech was well-written and persuasive, and she promoted him on the spot. Since, he had made her work life easier. Some people believed making things appear hard to do made them look good. She knew the best athletes—Michael Jordan, Peyton Manning, pre-scandal Tiger Woods—made things appear easy. Their talent masked the tremendous hard work involved. Landon was like that. He had the ability to distill complex legislation down to an understandable paragraph.

Life as a staffer on the Hill was rarely permanent. Not only did the staffer deal with the uncertainty of a legislator's re-election, the long hours and low pay often led to burnout. Most staffers used these jobs as a stepping stone to political office or the private sector, becoming influential lawyers or lobbyists. Landon, though, was dedicated and loyal to her. She wanted to keep him around for as long as possible.

Landon shook off his black leather briefcase. He removed his electronic tablet and sat down.

To Landon, she said, "Ted and I have been discussing poll numbers—surprise!—and which states I should be spending my time in over the next month."

Ted coughed. "Ohio, Michigan, Indiana, North Carolina, Virginia, and Florida. We're finishing up the TV spots for Ohio and Michigan."

"The public continues to believe," Whitney said, "that our party is weak on certain issues. I want these ads to show I am not weak."

After a silence, Ted said, "I'm on it," confirming to Whitney that he needed to reshoot the ads.

Ted shifted in his chair. "What about the serial killings? Is there some way we can use them to our advantage?"

Landon stopped typing and contemplated Ted with distaste.

"I don't want to be seen as capitalizing on this situation," Whitney said. "Rather, we should focus on condemning violence, sympathizing with the victims' families, and reiterating that freedom of speech is one of the pillars on which our democracy is founded."

Ted raised both of his hands to ward off the vehemence

of her reaction. "Okay, okay, I was just asking. I wouldn't be doing my job if I didn't."

"What else?"

"Nothing. That's it."

After a moment, Whitney said, "I made a decision."

The two men looked at her.

"I have chosen a running mate," she said, "and it's not Senator Paul Sampson."

CHAPTER FORTY-ONE

Detroit, Michigan

A WEEK AFTER THE Republicans monopolized the media and renominated President Richard Ellison in Columbus, Ohio, the Democrats descended on Detroit for their convention. The congregants took over the town: hotel rooms, restaurants, coffee shops, bars. Security was tight; a two-hour wait time—at least—preceded every event.

Inside Joe Louis Arena, the atmosphere was charged. Taking back the White House, a distant dream two years ago, was becoming a possibility. Earlier, Senator Sampson had stirred up the crowd by giving a good pro-Democrats speech, despite not being offered the vice presidency. He did not take the news well when Whitney called him last week. She smiled when his speech concluded, realizing he failed to mention her, the Democratic nominee for president. Touché.

Whitney waited in the wings as her future running mate concluded his speech and introduced her. When her name was called, she walked out and opened her arms to accept a hug from the Democratic vice-presidential candidate, Xavier "Xavi" Fernandez, the Independent governor from Florida. They stood together, facing the audience, one arm around the waist of the other. The other arm extended, each hand in a slow, royal wave. He gave her a slight kiss on the cheek and walked off the stage.

Whitney refrained from wiping her cheek, as she strode to the podium. She scanned the audience: different faces, different skin tones, different hairstyles, different modes of dress, different sexualities, different genders. America. The applause would not cease. She said thank you many times to quiet the crowd, a trick she learned from biographies about the Kennedys. The applause subsided.

She smiled.

"Is this a party or what?"

The wild cheers started up again and she clapped her hands once, laughing. She was enjoying this.

❧

After Whitney accepted the Democratic nomination with humility and grace, her husband, Grayson, and their two children, Chandler and Emma, joined her on stage, along with Xavi, his wife, and their four children.

She had not forgiven Grayson. But for the sake of the election, she was "standing by her man." She focused on smiling instead of cringing, his hand on her hip an unwelcome weight instead of a comfort.

The crowd was a sea of American flags, Our America, Our Future signs, and tons of confetti. "Celebration" by Kool and the Gang blasted from the speakers. The candidates and their families moved and clapped to the music.

Back stage, television reporters interviewed past and current members of the Democratic Party: senators, representatives, cabinet members, mayors, governors. Whitney was surrounded by her Secret Service team, including her new shadow, Josh

McPherson, his brown, bald dome glistening under the lights. She heard snippets of the interviews. Her party was staying on message for once.

As she passed a male reporter interviewing Ted, the reporter turned. He appeared stunned. Whitney slowed and stopped in front of him. He continued to stare. She had always wanted to meet him.

Whitney held out her hand. "Hello."

The television political analyst, Blake Haynes, stared at a spot up and to the right of her head. He stammered a "hello" and took her left hand in his, a belated gesture.

She smiled, trying to put the young man at ease. "I wanted to say how much I admire your work. I'm a big fan."

His eyes widened. "Thank you. I admire your work as well."

Whitney laughed with delight. The self-assured man she had seen on television had returned. He offered her a charming smile. "Seriously, I'm a huge supporter. Since we admire each other so much, perhaps you'll let me interview you on MSNBC. All softballs I promise."

"In that case, I am sure it can be arranged. Call my press secretary."

He extended his hand. "One day I hope to be an FOW."

She looked at him quizzically.

"Friend of Whitney," he said.

Whitney smiled and shook his hand. She left him, and moved on to shake the hands of supporters in a line that had formed in her path.

She attended the after-party at a popular restaurant in downtown Detroit, occasionally thinking about Blake Haynes and wondering why she had such a strong affinity for the young man.

CHAPTER FORTY-TWO

Washington, DC

THE PHONE RANG.

"Harrington."

"Uh . . . Agent Harrington. This is Landon Phillips from Senator Fairchild's office."

"Yes . . ."

"I was wondering if you'd like to go to dinner with me."

"Now's not a good time. I'm sort of . . . busy."

"I know. I thought you may need a break."

"I can't afford the time."

"We could discuss motives. I can provide a different perspective." She remained silent, so he continued. "You have to eat sometime, right?"

The offer was tempting. Perhaps talking to someone outside the case with a different perspective could generate new ideas.

"Right?" he asked, again.

She paused for another moment and then made a decision. "There's a restaurant across the street from my office called Social Revolution. I'll meet you at seven. I can give you a half an hour."

"I'll be there."

She hung up. She wondered whether having dinner with him was a good idea.

⁂

Landon sat at a booth in the back of the walnut-paneled restaurant, away from the other patrons. The lights were dim. Jade strode in his direction and stood next to him. He looked up at her, a smile starting to form.

"Is this all right?" he asked.

She didn't move. "Do you mind?"

He gave her a blank stare before grinning. "Ah, I get it. I saw *The Godfather*." He got up and motioned for her to sit in the vacated seat. He sat across from her, his back to the front door. He surveyed the restaurant and then the menu. "'Bi-partisan burgers,' 'The Lobbyist,' 'The POTUS,' 'The Bail Out,' and my favorite, 'The Balanced Budget-Sorry, we couldn't agree on contents. Please build your own.' I love this place." He glanced over at her. "What do you usually eat here?"

She straightened her silverware. "The Laissez-Faire. A burger with smoked bacon, cheddar cheese, and barbecue sauce."

He closed his menu. "A philosophy I agree with fiscally, but not socially. I'll get it anyway."

A waitress came to the table to take their order.

Jade spoke first. "Two Laissez-Faires, a Pepsi, and he'll have a—" She eyed Landon.

Amused, he said, "One of your craft beers. Something dark." The waitress left. "I've never had a woman order for me before." He paused. "I think I like it."

She smiled, but said nothing.

After a few moments, Landon said, "My sister played basketball, too. Do you still play?"

"Was she any good?"

"Pretty good. She got a free ride to a D-One school. So, as far as my parents were concerned, good enough."

"Did you play?"

He looked at his beer with regret. "Nah." He smiled at her, sheepish. "I sucked."

"Did you always want a career in politics?"

"Pretty much. My father was CIA, so I always thought I would follow in his footsteps. After a former president—who shall remain nameless—stole the election, I decided to go into politics instead. At the time, I wanted to change the system that allowed that to happen."

"You said, 'at the time.' You no longer feel that way?"

"Most days, no, but I'm going to keep trying."

"So what do you do?"

"Ha! It may be easier to describe what I don't do. My title is legislative director, but I act as Senator Fairchild's chief of staff. I help set her legislative agenda and priorities, develop strategies to help them pass, and evaluate their political outcomes. I manage the staff of assistants and correspondents and work with counsel to draft bills."

"Sounds like a lot of work."

"It is, but I love it."

The waitress brought their food and they began to eat.

"What's up with the pink wristband?"

He set his burger down, fingering the band.

"It says 'Strength,' for breast cancer awareness." He extended his arm across the table to show her. "My mother had breast cancer when I was in college." He noticed her expression.

"No . . . she survived, but I saw the courage and strength she demonstrated to beat the disease. I've worn this ever since."

"She must be quite a lady."

"She is. She's my hero. Her illness forced me to grow up fast." He took a bite of his burger and sipped his beer. "But we didn't meet here to talk about me. I've thought a lot about your case. Any leads?"

"Not many."

He clasped the beer mug in both hands. "Citizens on both ends of the political spectrum are upset about the direction of our country. The reason Senator Fairchild is so passionate about winning is she believes we must come together, if we want to remain a superpower. To quote Abraham Lincoln, 'A house divided against itself cannot stand.'" He chuckled.

"What's so funny?" Jade asked.

"I'm starting to sound like the senator. She's always quoting political figures. Anyway, I believe the two-party system has outlived its usefulness. It panders to the extremists in both parties and to special interests. Politicians no longer govern."

"What does this guy hope to accomplish?" she asked. "Does he really believe Congress will pass legislation to prevent further death?"

"He's delusional if he does. Then again, he may not want Congress to do anything. If he's true to his word, this will force him to continue killing conservative talk-show hosts. That may be what he wants. For him, it's a win-win."

"Good point," Jade said. "Why taunt us?"

Landon paused, trying to catch up with Jade's train of thought. "Ah . . . the email. Beats me. Death wish? Hates authority? Had a run in with the FBI? Thinks the FBI is out to get him?" He laughed. "Well, I guess the FBI is out to get him now. He also may be Machiavellian. The end justifies the means and all that."

"How so?"

"He'll do whatever it takes to save the country or save democracy or purify the country of those filled with hate or intolerance or all the above. He may believe he's the only one who can save us."

"That's a lot of responsibility for one person."

They fell silent. The waitress cleared their plates away, refilled Jade's Pepsi and brought Landon another beer.

"Given the killer's liberal politics," he said, "have you checked out blogs and op-ed pages written by liberal thinkers?"

"I hadn't thought of that." She made a mental note to check it out.

Jade and Landon lingered in front of the restaurant. A man on the street corner played the drums on several plastic buckets and a big overturned trash can. They stood watching him, listening to the reggae and African mix.

"He's pretty good," Landon said.

"We owe him a dollar," Jade said.

"Owe him?"

"Yeah. If a street performer is good enough to make you stop, you at least owe him or her a dollar."

Landon extracted a bill from his pocket. A five.

"He must be worth it," he said. He sauntered the ten yards to the near-full jar and returned. "I guess a lot of people stopped."

"Do you play an instrument?" Jade asked.

"I play a little guitar."

She nodded her head to the beat. "His music reminds me of my best friend."

"Who's your best friend?"

"Zoe."

"Zoe? First name only? Like Beyoncé, Rihanna, and Adele? Zoe and I worked together on several of Senator Fairchild's campaigns. She's a trip."

Jade nodded. No need to mention she already knew that. Zoe had given her Landon's phone number, but she hadn't used it. She'd called Fairchild's office directly. "I need to go."

"I know."

"Thanks for dinner."

"You're welcome. Maybe I can play for you sometime."

She eyed him with a quizzical expression.

"The guitar."

"Oh. Maybe. Goodbye." She turned toward her building.

"Wait!" He touched her arm. "Let me walk you."

Jade scowled, feeling the strength of his grip on her forearm. "I'm an FBI agent. I can take care of myself. Besides, it's across the street." She pointed to the employee entrance.

"Well, I'm a legislative aide and I would like to accompany you across the street."

She smiled at the spark in his eye. He was charming. And handsome. She checked her watch. Their thirty-minute dinner had lasted two hours. He offered her his arm. She peered at it and back at him.

"Thanks, but I got it."

A shadow of disappointment passed over his face.

Not her problem.

She crossed Ninth Street without looking back.

CHAPTER FORTY-THREE

Washington, DC

JADE HARRINGTON ENTERED the conference room for the task force's morning briefing.

"Kramer is the best QB prospect since RG3," Austin Miller said. "He runs like a running back."

By the earnestness of his expression as he spoke, Jade surmised they could only be chattering about the Redskins.

Christian, seated across from Austin, crossed his arms. "He throws like Billy Kilmer." He would know. Christian was an amateur Redskins historian and knew everything about the 1970s quarterback who led the franchise to its first Super Bowl. He knew the team's history, even as far back as when it was called the Boston Braves. "Start him on your fantasy football team, if you're so confident about his ability. I'll gladly take your money."

Jade laid her folders on the table, but remained standing. "No one understands better than I the importance of the Redskins and winning our fantasy football league, but I need to interrupt this discussion for something of equal importance. I received a phone call from the Pittsburgh PD."

She had their attention. Christian, Austin, Max, Pat, and

Dante stared at her, tense and expectant. Dante lowered the front two legs of his chair to the floor.

"We have a match. The hair located at the scene in Pittsburgh where Randy Sells was murdered matches the hair found on Taylor LeBlanc, the victim in Baton Rouge. Neither hair belonged to the victim."

Christian and Austin pumped their fists and said "Yes!" The same reaction Jade had made at her desk, when she heard the news a few minutes ago. They now had conclusive evidence two of the cases were connected. A small moment of triumph.

It didn't last.

There was a knock on the door. A male agent poked his head in and pointed at the blank projection screen. "Turn it on. Shakespeare struck again."

❧

One advantage of having a rookie on her task force: Jade had someone to go out and get lunch for her. The half-eaten Italian sub heaped with meat Austin had brought her lay next to her keyboard. Normally a bottomless pit, she was so pumped up now she couldn't eat. Almost. She sipped a Pepsi through a straw as she stared at her computer monitor, the latest email from TSK taking up the entire screen.

To Whom It May Concern,

I am disappointed. In my last email, I had asked politely for new legislation to address the monopoly of conservative talk radio in this country. To fill the airwaves with an equal share of inclusiveness and tolerance and equality, not hate. An ideology of tolerance that brings us together, not divides us. I want to be a part of an ideology that is greater than the sum of its parts rather than one of divisiveness. How about you?

Perhaps not. I have seen no evidence of pending legislation or discussions taking place within Congress regarding the issue of balance and fairness on the airwaves. Our government is not taking me seriously, so, as the old saying goes, if you want something done right, you must do it yourself.

There will be another murder.

To my clueless friends at the FBI, I shall give you a clue this time. Just one. Within the next week, a conservative talk-show host on the West Coast will be killed.

My hope is that this death will bring the much-needed attention to the issue of fairness, and facilitate discussion in our august halls of Congress to help us build a bridge to a better, more balanced dissemination of information in the future.

Sincerely,

TSK

P.S. FBI, I may bump into you on the West Coast. Catch me, if you can.

She wondered about a person driven to kill because of

ideology. An ideology of tolerance. How much sense did that make? She would have laughed at the hypocrisy, if the stakes weren't so high.

Jade's mood darkened.

What does he gain from taunting us? More exposure? Does he want to be caught? Is he one of us?

Why did she just think that?

She read the email again and sat back in her chair to think.

The tingle along her arms compelled her to look up from her monitor. Austin stood in her office doorway, his eyes shining.

"What is it?" Jade asked.

Although he seemed ready to burst if he didn't tell her, instead, he said, "You're going to want to listen to this."

≈

The CONFAB task force was back in the conference room. The group waited, restless, as Austin hooked up a laptop to two speakers.

"I've listened to hundreds of recordings." He glanced over at Jade. "I'm not sure what I ever did to you, but this was the worst assignment you could've ever given me."

Jade smiled, but said nothing, not bothering to hide her impatience.

"After a while," Austin continued, "I recognized a pattern by one caller whose vocabulary and speech were similar to TSK's writings." He paused. "And the same caller's voice talked to more than one of the victims."

The other agents glanced at each other, the tension in the room building the longer they waited.

Jade started to pace. "Get on with it, Austin."

Austin paused one more time for dramatic effect. "I heard the same voice today."

Christian sat forward in his seat. Austin began the recording and adjusted the volume.

"The Fairness Doctrine . . . are you kidding me?" asked a deep voice, born for radio.

"Yes. Why not?" asked the caller.

"Because we don't need it, you moron. If someone wants to listen to the other side, he can change the channel. I will never talk about liberalism on my show. My listeners don't want to hear about fantasy land. They want to hear about the real world. And this . . . TSK . . . wants minorities and women to own more broadcasting licenses? Haven't we done the affirmative-action thing? Haven't grievances been redressed enough? Minorities are already given too many breaks."

Silence, then: "You have no clue, you ignorant bigot, and no idea what it's like to be a minority in this country. You deserve to die."

Jade tensed and glanced at Austin. He was not trying to suppress the smile on his face.

"Oh, yeah? Am I talking to TSK? Hello? Hello?" The commentator's voice seemed to move away from the microphone. "Did we lose him?" A pause. "I guess we lost him. Shit. I hope I'm not next." The commentator laughed. A nervous laugh. He spoke into the microphone. "Well, uh, we're going to take a commercial break. Be right back."

Austin clicked off the recording. The room was silent.

"Could he be a minority?" Jade questioned Max, doubt evident in her voice.

"He doesn't sound black," Dante said.

"What does that mean?" Jade asked.

"You know . . ."

"No, I don't."

"It would be an unusual profile for this type of case," Max said, breaking the tension, "but, at this point, we can't afford to rule anything out."

"What station?" Jade asked.

"KSFC in San Francisco," Austin replied.

She turned to him. "This is good work."

He beamed.

Dante threw a sidelong glance at Jade. "West Coast."

She read a printed copy of the email again and sat up straighter.

"Last line . . . 'Build a bridge?' Could he be talking about the Bay Bridge?" She turned to Max. "Could it be that easy?"

Max shook his head. "I believe our UNSUB is too intelligent for that."

Christian shrugged. "I think we should check it out."

Jade turned to Dante. "Any luck with the yearbook photo?"

Dante's cheeks reddened. He shook his head. Under his breath, he said, "I think it's a dead end."

Jade wondered how hard he had tried.

Pat said, under her breath, "So's your love life, but you keep trying, don't you?"

"We don't have any other leads," Christian said. "Let's go for it. What do we have to lose?"

CHAPTER FORTY-FOUR

San Francisco, California

THE KSFC OFFICES were located in a gleaming glass skyscraper in the high-rent district of San Francisco. It was night. Jade, Christian, Max, Pat, Austin, and Dante were crowded in a van parked a block down the street, a computer repair company logo on its outside paneling. Monitors displayed multiple views of the intersecting streets in front of the building, the parking garage, and different areas of the radio station.

Arriving two nights ago, they had met with a team from the San Francisco Police Department. Men and women from the department were all around them outside now, dressed as businesspeople, tourists, and the homeless. Jade couldn't distinguish the cops from the civilians.

She had interviewed—twice—the radio commentator, Billy Stone, whose voice she had listened to on the audio recording. Although shaken, he agreed to continue his normal daily routine in the hope the killer would make an attempt on his life.

So far, nothing had happened.

MSNBC had not received another email from TSK.

Jade peered at her oversized, platinum watch. The talk-show host was wrapping up his broadcast. She scanned the monitors again. Nothing. Several people walked down the street, but they all seemed purposeful, with somewhere to go. More important, they strode by or away from the building.

"I don't like this," Max said, glancing at Jade. "I think he's sent us on a wild-goose chase."

Before Jade could respond, her radio crackled.

"I may have something. Parking garage. Second floor." Silence for a few minutes. "Our man just came out the door. Another man is walking toward him. I'm on it."

More silence. A grunt. Then, "Got him."

Jade, Christian, Austin, and Dante jumped out of the computer repair van, running, their FBI jackets flapping behind them with the wind. Passersby stopped and stared.

The team flashed their badges to the security guard in the lobby as they ran toward the stairs.

Jade's stomach clenched, uneasy. "I think Max is right. Something's wrong."

Right behind her, Christian said, "What?"

"Every crime, so far, has been in a different location: parking lot, alley, bedroom, parking garage. This one is like Houston."

From behind both of them, Dante said, "You're overthinking it. Sometimes, it is what it is."

Jade didn't turn around but kept running.

"With this guy?" Jade asked. "I don't think so."

They burst through a door to the garage's second floor, guns drawn but lowered as they ran. A cop squatted with his knee on the back of a prone man, struggling to handcuff him.

A few police officers surrounded him, guns leveled on the suspect. Jade, Dante, Austin, and Christian rushed up to them.

Jade stopped a couple of feet away, the officer subduing the man at last.

The suspect peered up at her and grinned.

Her shoulders dropped. “Shit.”

This kid appeared too young to be the mastermind of the TSK killings. Jade would go through the interrogation process, but she knew what they would determine.

They had the wrong man.

CHAPTER FORTY-FIVE

Washington, DC

HIS PRODUCER INDICATED the "Go" signal.

"Well, well, well . . . I would like to introduce to my audience my special guest: the Democratic nominee for the presidency of the United States, Senator Whitney Fairchild. Whitney, welcome."

"Thank you, Cole, it's good to be here, and, please, call me 'Senator' or 'Senator Fairchild.'"

"I stand corrected. Now, I must tell you, little lady, I do respect the fact that you crossed enemy lines for this interview."

"Well, Cole, presidential elections are important and I believe in fairness. Your listeners have the right to hear both sides of the issues in order to make better and informed decisions."

"Ouch. Nice plug for the Fairness Doctrine, but many conservatives would argue the mainstream media is already too liberal."

Senator Fairchild smiled. "Whom did we blame everything on before the media? Do you remember?"

Cole understood why women loved her. Men, too. She

was more attractive in person. So much class. Aristocratic. Cole would play up her elitism. His audience hated that.

"Now you're the confirmed nominee, how does that change your campaign?"

"It doesn't. Our focus has always been on the economy, education, and equal rights for women."

"Whitney, come on now. Haven't you won equal rights, already? Isn't that what the Title IX business was all about?"

"You would think. But we still do not have a federal law providing equal rights for women. And, now, women are re-fighting the battles we won forty years ago. Unlike other civil rights—for example, gay rights—women's rights are regressing instead of progressing. And, Cole, please call me 'Senator Fairchild.'"

"You're talking about abortion."

"Over the last decade, the opposing party proposed numerous bills that blocked funding for critical women's reproductive health, particularly for low-income women. A woman's access to a safe abortion should not depend on her ZIP code. But the issue is not only about a woman's right to choose, but equal pay, economic and educational opportunities for poor women and women of color, and protection against gender-based violence. But, yes, more women need to be in the room when women's health issues are discussed."

"We aren't going to agree on this one. I'm not qualified to discuss women's health issues with you, so I won't even try."

Senator Whitney Fairchild smiled. "Exactly."

Cole realized—too late—he lost the point. He needed to be more careful with this woman. "Let's move on to China."

The senator nodded. "As you wish."

"China slowed down on the amount of our debt it's

buying. Are you concerned, and, if so, what should we do about it?"

"'China is a sleeping lion. Let her sleep, for when she wakes she will shake the world.'"

Cole stared at her, perplexed. "Huh?"

"Napoleon said that." She smiled. "Of course, I am concerned. China had been a net buyer of US treasuries for a long time and is a significant and important trading partner of the United States. We're fortunate other countries took up the purchasing slack—namely, Japan—but the current situation is a warning about something we all realize. We must become more self-reliant."

"Finally, something we can agree on, my friend." Cole decided to switch topics, a tactic he used to rattle his interviewees. "Whit— Senator, tell me about your husband's affair."

The senator shook her head, pursed her lips, and wagged her index finger at him. "My husband made a mistake. And I don't believe we are friends, Cole."

"And a neighbor, of all people. Gives new meaning to the phrase 'borrowing a cup of sugar.'"

Senator Fairchild threw her head back and laughed. She had a pleasant laugh. "That's a good one."

"Uh, yeah." This woman couldn't be rattled. "You went to one of those liberal, Eastern schools—"

"I attended Northwestern undergrad and Harvard Law School, yes."

"—and you and your husband are extremely wealthy. How can you possibly identify with the struggles of the middle class in this country?"

"Because I know what's it's like to struggle. I grew up in a middle-class family in a small town in Missouri. My father was an insurance agent who owned his own small business; my mom was his office manager. They struggled to make ends meet for my two brothers and me. What I love about my party, Cole, is we are always fighting for the middle class and our ability to empathize. I don't need to be poor to want to raise the minimum wage to give people the opportunity to live a better life."

Walked into that one. Cole decided to change tack again. "What are your thoughts on TSK, the Talk Show Killer?"

"I think his actions are deplorable."

"Even though he seems to spout the same liberal B.S. you do?"

"I wouldn't describe my beliefs as B.S., but his acts are deplorable just the same and stem from the mind of a sick individual. Fairness on the airwaves and social equity are important issues and ones I care deeply about, but instead of killing conservative talk-show hosts, I ran for president."

Good answer. The interview ran for ten more minutes. After he signed off, he leaned back, tired, like a boxer who had been pummeled into the ropes for fifteen rounds. Still standing but barely. He smiled at her in spite of himself.

"I'm still going to do everything in my power to defeat your candidacy."

The senator smiled back. "And I am still going to do everything in my power to not let you."

The Democratic nominee picked up her purse and left the studio. Cole hesitated before turning to glance over his shoulder out the studio window into the hallway.

To his dismay, his smiling employees were lining up to shake her hand and take selfies with her.

CHAPTER FORTY-SIX

San Francisco, California

JADE SAT NEXT to Christian in an interrogation room at the local FBI office. Dante, Pat, Max, and Austin observed them through the one-way mirror. After confirming that the suspect in custody was not TSK, Jade had sent local agents to the home of Billy Stone, the San Francisco talk-show host, to make sure the incident in the garage hadn't been a diversion.

The man sitting across from them did not seem nervous.

She stated the date, case number, and her identification information. "Please state your name for the record."

"Kevin. Kevin Burke."

"So, Kevin, tell me, what were you doing in that garage?"

Kevin slouched in his chair, his arms folded across his slender chest. Dressed in all black down to his Chuck Taylor sneakers, he stared at her, but said nothing.

A criminal background check hadn't revealed much. Kevin was arrested six years ago for shoplifting a six-pack of Red Bull.

"Kevin, you could be in a lot of trouble unless you tell us what you know."

Kevin shrugged. "Walking."

She started to rise.

Christian stopped taking notes of the interview and put a hand on her arm. He asked, "Why did you happen to be walking in that garage at that particular time of night?"

"I was hoping to bump into the radio guy."

"Why?" Jade asked.

"I don't know."

"What do you mean you don't know?"

"I was supposed to bump into him."

"And then what?"

Kevin sat up. "Okay. Look. This guy I met on the street gave me fifty bucks to wait for the radio guy to get off work. All right? He told me to bump into him literally—the guy said he would be watching me—and afterward, we were to meet at the Starbucks on the corner and he would give me another fifty." Kevin slouched again. "Man . . . I guess this means I won't be getting the rest of my money."

"Which Starbucks?" Jade asked, knowing with a sinking feeling that there was one on every corner in San Francisco. Sometimes two.

Kevin told them.

Without a word from her, Christian left the room to send someone to check out the Starbucks. It was pointless. If TSK had ever been there, he was long gone. "What did the guy look like?"

Kevin surveyed the bare conference-room walls. Finding nowhere else to rest his eyes, he stared at Jade. "What's in it for me?"

"Reduced jail time. What did he look like?"

"I can go to jail for this?"

Jade said nothing. The silence stretched for a few minutes. She had learned over the years that sometimes silence was the best way to make someone talk. A lot of people hated silence. She did not.

Her patience was rewarded.

"White guy. Blond, brown hair, but I'm not sure. He was wearing a baseball hat. Sunglasses even though it was starting to get dark."

"Big guy? Little guy?"

"He was taller than me."

"I want you to work with a sketch artist to come up with a facial composite of him."

"If I help you, will you help me stay out of jail?"

Jade stood. "We'll see."

Kevin laughed.

This guy bugged her. "What's so amusing?"

"He told me I might get a visit from you, but he said not to sweat it. The FBI doesn't have a clue."

☙

Two agents led Kevin away. Dante, Christian, and the rest of the task force came into the room, along with some local agents. Jade leaned back in her chair staring at the ceiling. She had been wearing the same gray pantsuit for two days. She craved a shower, and they needed to head to the airport soon. But she didn't want to get up from this chair. She was drained: from the interrogation, from this case, from failing.

She lifted her head and turned to Max. "Well?"

Before Max had a chance to answer, Dante said, "You're not ready, yet. You don't have the experience to run a major investigation like this."

Jade counted to ten.

Before she finished counting, Dante continued, "You're

always so damn impulsive. When are you going to start thinking before you act?"

Christian slashed his forearm down like a traffic cop.

"That's enough, Dante."

"Why can't she defend herself?" Dante said. "Because she's a woman?"

Jade banged both hands on the table.

Everyone froze.

The rage, building within her for months, exploded. "I'm impulsive? Weren't you the one to suggest the West Coast? What is it with you? Is this all because I wouldn't go out with you when I first arrived at the Bureau? Is it because others are starting to realize you don't have what it takes?"

His eyes hardened. "Well, at least I didn't need affirmative action to get into the Bureau."

That was a lie. At the FBI Academy in Quantico, Jade recorded some of the highest scores ever for a woman. Her proficiency levels for firearms broke Academy records for both genders. A rare breed at the FBI—women accounted for nineteen percent of special agents, black women, a paltry one percent—everything she had accomplished, she had earned.

Her face burned. She didn't hesitate. She took two quick steps toward Dante and punched him in the face. The pain in her hand barely registered as Dante went down hard. He touched his nose and stared at the blood on his fingers. He popped back up and came after her. Christian sliced between them, his body as immovable as an oak tree. The other agents, taken aback at first, recovered and grabbed Dante. Breathing hard, Jade and Dante glared at each other.

"Shit, you two," Christian said. "Let's tone it down."

Jade would have smiled if she weren't enraged. Christian never cussed.

Christian faced her. "We're all frustrated."

Still pushing against Christian, she lifted a finger and pointed at Dante. "You crossed a line. You were wrong for that."

Dante's face was flushed, more from embarrassment at being decked by a woman in front of his peers than exertion. A smile played at his lips.

"Have you ever thought, Ms. Thing, that *you're* wrong for this?" He raised his arms to take in the interrogation room, the building, the Bureau.

Her life.

CHAPTER FORTY-SEVEN

Washington, DC

BACK IN HER office after the August recess, Whitney paused from catching up on her paperwork to enjoy the view outside her window. Hill staffers strode along the sidewalk to and from the Capitol. The tree leaves were still in full bloom.

She turned at the knock on her door.

Landon stood in the doorway.

"Yes, Landon?"

"I have something for you."

He crossed the room and handed her a slim, gift-wrapped package. He cocked his head, smiled. "Happy Birthday."

"You remembered."

"Of course. It's a little late, though."

She started to open it.

He raised his hand. "Wait! You can't open it until after the election."

"Then wouldn't it be an election present?"

She flipped the package back and forth, eyeing the note stating what he had just said. By the weight and feel of it, she could tell it was a book.

"I'm intrigued," she said and placed the book at the corner of the desk. "Sit down. We need to start prepping for the debate."

CHAPTER FORTY-EIGHT

Arlington, Virginia

JADE STEADIED HER hand and sighted her target, the outline of a man fifty yards away. She slowed her breathing. A calmness came over her. She stopped breathing and fired. She exhaled.

Fall was her favorite time of the year in Virginia. The days of ninety-degree-plus temperatures had finally abated. In college, however, she dreaded fall and the onset of pre-season, when all her basketball team did was run sprints and long distances in preparation for the upcoming season. She could run all day on the court, but believed running should be a means to an end and not an end unto itself. Like shopping.

A tingling sensation slinked down the back of her neck. Someone was watching her. She turned. Max. She removed her earplugs.

He gave her what she took for a smile.

"When you weren't at the basketball court or the dojang, I thought I might find you here."

"You should have been a detective."

"Must have missed my calling. Nice shot."

She glanced at the target and shrugged. She put the

earplugs back in, set herself, and went through her breathing ritual again. She fired five more times.

Max pushed off the wall he had been leaning against and moved toward her. He stepped across her to tap the SmartPad. She lifted her safety goggles, removed her earplugs again, and shook out her hair.

The target stopped about fifteen feet away. Six shots. All through the heart.

Max smile-grimaced again.

"Remind me never to make you mad."

She tried not to smile but failed. "I'll try."

He waited.

She scowled and gazed down at her .40 Glock 23, running her hand along the barrel. "I lost it."

"Yep."

"I let him get to me," she said, smoothing the top of her hair. "I'm so sick of his little comments."

"Dante takes pleasure in getting to you. You played right into his hands. But that's not where you lost it."

Jade avoided Max's eyes and said nothing. She knew what was coming.

"That interview. It wasn't like you. You didn't even try to build a rapport with the subject."

"The killer is going to strike again. Soon."

"Which is why you need to get your act together. Forget about Dante and focus on what's most important. The case. You don't always need to be in 'prove' mode. You don't need to prove yourself anymore. To anyone. Just because you ask for help, doesn't mean you're not in control. You're the best. Act like you've been there before."

"My college coach used to say that all the time."

"You're the only person I know who doesn't root for the underdog. You always want the best team to win."

"I like to win. What more can I say?" She glanced around the range and back at Max. "This guy is always one step ahead of me."

"He's one step ahead of *us.*"

Max touched her chin, forcing her eyes to meet his. "Jade, you're a beautiful, strong, intelligent, and amazing woman."

She tried to move her head, but he held firm.

He continued, his voice soft. "You're no longer the bullied, overweight kid with glasses."

After a moment, he let go of her chin. She stepped back from him and pushed the button to send the target back out.

Max started to walk away, but stopped and turned. "Leave some targets for the other shooters, okay?"

He hesitated, and left. She didn't watch him go.

Her phone vibrated against her hip. She answered.

"You can't let Dante bother you," Ethan said, without preamble.

"What is it, Dante Day?"

"What?"

"Never mind. Ethan, I can't work with him."

"He's off the task force."

"He undermines my authority. He creates dissension. I don't trust . . . Wait . . . What did you say?"

"He's off. I've re-assigned him."

"Just like that?"

"Just like that," he said. "Now, there's something I want you to do for me."

Wary, Jade said, "What?"

"Relax." He hung up.

She reinserted the earplugs and pushed the goggles back down.

Jade sighted the target, telling herself it was wrong to pretend it was Dante. She held her breath and fired. She kept firing until the chamber was empty.

She didn't need to bring the target closer. All the shots went straight through the heart.

This was how she relaxed.

CHAPTER FORTY-NINE

Arlington, Virginia

EARLY ON A Saturday morning, Jade and Landon strolled through the park near her house. She realized others had had the same idea. With the high humidity of summer finally breaking, the distinct sound of basketballs dancing on the pavement reached them. She loved that sound. It was music.

They arrived at the refurbished basketball court, the white lines painted fresh, the new rims and nets, a gift from a current Wizards player who grew up in the neighborhood.

Landon, wearing a t-shirt and baggy gym shorts, stopped a few yards behind the backboard and started stretching. Jade, in black sports tights and a sleeveless white Adidas shirt, dribbled onto the court and nodded at some guys on the adjacent court with whom she played occasional pick-up games.

She began shooting close to the basket to warm up. She went into the same shooting routine she had used since she was a young girl: shoot a couple of bank shots on each side, a couple of shots straight on, and then back up a few feet and do it again. She kept doing this until she was a foot behind the three-point line. She didn't miss many. After she had warmed up, she didn't miss any. When she was finished, she walked off the court to stretch, flipping the ball to Landon as he came toward her. He didn't catch it cleanly.

He gestured to the three-point line with his chin.

"Not bad."

She smiled, amused, and began stretching while he warmed up. His form was not good, his elbow at a twenty-degree angle to his body.

This should be easy. "I'm glad you called yesterday. This was a great idea."

"You were so reluctant," he said. "Thought you were scared."

She gave him a look in lieu of a response.

He shot the ball and missed. "How's your case going?"

"It's going."

He ran to retrieve the rebound. "Did you check out those liberal blogs I told you about?"

No. "Yeah."

"Did you find anything helpful?"

"Not yet."

He continued to shoot.

Jade stretched her hamstrings and looked down to the other end of the court. Some kids were playing three-on-three half-court. She loved listening to their laughter, the unadulterated joy of playing the game: no fans, no lights, no coaches, no refs, no money, no pressure. Just players, a hoop, and a ball. The way it should be. She lifted an eyebrow to Landon.

"Are you ready?"

"Bring it on."

"Okay."

She strode to the top of the key and he gave her the ball. She bounced it back to him to check. He twirled it in his hands, uncertainly, and then bounced it back to her. He positioned himself at the free-throw line.

She stared into his eyes. "Really?"

"What?"

Shaking her head once, she eyed the rim and shot the ball. Swish. Nothing but net. He retrieved the ball and bounce passed it to her again. He moved in a couple of steps closer.

She gave him an angelic smile. "Are you sure?"

He nodded his head, and raised his arms into a rigid, classic defensive position, one arm straight up to distract the shot, the other to protect against the drive. She pursed her lips and shot over his outstretched arm. Swish. Again.

He ran after the ball, handed it to her, and moved as close to her as he could.

"Now, you're learning." She faked a shot this time and blew by him for a layup.

"Damn it," he said.

After pulling out to a nine-zero lead, she finally missed a shot and Landon grabbed the rebound.

With the score at ten to three in her favor, he ball faked to the left and drove hard to the basket. Out of position, she ran at an angle toward the spot where he was going to be. He went up for a layup. She stepped into his path, crossing both arms over her chest to take the charge. His body plowed into hers.

She grunted and fell backward, using her arms to cushion her fall.

Landon scrambled up, the ball under one arm. He extended his other hand down to her. "Jade! What're you doing? Are you crazy?"

She grimaced. "Charge."

He pulled her up. "Are you all right?" He gazed into her eyes. "Your eyes are so beautiful."

Before she could react, he leaned down and kissed her.

His lips were soft. She responded.

The applause snapped her out of it.

She jerked her head back.

What was she doing?

She pushed him away and glanced over at the other side of the court. The six kids were lined up near half-court watching them. Clapping.

"Great defense, lady!" a girl yelled.

"Nice kiss, man!" shouted one of the boys. He pretended to kiss another boy and was pushed away for his efforts. The kids laughed and went back to their game.

Jade's face was hot. She grabbed the ball.

"Personal foul. My ball."

She dribbled to the top of the key, slapped the ball, and threw it back to him, harder than necessary. "Check."

"Jade, what's wrong?"

"I don't know. Just give me the damn ball. Game point."

CHAPTER FIFTY

Seattle, Washington

I HAD BEEN OBSERVING him for a couple of days, his routine always the same. At the appointed hour, I pressed the down button for the elevator. It stopped on the sixth floor—the one on which I was standing—a few times. A quick, cursory glance inside.

Empty.

I let the doors close and pushed the down button again. While I waited, I thought about Houston, Texas and my encounter with Pete Paxson. When he walked into the parking garage, I had been marveling at his BMW, wondering how much the vehicle cost and how many starving children in Africa—or in the United States, for that matter—it could have fed instead.

Shane Tallent was different than Paxson. He walked to work, minimizing his ecological footprint. At least he had one thing going for him. But it wasn't enough.

The elevator dinged open bringing me back to the present.

At last, the doors opened to a handsome man with dark hair and a high-wattage smile leaning against a corner.

My prey.

I avoided looking at him as I stepped in and moved to the other side. The man pressed the button for the lobby a couple of times and grinned at me, apologetic. "My son plays youth football. He's got a game tonight. I'm running late."

"No problem," I said.

His grin turned into an odd facial expression. The doors closed.

I did a double take, not quite meeting his eyes. "Hey, you are . . ."

The man grinned. "Afraid so."

"Wow. I love your show, man. I listen to it all the time."

"Thanks, I appreciate it."

I took a quick step forward and stabbed him in the stomach. I withdrew the blade and stabbed him again.

"Tallent cannot be your real name . . . right? Is it one of those stage names? You should have selected one more fitting."

Shane Tallent stared at me, uncomprehending. "Huh?"

I turned and pushed the button to stop the elevator. When I turned back to him, he was staring at his wounds, holding in his intestines with his hands. He started to slide down the wall. He reached the floor and stared up at me. "Why?"

I cannot be one hundred percent sure that is what he said. The word came out gurgled, as blood filled his mouth and began trickling down his chin. Articulation can be difficult after you've been stabbed.

It didn't matter.

She thinks I'm sick.

I pushed thoughts of her out of my mind. I bent down and stabbed him a few more times. It may have been more. I lost count. I did not like using a knife. Too messy. Too risky.

It was not as fun for me. I missed my baseball bat. I was glad I would not be around to clean up this mess.

It took a while to remove his tongue. Stubborn.

Out of my backpack, I grabbed my charcoal gray hoodie and put it on and zipped it up, pulling the hood over my head. I would fit right in walking the streets of downtown Seattle. I placed the knife and tongue in separate plastic bags and placed them in my backpack. The blood on my black jeans was visible to me, but probably not to someone else at a distance.

I pressed the button to restart the elevator.

Prior to the door opening, I knelt by the slumped body. Shane Tallent seemed so peaceful. And, once and for all, silent.

"By the way, I lied. I hated your show."

CHAPTER FIFTY-ONE

Washington, DC

JADE ARRIVED HOME from work Wednesday night, trying not to trip over Card as she walked to the kitchen.

She foraged in the bare refrigerator trying to scrounge up enough food from different leftovers to make a meal. As the food warmed in the microwave, she thought about playing ball with Landon last weekend.

While eating at her small kitchen table, she kicked herself mentally for allowing him to kiss her.

After dinner, she grabbed her journal from the wall. She settled into a corner of the couch and began writing phrases. After a few minutes, she had written:

Senator Fairchild

The next US president

My own match.com

Horrible. She read the poem again. She would never be published or win any prizes, which was okay. She wrote for herself.

Her cell phone rang. She swept it off the coffee table and eyed the display. Ethan. Ten-thirty p.m. Not good.

She answered. "Harrington."

"He struck again."

"Where?"

"Seattle."

"When?"

"About seven p.m. Pacific. The body was found about fifteen minutes later. I've booked you and your team out of Dulles. Your flight leaves in two hours."

⁂

A subset of the CONFAB team drove away from Sea-Tac airport onto I-5 North toward Seattle. With Max in the back seat and Christian driving, Jade surveyed the beautiful juxtaposition of the Olympic Mountains and the Cascades with the Puget Sound. Mount Rainier decided to make an appearance today. The rain did not. They stalled in traffic behind a blue minivan with a family decal on the rear window showing a stick figure of a daddy, mommy, three kids, and a dog. Jade shook her head; she believed those decals were road maps for predators.

Christian double-parked in front of an office building on Madison Street in downtown Seattle. Blue "12" flags—a tribute to the Seattle Seahawks' fans—were everywhere. They hung from poles, covered office windows, flapped on car antennas. Several police and unmarked vehicles were parked near the building's entrance, their lights and sirens off. On the sidewalk, a homeless man, his entire belongings wrapped up in a sleeping bag nearby, hopped past them, playing a game of hopscotch with imaginary lines.

A uniformed police officer met them inside the carousel doors and led them past a long marble desk manned by a security guard and through a modern lobby toward the back of the building. One of the four elevators gaped open, yellow crime scene tape draped across it.

A young man with shoulder-length hair came up to them and offered his hand.

"Agent Harrington? I'm Detective Kurt McClaine. I spoke to you on the phone."

He resembled Kurt Cobain—former lead singer of the famous Seattle rock band, Nirvana—and Jade almost did a double take. McClaine, with his slight frame and sporting a dangling gold earring in one ear and a tattoo snaking up his neck, appeared more like a rocker than a detective. Despite the crisp September day, he wore a black t-shirt with Don't Kill My Vibe in white letters on the front.

He shook her hand. "Yeah, I was named after him. My parents were into the grunge scene." He laughed. "They still are." He shook the rest of the agents' hands and said, "Good to meet you, man." Jade always thought the term "man" between men who were strangers brought an immediate intimacy and bond lacking in any expressions women used. McClaine gestured toward the elevators. "This way."

As they walked, Detective McClaine continued, "The victim, Shane Tallent, worked on the thirty-third floor."

McClaine pointed at the corner of the elevator. "He was found and killed here." Massive amounts of dried blood had congealed on the floor. "The UNSUB got on the elevator at the sixth floor."

"Camera?" Jade asked.

"He knew where it was. He averted his face."

Jade examined the blood spatter on the walls and the few drops on the ceiling. "The UNSUB must have got blood on him."

"Probably."

"No one saw anything? No witnesses?"

"No. It was after work hours, and the security in this building is pretty lax. We interviewed the guard on duty. He was reading a book at the time, but he remembered someone wearing a dark hoodie leaving around the time of the murder. He couldn't be sure whether it was a man or a woman, but thought the former. The camera by the guard's desk confirmed his account. We haven't determined, yet, when the perp entered the building."

"How many stab wounds?" Christian asked.

"Twelve."

Christian whistled.

McClaine nodded. "The perp obliterated the vic's internal organs—arteries, major muscles. The guy was butchered."

She glanced down at the bloodstain on the floor and then at Max. She murmured, "This isn't his usual MO."

Max nodded, apparently lost in thought.

McClaine's eyes shifted from Max to Jade. "What do you see?"

"Nothing. It's just—"

The detective's phone rang. "Yeah." He listened. He glanced at Jade. "We'll be right there."

The agents followed Detective McClaine down a wide alley two blocks away from Shane Tallent's office building. Evidence of America's number-one "green" city, according to Jade's brief research on Seattle she conducted on the flight, was absent: dirty food wrappers, bottles, napkins, soft-drink cups, and Styrofoam containers littered the alley. The stench was overpowering.

A police officer walked up to them. "Over here, Detective."

The officer guided them down the alley. "The owner of a Chinese restaurant," the officer continued, pointing to a black door with peeling paint, "witnessed a man throwing something in her dumpster."

Jade's pulse accelerated. "Did she get a good look at him?"

The composite they had received based on the information provided by the San Francisco witness, Kevin Burke, turned out to be garbage. She hadn't bothered to send it out to anyone.

The officer shook his head. "Unfortunately, no. The establishments around here have an understanding they don't use each other's dumpsters. She was ticked off and dug through the trash, coming up with this bag. She decided to open it."

They all leaned in to peer inside the bag. A knife greeted them, coated with a massive amount of blood. It appeared to be eight inches long, and thick. A blanket and a few other items lay underneath.

Detective McClaine surveyed the alley. "The perp didn't try very hard to hide the evidence, if this belonged to him." He paused. "It better belong to him. Otherwise, I have two major crimes on my hands instead of one." He laughed without humor. "There are a million places in this city to hide this bag and it would've never been found."

Christian stood with his hands on his hips. "Maybe he was in a hurry."

A quiet interjection from Max: "Or maybe he wanted it to be found."

McClaine glanced at Max and then stared at the bag,

unconvinced. The three agents—Jade, Christian, and Max—McClaine, and the police officer continued to stare at the bag, as if it would divulge the answers if only they were patient.

Finally, the officer cleared his throat. "That's not all." He guided them to the back door of the Chinese restaurant, bent down, and—with latex gloves—opened a carton of takeout Chinese food. With uncomfortable closeness, everyone again bent over to peer inside the small carton.

A coiled tongue lay within.

Christian stepped back. "Jesus."

The officer tilted the carton at a forty-five-degree angle. *Tongue Lo Mein to go* was scrawled in black magic marker on the side of the carton.

"I presume that's not on the menu," Jade said.

"The UNSUB has a sense of humor," Max said, "and he left us a calling card."

&

Despite it being midweek and late at night, the Sea-Tac airport was crowded. Jade, Christian, and Max sat next to each other, seats far away from the gate, each deep in thought as they waited for their red-eye flight back to DC to be announced.

Jade leaned back in her chair with her eyes closed.

"What about the switch of MO? A blunt object in the first four killings, which he either took with him or disposed of. In this one, a knife. A knife he left for us to find."

Christian, seated across from her, bent forward to rest his arms on his thighs. "Copycat killing?"

Next to her, Max stirred. He hadn't been sleeping, but thinking. Always processing. "Not necessarily. It's not unusual for a serial killer to change his modus operandi. In the seventies, Gary Taylor started off by hitting women over the head with a wrench at bus stops before moving on to shooting them. He then moved on to machetes."

"Nice," Christian said.

Jade, eyes still closed, grimaced. "Max, maybe you do need a hobby."

Max continued, as if they hadn't said anything. "This killer studies his victims and their habits. He does his homework."

"He seems to be able to travel wherever and whenever he wants," Christian said.

"Which leads me to believe he has means and a flexible occupation," Max said. "He also diverted us with the San Francisco incident."

Jade yawned, but cut it short as her phone vibrated. "Harrington."

It was McClaine. "We got a hit on the knife. It was purchased two days ago from a Federal Army and Navy Surplus store on First Avenue. The knife is a Columbia River eleven-twenty-one Elishewitz Anubis."

Jade balled her hand into a fist. "Any description on the perp?"

"The owner remembers the buyer well: He was wearing a hoodie, but the owner observed he had short, light brown or dark blond hair. Here's the interesting part. The guy wasn't a local. He had an accent. The owner couldn't place it, but guessed East Coast. The buyer told him he was going camping and purchased the knife, blanket, a flashlight, and a few other items."

"Were all those items found in the bag?"

"Yes. All unused. Except for the knife, of course. The

owner is coming in tomorrow to ID the items and to assist us with a facial composite."

"Thank you, Detective. Feel free to call me anytime."

"You're welcome. Good night and have a nice flight."

She called the local FBI office in Seattle, conveying the information to the special agent in charge with follow-up instructions. Jade hung up, as their flight to DC was called.

Was the UNSUB getting sloppy or playing games with them? And, if the latter, why?

CHAPTER FIFTY-TWO

New York, New York

THE MODERATOR STARED into the camera.

"Good evening. This is Blaine Jones and welcome to Radio City Musical Hall in New York City. The candidates have agreed to new rules for this election. Tonight will be the first, last, and only presidential debate between the Democratic nominee, Senator Whitney Fairchild of Missouri"—Whitney smiled for the camera while Jones paused for the applause—"and the president of the United States, Richard Ellison."

While the camera stayed on Ellison, Whitney admired the grandeur of the historic hall built in the 1930s and its art deco interior. Ted had created a similar setting yesterday for her debate prep, but the imitation was nothing like reality. She and Ellison stood at separate, stainless-steel podiums each with a thin free-standing microphone. They each had a glass of water, notepad, and pens.

Jones continued. "Since this is the only debate, we're going to make this an open forum. I may ask a question regarding any issue to one of the candidates, who then has three minutes to answer. The other candidate can respond. If the second candidate mentions the other candidate, the first candidate may have an additional one-minute rebuttal." Jones eyed both of the candidates in turn to make sure they understood.

"The first question pertains to unemployment. Five percent is considered the normal unemployment rate. The current rate stands at six percent. Some would argue the real unemployment rate, though, is twice that, if you include those who want and are able to work, but have become discouraged from looking. How would you reduce the real unemployment rate further? Mr. President?"

Ellison wrote as the moderator spoke. Whitney wondered what he could be writing already. The president put down his pen and stared at Blaine Jones.

"It's not the government's role to create jobs. The only action we can take is to create an environment in which business owners can be successful by eliminating onerous regulations and decreasing taxes so more money is pumped into the economy. Lower taxes give people the incentive to work harder, save, and invest, which improves living standards for all. We must continue to reduce the size of government and the role it plays in our lives. The free-market system works."

"Senator Fairchild?" the moderator asked.

Whitney faced Ellison. "When?"

Some members in the audience chuckled. After a few moments, Ellison shifted on his feet. When she realized he wasn't going to respond, Whitney turned back to the moderator. "I believe in capitalism as well, but the free-market approach in itself is not working and hasn't worked for many years. Businesses exist to make money for their owners. That's why, despite the turnaround in our economy, the pay for the average worker has remained flat.

"My goal is to spur economic and employment growth.

One of my first initiatives after I am elected president will be to enact a significant training tax credit to businesses. There are millions of jobs available, but workers aren't trained to do them. In my first year of office, I will also propose a National Infrastructure Bank. The bank would work with local, state, and federal entities to provide financing and grants to build and repair roads and bridges, create rapid inner-city rail in all major cities, and modernize our air-traffic-control system. This proposal would put even more Americans back to work and increase worker productivity. Delays from congestion and damaged roads will cost two hundred and ten billion dollars over the next five years. There is nothing fiscally responsible about deferring maintenance of our crumbling infrastructure to future generations."

Whitney paused while the audience clapped.

Ellison shook his head. "How will you pay for that?"

Whitney faced him. "By ending tax subsidies for big businesses." Turning back to the camera, she continued. "We don't need to shrink the government. We need to modernize it. A limited government made sense when we were an agrarian society back in the days of Thomas Jefferson. People were self-sufficient. Today we are interdependent. Our government must change as our society changes. We have done this before. In the nineteenth century, we changed from an agrarian society to an industrial one. We became a superpower in the twentieth. The question is, 'What do we want to be in the twenty-first century?'"

"Time," Jones said.

"We can, however, streamline our government," Whitney continued, ignoring Jones. "The financial industry has proven time and time again that it is incapable of regulating itself.

Bernie Madoff bilked investors for sixty-eight *billion* dollars. I plan to consolidate all of our financial agencies into one agency, the Federal Financial Regulatory Authority, making it more efficient and more effective in enforcing the law and protecting investors and consumers.

"I will propose a committee to review all current regulations: to revise those that do not make sense, to eliminate those we no longer need, and to create regulation that protects our citizens while encouraging innovation. Your party, Mr. President, transformed regulation into a dirty word. It is not. Regulation protects consumers: from the foods we eat, to the water we drink, to the drugs we take, to the safety of our highways."

"Can I talk?" Ellison asked.

The audience clapped, many of them laughing. Whitney joined in the laughter. The moderator waited for the clapping to subside. "Senator, may I remind you to limit your responses to three minutes?"

"Yes, you may."

Blaine Jones hesitated before realizing she was teasing him. Charmed, his cheeks reddened.

"Senator Fairchild, can you outline your tax plan for the audience?"

"Sure, Blaine. We must decrease income taxes for the middle class. For American couples making less than one hundred thousand dollars, I am proposing a flat fifteen-percent tax and elimination of all loopholes, exemptions, and deductions. This plan will lower the tax burden for most taxpayers and simplify tax preparation. I want to eliminate special tax breaks. To that end, I intend to raise rates for taxpayers making over one million dollars per year to the same levels as the Bill Clinton administration, aligning our tax system to better serve our economy and our planet."

"Mr. President?" Jones asked.

Ellison screwed up his face. "Your party, Senator, always wants to engage in class warfare, pitting the wealthy against everyone else. They forget who creates the jobs and the opportunities in this country. My plan calls for a flat ten percent tax for everyone. Further—"

"Your plan," Whitney said, "would not raise sufficient revenue to offset current spending."

"According to the reports I've received, it will."

"Well, as Hillary Clinton once said, 'I think the reports you provide us really require a willing suspension of disbelief.'"

Scattered laughter filled the hall like wind chimes.

Jones waited for the laughter to subside. "Mr. President, when you were elected, you promised to build a fence between our country and Mexico. Why haven't you done so?"

"These things take time, Blaine. I'm more committed than ever to building a fence to protect our borders. We spent a few years conducting feasibility studies on the terrain that can't be fenced easily. Once those studies are completed, the fence will be built."

"Senator?" Jones asked.

"Blaine, twelve million so-called illegals live in this country. Every year, five hundred thousand more cross the border. Instead of wasting our time discussing a fence that will never be built, we should devote our energies to a solution in keeping with a nation *founded* by immigrants and created by the rule of law."

"The next question is for the president." Blaine Jones looked up from the paper in front of him. "Your campaign promised four years ago to repeal health-care reform, which you've not done. If you're re-elected and repeal of the entire act is not possible, what parts would you repeal?"

Ellison stared into the camera and ticked off the points on his finger. "First, I'd do away with the individual mandate; a person shouldn't be forced to buy health insurance. Second, I'd lower the age that children could remain on their parents' insurance to eighteen. Third, I'd eliminate the penalties on companies who don't insure all of their employees."

The last statement was met with polite applause. The moderator turned to Whitney. "Senator?"

"First, as for the individual mandate, who pays when the uninsured go to the hospital? The insured. Why not put the burden on the individuals who use it? Isn't that what the free-market system is all about? Second, I would resurrect an idea proposed by the president's party"—she gestured at Ellison—"an eventual complete transition away from employer-provided health insurance. Why should companies be involved? Employer-provided health insurance began as a response to World War II wage and price controls, giving employees greater benefits and a sense of security. This made sense when employees stayed with a company for forty years, but how much sense does it make now when the average employee's tenure is three years? Exchanges or portable health insurance allow employees to change jobs without worrying. This will provide individuals with greater choice, and employers, as President Ellison always says, can then concentrate on their businesses.

"Third, President Ellison knows as well as I, health-care reform prevented many families from going bankrupt and children and young adults from joining the uninsured. These same children cannot find good-paying jobs. Throughout this campaign, I have talked with many college graduates—Michael in North Carolina, Jessica in Ohio, Matthew in Florida, bright and intelligent young men and women—who are working in fast-food establishments. I have two college-aged children. Is this any way to take care of our children? I don't think so. This is America. We are better than this!"

The audience rose to a standing ovation.

When the applause subsided, the moderator turned to Ellison.

"Mr. President, your turn to respond."

"Children? A twenty-six-year-old is not a child. Our young adults must start taking personal responsibility for their own care and learn early in life the government can't solve all of their problems. Third parties make costs go up. To bring down the cost of health care, we need to eliminate the middlemen. Health care should be between a doctor and his patient. If you break your leg, you should be informed of how much it's going to cost to fix it. This cost should not be disclosed to you for the first time when you open the bill."

Tepid applause followed.

Whitney scanned the audience and smiled. President Ellison's face was flushed and he gripped the podium as if he were holding on for dear life. Whitney understood if she did not make any major gaffes the rest of the debate, the night was hers. She focused on the moderator, Blaine Jones.

He looked at both candidates with a grave expression. "Let's talk about China."

CHAPTER FIFTY-THREE

Washington, DC

JADE STARED AT the blank wall on the opposite side of her office. She was back at the Bureau, two days after returning from Seattle.

The owner of the Federal Army and Navy Surplus store had provided a good description of the man who bought the knife. So far, nothing had come back from showing the composite to every airport, train station, bus terminal, hotel, rental car agency, and bed and breakfast within one hundred miles of Seattle. The facial composite had also been sent to every known victim's employer. No one remembered seeing the suspect. Her team had checked out every lead provided by the public. None credible. Austin called MSNBC and no one fitting the description had ever worked there. No one fitting that description had ever worked at the Bureau. Dead end after dead end.

She had been avoiding Ethan. Although he was still supportive, he was under pressure, too. She had grown up with demanding parents who only wanted to hear good news. She didn't want to see Ethan until she had something positive to report.

She started aligning the items on her desk. After she

finished aligning her files, she selected one to review. Her phone rang again. "Harrington."

"Agent Harrington, Detective McClaine, Seattle PD. I wanted to let you know the evidence reports came back. I'm sending them over to you now."

"Hair?"

"No, but we found carpet fibers. We checked the victim's residence and car, and they don't belong to him."

Jade had opened his email during the conversation and scanned the report. Now, off the phone, she read it in detail. Jade started rifling through the files on her desk, grateful that she had just organized them in alphabetical order. She located the correct folder and flipped pages until she found the fiber-analysis report. Carpet fibers were also found at the LeBlanc scene in Baton Rouge and the Paxson scene in Houston. Unlike DNA and fingerprints, a national database didn't exist for fibers.

The color, diameter, shape, dye content, and chemical composition of the carpet found at the LeBlanc and Tallent scenes—as analysts would say—were consistent with each other.

Jade would say it was a match. She did a fist pump.

Yes!

The fibers were not consistent, however, with those found at the Paxson scene. Why not? The killer must have brought the fibers with him from his house or car. Perhaps he moved to a new residence between the Houston and Baton Rouge murders. Maybe he had bought a new car. No hair samples this time. Why not? Why did he switch modus operandi? How was he selecting his victims? Questions, questions, and more questions.

CHAPTER FIFTY-FOUR

Washington, DC

IN HER OFFICE the next day, Jade clicked open the PDF on her computer. A composite of a young white man with short-cropped hair and nondescript face stared back at her. The face of a killer.

MSNBC had received another email from TSK. She printed out several copies and called her team together for an emergency task force meeting. A few minutes later they were all assembled in the conference room.

Jade passed around the copies.

To Whom It May Concern,

Or should I ask, does it concern anyone? I told the world what would happen if my demands were not met. They should not even be called demands, because balance and fairness on the airwaves is what we deserve. What we should all want. The left and moderate views must be heard. How many more people are going to die before you start taking me seriously?

I gave the FBI a clue last time, albeit with some

misdirection. This time, the Bureau will need to figure it out on its own.

I hope the death of poor Mr. (lack of) Tallent will propel our members of Congress to act. If not, you will be hearing from me again soon.

Sincerely,

TSK

Christian dropped the paper on the table. "Motive, means, and opportunity."

Jade slipped a yellow peanut M&M into her mouth.

"Any hits on the sketch?" Christian asked.

Jade shook her head. "Nada. We sent the facial composite to every radio and TV station and all transportation possibilities in the victims' cities."

"The UNSUB's like a ghost," Austin said.

Jade turned to Pat, clicking away at her laptop. "Circulate the facial composite to former students, teachers, radio station employees, student housing, and restaurants in Chattenham. And send it to OPA"—Office of Public Affairs—"to add him to the Most Wanted list."

Pat nodded her assent without ceasing her typing.

"Christian, have someone from our Baton Rouge office interview the girlfriend of LeBlanc again. Ask her if she recognizes the sketch. Perhaps her memory can be jarred further."

"Got it."

"And run the facial composite through the database again."

Christian flashed a look at her.

"Do it again," she said. She turned to Max. "Thoughts?"

Max cleared his throat. "I studied every photo, autopsy, police report, witness statement, and pattern of the offenses again. The perpetrator is under a lot of stress and will become more frustrated and angry by the growing media attention and lack of action by Congress on his demands, evidenced by the overkill and concentrated knife wounds in the Tallent killing.

"He is trying to save our country and society isn't listening to him or giving him the respect he deserves. He'll start to believe the situation is hopeless. At the same time, he receives intellectual satisfaction from outsmarting the FBI and local law enforcement. It's a game. The inadequate part of him wars with the superior, grandiose side."

The other agents stared at him. Pat stopped typing. They had never heard Max say so much in one breath. He was in the zone.

He pushed his glasses up farther on his nose. "This guy isn't going to stop on his own."

CHAPTER FIFTY-FIVE

Washington, DC

A MONTH BEFORE THE presidential election, Senator Whitney Fairchild worked at her desk in the Russell Senate Office Building. She had finally succumbed to Landon's suggestion of installing a TV in her office to keep up with current events. She glanced at the flat-panel television hanging on the wall across from her. The portrait of Eleanor Roosevelt had been relegated to storage.

Another Breaking News flash filled the bottom of the screen. News today, for the most part, was neither "breaking" nor even news, but this time, a TSK logo popped up in the top right corner. As time went on, the logo had become more elaborate. A facial composite of the killer was lodged in the bottom of the screen.

She came around her desk for a closer inspection. She wondered how someone could kill another person, especially over politics. What must be going through his mind? The face seemed familiar. Something in her stirred. She dismissed the feeling. The guy looked like a lot of young men today who wore hoodies. She turned up the volume.

"Moments ago, this network received what TSK is calling

his *Manifesto for America,* a hundred-page document detailing his solutions to our country's problems. He demanded we post a link and the document itself on our website. We understand similar demands were made to the print and online departments of *The Washington Post* and *The New York Times.* Executives for MSNBC are not commenting whether they will honor the request. We have also been unable to reach the Director of the FBI or the Attorney General. We will continue to keep you updated on any further developments."

The talking head went on, "What has Kim Kardashian been up to and what is happening with her latest marriage? You'll find out after—"

Whitney muted the volume and returned to her desk. She pressed a button on her phone. "Landon, I need a copy of the TSK manifesto."

"What manifesto?"

"Turn on the news." She hung up.

CHAPTER FIFTY-SIX

Westchester County, New York

THE WOMAN WAS late for work. At fifty years old, she believed she was too old to have just picked up her child from an elementary school and taken her home. Hence, why she was late for work. She brushed back her hair as she yelled out the window at her ten-year-old.

"Daddy will be home soon. You can watch TV after you've done your homework. Listen to Isabella. I love you!" She blew her daughter a kiss as their au pair, Isabella, opened the door, allowing the woman's daughter to pass under her arm. Isabella waved. The woman waved back and put the car into drive.

The woman was Liz Holder. A former lawyer, she was now the most powerful woman in conservative politics. Born and raised in New York City, Elizabeth Holder, née Dolan, grew up in a Democratic household. She embarked on the typical liberal route, attending Brown University for undergrad and the University of Pennsylvania for law school. During her college years, she fell in love with the cheery optimism of Ronald Reagan and became a Reagan Democrat. She felt chills when Reagan told Gorbachev to "tear down that wall." Now, the lone Republican in her extended Democratic family, she was hardly tolerated by them. She didn't care.

After law school, she clerked for a forgettable federal judge in New York City, and then went to Washington for many years to work as a legal aide for a senator from New York. During the presidency of George W. Bush, she wrote a book defending his decision to invade Iraq. The book was a surprising best seller for a first-time author. She quit her day job, moved back to Westchester County, New York, and became an author full time. She began to receive numerous offers for guest appearances on all the cable-news networks. The networks loved her because she was smart, attractive, and controversial. When Liz Dolan spoke, ratings went up. After years of guest appearances, Patriot News created a show for her. They allowed her to broadcast from a satellite studio not far from her home.

She was hated by Democrats and liberals across the country, and even some conservative politicians distanced themselves from her. Nevertheless, people read her books and tuned in to her show. She was second only to Cole Brennan in influencing conservative thought and ideals.

Still single into her late thirties and needing to quiet the budding lesbian rumors, she married Adam Holder, a partner with a New York City law firm. Theirs was a marriage of mutual respect and companionship, not love. Thus, while she was at the age she should have been traveling or enjoying her grandchildren, she was instead dropping off her young daughter at home after elementary school.

She pushed the speed dial on her Jeep's phone.

Without preamble, she said, "I'm running late, but I should be there before the show starts."

"Hurry," her producer, Aaron, said. "By the way, we lost another advertiser."

"Who?"

"GE."

"I wonder why."

"You know why."

"I'm not going to apologize for saying what I think. I'm not going to be politically correct. I never claimed to be impartial, fair, and balanced. I only claimed to be right."

"Well," Aaron said, "some of their customers complained about your comment last week that if the Nazis had exterminated six million liberals instead of Jews, the world would be a better place. The comment about putting a numbered tattoo on liberals' arms in the event we wanted to round them up later didn't help. Oh . . . and what you said about white liberals being only slightly better than minority liberals put them over the top."

"I've not kept it a secret I hate liberals. They're Godless and moral-less. They won't be happy until the queers and minorities take over this country, which will be sooner than you think. Whites in the Sixties made up ninety percent of the population. By the year 2050, we will be the minority. Am I supposed to sit around and let them extinguish our race as we did to the Indians?"

Aaron ignored her rhetorical question. "Remember, President Ellison will be on the show tonight. Please try to control yourself. And get here."

"Are you afraid I'm going to endorse Whitney? Wouldn't that be a hoot? That would shake up Ellison's pseudo-conservative ass. I still think I should have convinced Cole Brennan or another true conservative to run against him in the Republican primary. Aaron, hold on a minute."

She pressed a button and her window lowered.

"Welcome to Starbucks. What can I get started for you?" came the tinny voice from the drive-thru microphone.

"I'll take a venti low-fat caramel macchiato."

"Will that be all for you today?"

"Yes."

"Please drive around. I'll have your total for you at the window."

An uncharacteristic foreboding preceded the shadow reflecting off the Starbucks menu.

Before she had time to press the button to slide up the Jeep's window, a flash of black—a coat sleeve?—and a glint from an object slipped through.

An excruciating pain began at the base of her throat. She reached up and touched her neck. She pulled her hand away. It was bright red. She thought of her daughter. She tried to turn her head to face the person who had done this to her, but her head fell forward and landed on the horn of her steering wheel.

In the passenger seat next to her, Aaron's voice was yelling from the cellphone she had dropped. "Liz, what's going on? What's happening?" Pause. "Are you all right? Liz!"

Through the drive-thru microphone, the Starbucks employee said, "Ma'am, would you like to order anything else? If not, please proceed to the window."

After that, she didn't hear anything at all.

CHAPTER FIFTY-SEVEN

Washington, DC

"WELCOME BACK. I'VE saved the worst for last. Now, we're going to talk about this so-called *Manifesto for America* written by the Talk Show Killer, aka TSK, which he sent to MSNBC. Yes, the executive folks over at MSNBC, after two minutes of intense deliberations, decided to post the document on its website. You can now find it on mine as well at www.theconservativevoiceonline.com.

"I read all one hundred pages of this liberal, Socialist crap and I can tell you all I want to do now is throw up. The killer doesn't even need to try to kill me. Just make me read this sh—stuff again and again and I'll kill myself. Folks, if you want to understand why our country is going to hell, read this thing. Why do these Commiecrats write these manifestos anyway? Who cares? Who does this guy think he is? The Unabomber?

"All right. Let's get to it. He starts off by writing about regulation and how we need big government to protect us from the greed of big, bad businesses. Have you been to a DMV lately, TSK? Who is it protecting you from? Getting a license? Keeping you off the road for a few hours?

"He writes about our efforts to abolish abortion in this

country. The only lives we care about are the unborn. What about the women who bear them? What about a woman's freedom of choice of what to do with her own body? All that Seventies feminist crap. He states a fetus isn't a human life, yet, so it shouldn't be granted separate and individual rights. Wrong! Life begins at conception, folks, and abortion is murder.

"He complains the federal government slashed programs that helped lower-income young mothers care for their children. So, we force these women to bear children, who then die of malnutrition. Well, I can turn this argument around, Mr. TSK. Why do all of you liberals support children's health, nutrition, and education programs, but support the abortion of these future children? He doesn't understand why our party is pro-life and pro-death penalty. 'Is that not a contradiction in terms?' Yes, folks, that's how he writes. Probably went to an Ivy League school. He ends this section by arguing the abortion debate would be different if men instead of women were the ones who got pregnant. I don't even know how to respond to that.

"He opposes the death penalty, calling it unjust, inhumane, and cruel and unusual punishment. With every execution, the government takes a chance of killing an innocent person. The United States is one of the top five countries in executions along with China, Iran, North Korea, and Yemen. Okay, not good company, but executing a murderer for taking an innocent life is still okay in my book.

"I'll skip the part about the Fairness Doctrine and income inequality, since we've discussed them ad nauseam on this show. The killer condemns capitalism. Calls it evil. How did he type this manifesto? I would guess with a computer.

How was the computer created? By the computer fairy? These Socialists complain about capitalism, but they don't mind using the products of capitalism.

"He yawns on about increasing the safety net for the poor and the elderly. Where is the money going to come from, big guy? One solution, of course, is to increase taxes on oil companies and the rich. On the one hand, we encourage entrepreneurship in this country. On the other hand, as soon as you become successful, we want to tax and regulate the hell out of you.

"Next, illegal immigrants should be granted amnesty and bestowed the same rights as American citizens. They should be given driver's licenses and their kids should be allowed to go to college at in-state tuition rates. I disagree. I think they should be paying out-of-country rates. He believes in the Dream Act, allowing illegals to attain permanent residency if they demonstrate good character—according to whom?—and get a college degree or serve two years in the military. The Dream Act is a nightmare, folks. We are a nation of laws and should only accept legal immigration. Let's secure our borders, President Ellison, by building that fence!

"Mr. TSK believes America needs to stop being so nationalistic and take a more global view. We are citizens of the world and through tolerance, diplomacy, and disarmament, we can achieve global peace in our lifetime. He wants to re-establish foreign aid to previous levels to help educate citizens in other countries on the virtues of democracy. If citizens of other countries understood democracy and became less hostile, they will be less likely to attack us.

"What friggin' planet does this guy live on? Does he want us all to gather around a global campfire and sing Kumbaya?"

Cole dropped the hundred-page manifesto on the table.

"Folks, that's about all I can stomach for today. There is a lot more in here—affirmative action, global warming, gay marriage, welfare—it's all in here. If you're suffering from constipation, grab this manifesto, and head to the toilet. I guarantee you'll feel better fast."

Cole signed off.

CHAPTER FIFTY-EIGHT

Washington, DC

JADE TURNED THE final page of TSK's *Manifesto for America*. She leaned back in her office chair and rubbed her eyes. She had read the document all the way through three times. The killer's writings didn't seem crazy to her. This was not the work of a raving lunatic. The writing style was coherent, methodical, and logical. What kind of person were they dealing with? What was driving him to kill? How did he continue to elude them? Who was he going to strike next? *How can I get there first?*

She must have gone into a trance, because her phone was ringing. Normally, she picked up on the first ring.

"Harrington."

"Hey you. It's your best friend, Zoe. Remember me?"

"What's up?"

"Do you need me to swing by and take care of Card?"

"Yes, thank you. I don't think I'll make it home tonight."

"Anything else? I can bring dinner."

"No, I'll pick something up." She paused. She could tell Zoe, couldn't she? "By the way, I've been sort of hanging out with your friend, Landon Phillips."

"Sort of hanging out . . ."

"Yeah. During my meeting with Senator Fairchild, she sort of set us up."

"Huh," Zoe said. "And?"

"We had dinner. Played a little ball."

"How romantic."

"You didn't tell me he was so handsome."

"I didn't? Hmph. I mean, he's okay . . . for a guy."

"Listen, I gotta go. My other line is ringing."

Jade punched the lighted button on her phone. "Harrington."

A pause. "Jade, this is Landon."

"Landon." She was caught off guard. He must be telepathic. "Hi."

"I'm calling to apologize."

She stayed silent.

"For the kiss. I'm not sure what came over me. Well, I know what came over me. You did. But, still, it was out of line."

"I kissed you back."

"Yeah, there's that."

After a few moments of silence, he asked, "I'm also calling for the Senator. Any update? On the case?"

She hesitated. "Did you read the manifesto?"

"Sure. No real surprises. No new solutions. Solid liberal positions. As a Democrat, I can't disagree with a lot of them, although in practice I'm more of a progressive than a liberal."

"What's your distinction?"

"Some say there isn't one. Some liberals call themselves progressives, because Republicans have painted 'liberal' as a dirty word. If I had to distinguish between the two, I'd say a liberal is someone who uses taxpayer money to help society—improving health care and giving subsidies to help people—whereas a progressive uses the power of the government to make large institutions and individuals play by the rules. Both believe in using the government for social change, such as improving food safety, instituting minimum wage and labor laws, and creating financial rules to make sure corporations don't hurt workers or consumers in their pursuit of profit."

He waited. When she didn't say anything, he went on.

"Progressives created the FBI. During the Progressive Era in the early twentieth century, Attorney General Charles Bonaparte formed the FBI from a force of special agents under Teddy Roosevelt's administration. Bonaparte believed government intervention was necessary to provide justice in an industrial society. The FBI also had a major role in integration and giving African-Americans the right to vote. Its investigation into the murder of three voter registration workers in Philadelphia, Mississippi was a key turning point in the civil rights movement."

"Thanks for the history lesson."

"You're welcome," he said, his tone embarrassed. "I guess you know all that, working for them and all."

"Listen, Landon, I need to go. 'And miles to go before I sleep.'"

"'The woods are lovely, dark and deep. But I have promises to keep.' Frost is one of my favorites. Maybe we can get together . . ."

"Landon, I need to go."

During her conversation with Landon, she had been turning the pages of the manifesto. Midway through the document, the killer had drawn a caricature of congressmen and congresswomen standing on the Capitol Hill steps. She traced the drawing with her finger. It spoke to her. And seemed familiar. Had she seen it before?

She opened up her web browser and entered "Congress standing on Capitol Hill steps" into the search bar to find the image online. She came up empty. She typed variations of the phrase. Still nothing.

She rolled her shoulders and moved her neck to loosen them up. She clicked on the television and turned to MSNBC. A four-person panel discussed the manifesto, all the panelists young, attractive, and dressed in the latest style. The most stylish was the handsome Blake Haynes. He was smooth. She loved to hear him talk; she could listen to him all day.

She remembered telling Landon she had checked out liberal bloggers as he suggested. She might as well do that now, in case he asked her again. Maybe she would find one that had the same writing style as TSK. With reluctance, Jade turned her attention from the TV screen to her computer and typed "liberal bloggers" into the search bar.

She began to read.

ɞ

After two hours of reading liberal blogs, Jade was no closer to finding a writing style that matched the manifesto's. She pushed back her chair and bent over, her head in her hands. She breathed in and out slowly for a few minutes before lifting her head, her heart rate steady. She needed to work out before she hurt someone. Something blinked red out of the corner of her eye. She gazed at the television, her stomach dropping at the sight of the now-familiar TSK logo and the breaking-news bulletin. *What now?* She turned up the sound.

A pretty Asian-American stared into the camera. "That's

right, Joe. An anonymous source within the Seattle Police Department confirmed that radio host Shane Tallent's tongue had been severed."

"Was the tongue found?" asked Joe, the show's host.

"Yes. The tongue was found a short distance away from the scene of the crime in an alley behind a restaurant in downtown Seattle. The source didn't divulge the name of the restaurant. But Joe . . . there's more. Another source told me this isn't the first time. All the victims had their tongue removed."

The host thanked the on-the-scene reporter and the panelists in the studio began giving their thoughtful, compelling analysis of the significance of this new evidence. Their chatter, though, had an underlying tinge of nervousness.

Jade turned off the television and started to pace. *Shit!* The leak of the severed tongues was going to cause a media frenzy. She needed to brief Ethan.

She headed toward his office, dialing McClaine's number on the way to find out what the hell was going on in his police department. She realized, though, she had a leak at her end as well. McClaine didn't know about the other victims' tongues.

When she entered, Ethan hung up the phone.

"You saved me a call."

"What?"

Ethan only looked at her.

Her shoulders dropped. "Again?"

CHAPTER FIFTY-NINE

Westchester County, New York

CHRISTIAN, MAX, AND Jade drove in silence from the airport. The Starbucks was easy to spot long before they saw its sign. Yellow Police Line Do Not Cross tape encircled the parking lot entrance, the drive-thru lane exit, and the perimeter of the store. Christian parked the car, and they exited the vehicle. A huge man left the others he was speaking to and walked over.

"Agent Harrington?"

Jade nodded.

"John O'Shaunessy. I spoke to you on the phone."

As they shook hands, Jade gave him the once-over. This man had played professional football, or at least tried.

He acknowledged her appraisal. "Yep. Spent five years in the league. Defensive tackle for the Eagles."

"I thought so!" Christian said.

By the extended belly and the broken capillaries on his nose, Jade guessed he spent more time these days chasing pints of Guinness with shots than chasing running backs. She introduced Christian and Max.

Detective O'Shaunessy led them over to the drive-thru

microphone. "The victim ordered her drink right before it happened. The employee who took her order asked her to come to the window a few times. When the victim didn't respond or move, the employee told his manager. The manager had already received complaints from drive-thru customers who had come inside the store to order. Other customers came inside when the victim's horn went off. None of the customers in line bothered to check out what was going on in her car. They needed their caffeine, I guess. The manager came out and found the victim's head on the steering wheel. The horn, still blaring. She saw blood everywhere and ran back into the store to call us."

Jade scanned the surroundings. "This happened at what time?"

"About four-thirty p.m."

"So, it was still daylight," Jade said. "With no trees or anything else around, how come no one saw the UNSUB?"

"The teenage girl in the car behind the victim observed her ordering, but began texting with a friend and stopped paying attention. She looked up when the horn started going off. She thought she saw a guy walking away, but couldn't be sure. There were cars behind her so she couldn't back up. She began taking selfies and Snapchatting her story that she was stuck in a line at Starbucks, but didn't think to get out of the car to find out why."

"No one else in line witnessed anything?" Jade asked.

"They were all on their cell phones," O'Shaunessy said.

"Unbelievable," Christian said.

"Not really," O'Shaunessy said. "How many times do you go to a restaurant and most of the customers are staring at their phones? Bus stops? Coffee shops? People would rather communicate with anyone else besides the people they're with."

"How did the UNSUB know Holder would be here?" Jade asked.

"The victim came to this Starbucks every day at about the same time. Ordered the same thing. She was running a little late yesterday, though."

"Any evidence?" Christian asked.

"We lifted a shoeprint over there," O'Shaunessy said, pointing toward a grassy median that separated the Starbucks from a nearby Wendy's. They walked over to where he had pointed.

Jade crouched for a closer view. "Pretty big feet. He was walking away from the car. Someone must have seen him at the Wendy's. Any results back, yet, on the shoeprint?"

O'Shaunessy shook his head. "Seen enough?"

Jade glanced at Christian and Max. Max held her gaze, but said nothing.

As he walked them back toward the car, Jade asked, "Have you interviewed her co-workers? Any enemies? Any threats?"

O'Shaunessy nodded. "We're in the process of doing that now."

"And?"

"Our problem isn't determining whether she had any enemies. It's narrowing down the list."

CHAPTER SIXTY

Bethesda, Maryland

COLE BRENNAN RELAXED with his wife and six children in their family room. He loved the term "family room." How appropriate.

He took a sip of his drink. Cole was stressed. Between the election next week, Liz Holder's murder, and someone wanting him dead, he had about all the anxiety he could take. Not to mention trying to save this damn country from the Socialists.

Was it worth it? Was saving the country worth risking his life? Maybe he should give the Democrats what they want. *Atlas Shrugged* them. When the nation drowned from runaway debt, twenty-five percent unemployment, loss of morals, and lost its superpower status, would the liberals be happy? The US would become the Great Britain of the twenty-first century—the former superpower of the eighteenth and nineteenth centuries, now reduced to being the obedient lap dog of the United States. The US, however, would be licking Chinese boots. Boots Made in China.

He laughed out loud.

His daughter, Kaitlin, raised an eyebrow. "What's so funny, Dad?"

"Nothing, sweetheart."

"You're doing it again, Dad. This is supposed to be family time."

He smiled at her. "You're right. I'm sorry."

His son, Ryan, came to stand before him. "Dad, guess what!"

"What, Sport?"

"I scored today!"

"You did? Wow! I wish I could've been there. I had to work late. That's awesome. High-five!" Cole reached his arm out to his son.

Cole Jr. groaned. "Dad, high-fiving is so out."

Cole retracted his arm. "Oh?"

"Try a fist bump," Cole Jr. suggested.

"That's okay, Dad," Ryan said. "Wait! I forgot to show you something!" He sprinted out of the room.

The running and yelling would annoy a lesser man, but Cole loved it. He wasn't a lesser man.

Ryan returned carrying a soccer ball.

Cole gazed into his son's beaming face. This face was what he was fighting for. "What do you have there, Sport?"

Ryan offered the ball to him, as if it were a Fabergé egg. "One of the dads gave this to me for scoring a goal!"

"Wow! That was nice of him."

Cole spun the blue and white soccer ball in his hands. In one of the white panels, the letters "TSK" were scrawled in black magic marker.

Pain tore through his stomach and his hands started to shake.

Cole dropped the ball.

CHAPTER SIXTY-ONE

Arlington, Virginia

JADE ENTERED WON Ho's Tae Kwon Do Academy, which was located a few miles from her house. She was dressed in a gray sleeveless sweatshirt and black workout tights. Master Ho had given her a key.

The place was empty at this time of night, as it should have been. She went through the small lobby and performed a slight bow before entering the dojang (school), not caring whether anyone else was present to ensure she obeyed the rules. She placed her gear bag against the wall and ran some laps and stretched to warm up.

Master Ho entered the dojang and walked over to her. She jumped to her feet, and they bowed to each other. Bowing in Tae Kwon Do was a sign of respect. She bowed to show respect for her instructor, the art, and herself.

"Good to see you, Ms. Harrington. It's been a long time."

"I've been a little busy, sir. I didn't think anyone would be here."

He shook his head. "Paperwork. Always paperwork."

"Do you mind if I work out?"

"Not at all. I'll come out and spar with you in a little while."

Jade gazed down on his short-cropped silver hair. As a fourth-degree black belt, she didn't require an instructor to work out with her.

"You don't have to, sir. I know it's late."

He shot her a look and left.

She started off doing *poomsae* (forms). She loved performing the predetermined patterns of movement, kicks, punches, and blocks, and the concentration, strength, coordination, and flexibility required to do them well. She tried to execute the form for her rank better each time, competing with no one but herself.

Master Ho returned twenty minutes later in his sparring gear. She ran to her bag and put on her gear and moved to the middle of the mat. They bowed to each other again.

She went into her sparring stance and—

He kicked her in the head with a round kick.

Although over sixty years old, Master Ho had the physique of a man twenty years younger. He could still fight. Despite the headgear, the kick stung. A lot. While her head rang, she spun and landed a side kick in his kidney. He grunted and nodded, pleased. Counterattacking was the key to being a good fighter.

They exchanged punches and kicks until Jade punched him, hard. But missed.

"Damn it!" She took off her headgear and slammed it to the mat. The gear rolled away from them.

Master Ho walked over, picked it up, and returned it to her. He stared into her eyes.

"A good fighter never loses control. You cannot control

every situation, but you can always control your body and your mind." He pointed to his temple. "The circumstance is not of consequence, but how you react to it is. Being still and doing nothing are two very different things."

She nodded her head, then stopped. "Wait . . . isn't that a line from *The Karate Kid*?"

The lines around his eyes twinkled. "No one can be endowed with all wisdom." He stared into her eyes, as if trying to see into her soul. "Ms. Harrington, trust your training."

"Yes, sir. Thank you, sir." She bowed.

Master Ho bowed. He hesitated before touching her shoulder, a brief yet comforting gesture. He nodded and left.

Jade had never noticed physical affection from him to her or any of his students. She stood there for a moment, assuring herself it had happened before splaying out on the floor and removing her gear. She stuffed all of it into her bag. Crossing her legs Indian-style, she closed her eyes.

For years, Zoe had tried to interest her in Zen Buddhism and meditation. At first, Jade didn't care much for the meditational aspect of Tae Kwon Do. She would rather hit people.

She focused her mind on her breathing. In, out. In, out. In, out. As often happened when her mind was quiet and her body stilled, thoughts of the past came forward unbeckoned. Growing up as an Army brat, the only mixed-race kid in her neighborhood, and a bullying victim made for a lonely childhood. She had thought then she was the only person in the world who lived like that. Besides Zoe, she had never had any friends. What was the point when her family could move away at any time? She felt disconnected from others. No one *got* her. Or she didn't get them. Now, she preferred to be alone.

She had a greater connection to athletes or actors on television than people in the real world.

Jade had no time or need for romance. Never did. After three years of playing professionally in the WNBA and overseas in Japan, she started later than other agents at the Academy. She not only had to catch up, but she had to be better. Her work was her love. Being the best, her mission.

She did not have time for Landon Phillips.

Several thoughts swirled around in her head at once: the killer, the leaks, the slow progress of the investigation, all interwoven with pictures of the victims adorning the walls of the conference room at the Bureau.

After fifteen minutes, she gave up, realizing the meditation had failed to calm her mind. Or, maybe, she failed to let it. She opened her eyes and studied herself in the full-length wall mirror. She looked away.

She toweled off her face, stood, and started to zip her bag. Her phone indicated she had received a text message. She snatched it out of the bag.

Christian had texted an address and told her to meet him first thing in the morning.

TSK had sent Cole Brennan a gift.

Early the next morning, Jade knocked on a massive red door. She had already rung the bell. The door swung open to the big man himself.

"Mr. Brennan, I'm Special Agent Jade Harrington and this is Special Agent Christian Merritt. We'd like to talk to you about the soccer ball your son received. May we come in?"

Cole Brennan's eyes did a quick survey of her body before moving aside. "Come on in."

She stepped into the foyer and marveled at the two curved staircases with black iron railing that led upstairs. Brennan led them toward the back of the house. She stopped at the door to a large room. Inside, chaos. She had heard he had six kids, but now she *knew* it. A woman sat on the sofa, her smile vacant, the skin around her eyes tight.

"This is my wife, Ashley. Ash, this is Agent Merritt and Jade."

"Agent Harrington," Jade corrected, shaking Ashley's hand.

Brennan addressed the room at large.

"Kids, these are our friends. We're going to go chat with them."

The younger children paid little attention and continued to play. Not fooled, the teenagers eyed Jade and Christian from their spots on the floor in front of the TV.

"Follow me," Brennan said.

He led them to a room off the great room. His home office. He waved for them to sit as he settled into a leather chair behind the grand desk. He nodded to his wife to close the door. She came up and stood beside him, placing her hand on his shoulder.

Brennan's demeanor changed as soon as the door closed, his face darkening.

"What are you doing to catch this liberal freak? He talked to my son!"

Ashley pressed down on his shoulder. "Keep your voice down, sweetheart."

Brennan ignored her. To Christian, "Are you any closer to catching this guy?"

Jade stared at Brennan waiting for him to turn to her. He didn't.

"Mr. Brennan," Jade said. "First, we need to make sure it's him. We're pursuing several leads. We had the soccer ball dusted for prints. The only prints on it were yours and your son's."

Brennan addressed Christian.

"Of course, it's him. TSK. The other parents don't hate me enough to play a joke like that." He paused. "I don't think. What are you doing to protect my family?"

Christian pointed at Jade, his eyes not leaving Brennan's.

"She's the boss, sir."

Brennan sighed and faced her as if it were painful.

"Your house is under surveillance," Jade said, "and agents are covering your office building. We're shadowing all of you to the best of our ability with the limited resources we have."

"Typical. The FBI is a stupid and useless government agency that should be eliminated."

Jade stood. "Then, we should be going. I trust you can find someone else to protect you and your family and to catch this killer. Good day."

She eyed Christian and they both moved toward the door.

"Wait! Come back!"

Jade paused.

Brennan gestured to the chair. "Sorry. Please sit. I'm just stressed out."

After Jade resettled in her seat, she looked past him. "Mrs. Brennan, may we talk to your son?"

Cole Brennan, stunned at the rebuff, glanced over his shoulder at his wife. She gazed at him. He nodded absently and she left.

"Mr. Brennan, have you received any suspicious calls lately? At work or home?"

"I don't think so. Socialists know better than to call me."

Jade eyed Christian again, willing herself not to roll her eyes.

Ashley came in with a young boy. Christian stood and moved to the credenza underneath the window, leaning against it. Jade smiled at the boy, patting the chair Christian vacated.

"Hi, there. Why don't you sit next to me?"

The child looked at his mother and she nodded. He sat.

"What's your name?" Jade asked.

"Ryan!"

"How old are you, Ryan?"

"I just turned seven!"

"So, you like soccer?"

Ryan's face broke out into a grin. "Yeah!"

Jade flinched, not sure why he was yelling. She glanced at Christian, who was trying not to laugh.

"I played soccer, too."

"It's so much fun!"

"I think so, too." She leaned forward, elbows on her knees. In a soothing voice, she said, "Tell me about the man who gave you the soccer ball."

"After the game, he told me 'Awesome goal!' and he said, 'Here's a present for scoring.'"

"Can you tell me what he looked like?"

Ryan thought for a moment.

"He was tall."

"Do you remember anything else, Ryan? Anything at all?"

Ryan scrunched up his face, deep in thought. "No, that's it." After another moment, "Wait!"

"What? What do you remember?"

Ryan tilted his head to the side. "He was skinny. Not fat, like my daddy."

ൿ

The October air was cool, the leaves beginning to change color. After the interview, they had spoken to the agent in charge of Cole Brennan's security detail. Now, Jade and Christian walked the perimeter of his home, checking on security.

Christian surveyed the property as they walked. "Did you check out the wife?"

"Yes."

"She was creepy. With that plastic smile and those glassy eyes, and how she stared straight ahead, it was almost as if she were—"

"A Stepford wife."

"Yes!"

The leaves crunched underneath their feet.

Christian smiled at her. "He sure doesn't hold back, does he? Everyone's a Socialist. He wants to eliminate the FBI."

Jade shook her head. "It's no wonder someone wants to kill him."

CHAPTER SIXTY-TWO

Philadelphia, Pennsylvania

COLE BRENNAN STOOD at the podium. He scanned the auditorium audience, the place packed, expectant faces waiting for him to begin. Wearing a white dress shirt opened at the collar and tan slacks, he was sweating under the lights. It didn't help that the shirt felt a little snug after fitting only a few months ago.

He didn't feel right being here. He should have stayed home, to be there for his family. But he had made a commitment. And this election was too important.

Cole began to speak.

"We had our only presidential debate last week. Today, I want to provide answers to our most pressing problems for which there is no debate. You see, politicians tend to fill their speeches with highfalutin ideas and beautiful prose. I want to talk about the specific common-sense things I would do if I were president of this great country." He paused and smiled. "But don't get any ideas, folks!" He waited for the laughter to die down.

"No, I'm not running for president, but I do love my country. At the rate we're going, though, the debts of the

Greatest Generation, the Baby Boomers, and Generation X will be repaid by the Millennials and the next generation. And because of that, those generations will not have a chance at the American Dream as we had, unless we do something about it now.

"We need to eliminate federal agencies by privatizing or moving their functions to the states, or relying on private businesses or charities to perform them. I volunteer a lot of my time to raise money for learning-disabled children. I choose to donate my hard-earned money to people less fortunate than me. To me, that is much better than the government giving it to low-income folks to pay for their flat-screen televisions.

"All right. Do you want specifics on how we can reduce the deficit?"

"Yes!" the audience yelled.

"First, we need to eliminate the Department of Energy. We don't need a national plan to address our energy needs. We possess plenty of good sources of energy right here: oil, gas, and coal. The DOE—it should be D-I-E—has been poorly managed and wasteful from the get-go. It is counterproductive to fund wrong or inefficient energy companies. Let the private sector fund research into alternative energy. We need to shut down the DOE!

"During the first half of the last decade, we gave one-point-two billion dollars to farmers who no longer farm and a bunch of money to large farming companies who don't need it. Agriculture subsidies never made sense and they don't make sense now. Shut it down!

"Fraught with scandals since it came into existence, the Department of Housing and Urban Development should be eliminated. Understand this folks, federal subsidies help people buy homes they can't afford. Federal rent subsidies make people reliant on the government to pay for something that is their responsibility. Shut it down!

"As for the Department of Labor, unemployment insurance should be the responsibility of the states and OSHA downsized. Eliminate the federal minimum wage and job training . . . what in the world does the government know about training? Have you called the IRS lately? Shut it down!

"We need to privatize air traffic control. Canada created a private nonprofit organization to manage its air traffic. Our Federal Aviation Administration is poorly funded and has no idea how to innovate. Let's be more like Canada, eh? Shut it down!"

On a roll, the sweat poured down Cole's face, but he didn't care. He didn't wipe it away. Some members of the audience were standing up now and shouting "Shut it down!" with him, transforming the auditorium into an evangelical experience. The Department of Commerce, Federal Transit Administration, Federal Highway Administration, Department of Transportation, and Amtrak were all on his chopping block. Cole decided to wind down his speech. He could talk about this stuff forever.

"Assistance for needy families, children's health insurance, and Head Start can all be provided by the states or funded privately. We don't need the federal government to do these things."

By now, every single person in the audience was standing and applauding and cheering. The crowd flowed out into the aisles. He took a deep breath. He finally wiped his forehead with a hand towel and placed it back down on the podium.

"The federal government can slash the deficit if it has

the will to do so." He paused. "If it has the will to do so." He repeated. "This is what's at stake in this election. A feminist Socialist who hasn't done much in the Senate is trying to unseat President Richard Ellison, a strong, conservative Republican and a good family man. Don't be fooled by Whitney's new moderate attitude. Once she's elected, she'll pull out Karl Marx's Communist Manifesto and turn America into twentieth-century Russia. If you don't believe me, folks, go back and read the papers she wrote in college. You'll receive a Socialist education. For your convenience, we've posted all of her undergraduate and graduate papers on my website, www.theconservativevoiceonline.com.

"Now, Richard Ellison is a man we can trust. Didn't he re-enact 'Don't Ask, Don't Tell, Don't Worry?' He's done more for America's families than any president since the late, great, President Ronald Reagan. Have you seen Whitney's family? She lives in Washington, DC. Her husband lives in Missouri in a very friendly neighborhood. What kind of marriage is that? Do we want a long-distance, open marriage in the White House? What kind of example does that set for our kids? Also, if she's that hands-off in representing her constituents in Missouri, what will happen if she becomes the president of the good ol' US of A?

"Whitney Fairchild is untested, untried, and unfit to be our president.

"I want my posse to get out and vote and get your neighbors out to vote. We can't leave this election to chance. We can't allow the Commiecrats back in office. Your children's future depends on it. Help me to re-elect President Richard Ellison, who has the will to give our children a future of prosperity and freedom rather than one of paying off the previous generations' debts.

"Thank you for having me tonight. God bless you and God bless the United States of America."

The applause was deafening.

Cole had given it his best shot. The rest was up to Ellison.

CHAPTER SIXTY-THREE

St. Louis, Missouri

YESTERDAY, WHITNEY, TED, and the road show flew across the country for last-minute campaigning, chasing the sun from east to west. She arrived home from California late last night. It had been a while since Whitney had been home. Her real home. She rose at six a.m., as if it were any other day. Grayson slept.

She pumped away at the elliptical machine in their home gym in St. Louis while watching a simulated bike ride through the mountains on a massive projection screen. She pushed herself hard, not sure when she would be able to work out again. Forty minutes later, she went back to their bedroom.

She watched him sleep for a few moments.

After learning about the affair five months ago, she still felt like crying every time she looked at him. She had thought long and hard about him, their marriage, his mistake. When she transcended the most difficult part of the pain, she thought about the role she had played in what happened. She hadn't been there for him or her family. In some ways, she still wasn't. She wasn't excusing what he did, but she believed she had to own her part of it. Grayson was human, and that's why she ultimately decided to forgive him.

She woke him. Head on the pillow, his hair grazing his forehead, he gazed up at her and smiled. The same smile that made her fall in love with him all those years ago.

He searched her eyes. "Is it time?"

"It's time."

"Okay, I'll get up."

He pushed up on one elbow, and she took his face in her hands. "Let's take a shower."

"Together?"

She nodded. They hadn't made love since she found out.

"Are you sure?" Grayson asked. "Do we have time?"

Whitney took his hand and helped him to his feet.

Afterward, she walked down the hall to the children's rooms. Emma's room was white: white bed, white dresser, white walls. Posters of the singers Adele and Bruno Mars adorned her walls. Whitney touched her daughter's shoulder.

"Are you ready?"

Emma sprang up and gave her mother a hug. "I love you, Momma. I'm so proud of you."

Whitney, surprised at her own tears, hugged her back, tight.

She didn't go into Chandler's room. When he turned fourteen, his room began to take on a locker-room odor that nauseated her. She knocked several times, before he grumbled, "I'm up!"

"Are you ready?"

"I will be."

She went back to her bedroom. She sat in front of her vanity mirror in the sitting area adjacent to the bathroom to apply her makeup—not too much—before moving to her dressing room to put on a new suit designed by the up-and-coming female American designer Ashley Smith. She admired herself in the full-length standalone mirror and nodded.

Grayson sat on the off-white upholstered chestnut bench at the foot of the bed. Dressed in a dark blue three-piece suit, white shirt with a spread collar, light blue tie, and polished black dress shoes, he had his coat draped over one arm. He held a fedora hat in his other hand. She loved fedora hats.

"You look nice."

He gave her a smile, tinged with regret. "And you look beautiful, darling. Oh, and presidential."

She peered down at her suit in the same shade of blue as his, wiping away imaginary lint. She took a deep breath, exhaled, and held out her hand. "I'm ready."

He rose and took her hand in his strong, firm one. He squeezed. It did not give her the feeling of comfort, of safety, that it once did. Forgiving and forgetting were two different things.

They walked down the stairs. At the bottom, her children, dressed up, smiled as they looked up at their parents. Sarah, her body woman, and a few other members of her staff and Secret Service agents waited with them. As she reached the bottom stair, Josh McPherson, her lead Secret Service agent, slid in beside her.

"Are you ready, ma'am?"

She nodded.

He brought his wrist to his mouth. "Twilight is ready to move."

"Twilight?"

"I noticed that you read young-adult novels when you think no one is around."

Whitney laughed. "I like it."

Whitney and Grayson stepped onto the porch. A large crowd had assembled beyond the wrought-iron gate of their front yard. They gave each other much-practiced smiles, as the cameras clicked, turned to the crowd and waved.

It was a beautiful, crisp Tuesday in November.

Election Day had arrived.

❧

Whitney turned to her husband. "I forgot something."

She came out a few minutes later carrying a box.

Grayson shook his head, mystified. "Sweetie, what are you doing? Do you need some help with that?"

To Josh, she said, "Come with me. And bring some of your friends."

"Where are you going?" Grayson asked.

As Whitney headed out the gate enveloped by Secret Service agents, the crowd parted and then followed behind her. She strode to the front door of the house and knocked. A minute later, her neighbor answered the door. Although it had been two years since Whitney had seen her, the woman had aged ten. *That's what being hounded by the paparazzi will do to you.* When once Whitney regarded her as Midwestern cute, now she only looked plain.

The neighbor peered around Whitney at the large men in suits and sunglasses and the crowd beyond. She shrank away from Whitney's gaze. "What do you want?"

"You left these dishes at my house. Your services are no longer required."

❧

Standing with her hands on the railing, craving a cigar, Whitney admired the spectacular view from the luxury suite's balcony at the Ritz Carlton in Clayton, a suburb of St. Louis. She welcomed the cool night air on her face after being surrounded by people all day. She and Grayson had voted early in the morning and spent the rest of the day crisscrossing the state, shaking hands at as many polling places as possible.

Competing with the election coverage on television and social media, was Whitney's visit to her neighbor. Not only the television cameras, but many of the people in the crowd caught the exchange on video for posterity. #NeighborBoom was the number-one trending topic on Twitter for most of the day.

She drifted back into the living room. Ted, Landon, Grayson, Sarah, vice presidential candidate Xavi Fernandez and his family, friends, and others sat or stood near the television, their eyes fixed on the electoral map on the screen.

The returns had started to come in.

Maine, New Hampshire, New York, and all the northeastern states had gone to her. Georgia, South Carolina, Alabama, and the rest of the Southern states went to Ellison. No surprises, yet.

They split two of the battleground states. Ellison won North Carolina. She smiled to herself. She had eaten all that barbecue and potato salad for nothing.

Whitney took Virginia.

Thank you, high school kids.

The Midwestern states started coming in for the president: Nebraska, Kansas, Oklahoma, and—no surprise—Texas with its thirty-eight electoral votes. She picked up the key states of Michigan and, of course, her home state, Missouri.

The lead changed hands all night. And, then, she won Ohio.

As Ohio goes, so does the nation. She turned and gazed into Grayson's eyes.

Are we really going to do this?

He patted her hand, but didn't say a word.

They had never discussed what they were going to do if she won the presidency. Would he relinquish the CEO position to one of his brothers? Would he take a leave of absence? Or would he continue to work? Had a president ever had a long-distance marriage? Not in recent history. She had not wanted to jinx her chances by speaking to him about it.

A couple of her staffers shushed the others.

Someone turned the volume up on the television.

Blaine Jones, who had moderated the presidential debate, anchored the election coverage for CNN. He stared into the camera, and Breaking Results flashed at the bottom of the screen. A picture of Whitney popped up next to a picture of Florida. A big, blue check mark next to her face.

"This just in, CNN is now projecting that the state of Florida will go to Senator Whitney Fairchild."

The gathering in the room erupted in cheers. With the explosion of Florida's population over the past sixty-five years, its importance in presidential elections had grown. The sunshine state not only had the third-largest number of electoral votes, but also its diverse population represented a microcosm of the United States. Whitney was glad Florida now had its voting act together. The people should decide elections, not the Supreme Court.

She eyed Xavi Fernandez, the governor of Florida, from across the room, and nodded her thanks. He smiled and raised his glass of champagne to her. Adding him to the ticket had paid off, but she wondered at what cost. He wanted to be president. Now. Not eight years from now. She would need to watch her back.

Whitney grabbed Grayson's hand while continuing to stare at the television.

One more.

She needed one more.

California.

Several minutes passed with no results. The staff parked in front of the television became antsy and started moving around the room.

Whitney did not move. The polls for California closed at 10 p.m. Central. The time was now 10:05.

CNN cut from a commercial.

She glanced at the Breaking Results at the bottom of the screen and at Blaine's face. He had a slight twinkle in his eye.

And she knew.

Her face appeared on the screen next to her name. Underneath her picture were the words Elected President. The living room was quiet for the first time that evening, except for the tinkling of ice in someone's glass.

"CNN has projected the states of California, Oregon, Washington, and Hawaii for Senator Whitney Fairchild. Whitney Fairchild, the Democratic Senator from Missouri, will be the next—and the first woman—president of the United States."

All around her, friends and campaign staff jumped up and down while trying to hug each other. Some cried. CNN cut to different cities across the country and around the world where crowds celebrated her victory.

She stared at the screen, hand over her mouth, in shock. Ted had told her the polls indicated it would be close, but she should win. She had found it hard to believe him. She faced Grayson. He smiled and held his arms wide. She fell into them.

He whispered into her hair. "I love you. I have always loved only you. I'm so proud of you, darling."

She clung to him, but did not respond. After a while, the others gathered around her, waiting. She stood to make it easier for them to hug her. She raised both arms.

"We did it!"

Everyone started cheering. She accepted the hugs from her family, staff, and members of the road show who had been with her every step of the way during the last two years. All of them felt like family. And this would be the last night they would all be together. Some of them would join her transition team and the administration. Most would not.

Whitney gazed out the window at the Gateway Arch, a monument to westward expansion and now a milestone in the country's history.

In a few minutes, she would be leaving for the Arch to deliver her acceptance speech as the first female president-elect of the United States of America.

CHAPTER SIXTY-FOUR

Bethesda, Maryland

A COMMENTATOR FOR THE Patriot News television network insisted that all the votes weren't in for Ohio. But with the loss of California, it didn't matter. It was over.

Cole Brennan stared in disbelief at the television in his family room.

This did *not* just happen.

His wife, Ashley, patted his back and said soothing words to him he couldn't, wouldn't hear.

The tall, lanky, former cowboy—and soon-to-be former president—stood with his wife and two children on a stage somewhere in Wyoming and spoke about what he had accomplished over the last four years. That this wasn't the end, but only a setback. The beginning of the next phase of the journey. Their party was stronger than ever and its ideals would endure.

The son of a bitch doesn't even appear upset that he lost.

Cole dropped his head into his hands. He felt sick to his stomach. When he looked up, the scene on the television screen changed to the imposing Gateway Arch. The camera cut to Whitney's beaming face.

Cole couldn't take it anymore. He swept the remote off the coffee table and pressed the power button.

He got up and left the room to go to bed without a word to Ashley.

CHAPTER SIXTY-FIVE

St. Louis, Missouri

IT HAD BEEN a long night. I finally got back to the hotel and now sat on the room's couch, my eyes rarely moving from the television screen. A bottle of Ketel One kept me company on the side table. The hotel room was dark except for the light from the TV. The election coverage had been on nonstop; I even had a chance to watch the best parts again: Ohio, Florida, California. I poured a generous portion of vodka into a glass and placed my stockinged feet on the ottoman. As always, I had removed my shoes at the door. I do not like elements from the outside world contaminating my home or anywhere I slept.

An estimated one million people witnessed President-Elect Whitney Fairchild's election speech in person. The place was electric. Spectators in the crowd interviewed by on-the-scene reporters provided a consistent response; they were blessed to be given a once-in-a-lifetime opportunity to witness history.

The network was broadcasting her speech again.

The camera angle descended from the Gateway Arch to a close-up of Whitney's face. Her shoulder-length, light brown hair, with a tint of auburn, stirred in the wind. She gave her speech without notes or a teleprompter. Although she had a speechwriter, it was public knowledge that she wrote the major revisions herself.

Whitney scanned the crowd. "I am standing here, in my home state of Missouri, the geographic center and heart of the United States. Missouri is called the 'Show Me' state for a reason. Our residents are hardworking, independent, stubborn, conservative, and prudent. Like me . . . well, except for the conservative part." She smiled, as the audience laughed.

I did not.

"America was once a great country," the president-elect continued. "A place where you could raise a family, get a good job, enjoy your civil liberties, and retire after many years of service. A country you could be proud of, respected around the world for its leadership, diplomacy, innovation, and economic might."

President-Elect Whitney Fairchild fell silent.

"I promise you. We will make America great once again."

The crowd went wild. After a few seconds, Fairchild held up her hand for silence.

"America will once again be a place where individuals of all faiths, all races, and all walks of life can live together, work together, and use our differences to make us stronger rather than to divide us. We need to stop the discrimination against our Muslim-American brothers and sisters. We should not judge them by the acts of a few terrorists, as all Christians would not want to be judged by the acts of Timothy McVeigh.

"We must find a balance between safety and liberty. A liberty that allows fairness and unity. A former president once said, 'Tyranny is no match for liberty.' For those who want to cause harm to the United States, please listen and understand. We will continue to fight and defeat terrorism wherever we may find it. I warn you not to mistake our diplomacy for weakness.

"The United States, however, is not united now. We are a house divided. Our Pledge of Allegiance asserts we are 'One nation, under God, indivisible.'" She scanned the crowd. "Indivisible." She repeated.

"Today our country is like a large family with a big inheritance and our politicians are its children fighting between themselves to squander our money, our prosperity, and our liberty. So, what can we do about it?" She paused and pointed to the crowd. "We write the politicians out of the will!" She waited for the shouts of agreement to subside. "We need politicians who will work together, not at odds with each other. After this Congress and I take our oaths of office, we must put partisan politics aside and do what is best for this nation. Compromise is not a dirty word, but a necessity to govern." She paused for a few moments to gather herself for her concluding remarks. She scanned the crowd again and smiled.

I loved that smile.

Our next president did not mention me. With less opposition in the media—thanks to me—the divide should close and the country will become great once again.

Whitney continued. "During a campaign, politicians talk about everything they are going to do on 'day one.' But there are not enough hours in one day to resolve all the problems in this country. Our problems were not created in a day, and they will not be solved in a day. The solutions will take time, and they will not be easy. I remember hearing the stories from my parents about the race riots in the Sixties, and how they chose to be involved and fight for what is right and what is fair, even though their lives would have been much easier if they had stayed silent and lived a peaceful middle-class existence in the suburbs. Like my parents, I refuse to stay silent.

"I stand before you humbled and honored by your faith in me to lead this nation. Yes, we have a lot of work to do, but on this night, let us take a moment to celebrate and rejoice. I believe in this country. I believe in you. We can do this together. God bless you and God bless the United States of America!"

The crowd erupted again. Fireworks went off, lighting up the midnight sky. Everyone was so happy. Some people had tears streaming down their faces. It was as if Jesus Christ himself had been elected our Lord and Savior. I hugged the near-empty glass of vodka to my heart.

Whitney Fairchild summoned her husband and their two handsome grown children next to her behind the transparent, two-inch thick, bulletproof glass. They had their arms around each other's waists and bore huge smiles as they waved to the audience.

Using the remote, I froze the picture.

I walked around the ottoman and stood in front of the television, holding my glass. I traced each of their faces from their foreheads to their noses to their chins. I touched their cheeks. It was not lost on me that I had traced the sign of the cross over each of them.

I started to return to my chair and stopped. I finished my drink.

And I threw the glass at the television screen as hard as I could.

Nothing happened at first. And then a tiny crack formed. The crack made a slow, formal march downward.

I unpaused the screen. Whitney's family continued to wave and smile, now with a jagged line dividing them. How fitting.

Why is no one listening to me? Why am I not being taken seriously? Do they not realize who I am? Why am I not receiving the credit I deserve?

She ignored me. Congress ignored my demands. I must not be doing enough to get their attention. To get her attention.

After the long wave session, the network commentators began analyzing the president-elect's speech. This blather would take hours. The program cut to a commercial. Cole Brennan filled my screen holding his latest book.

That was the last straw.

I turned off the television, poured myself another drink, and walked over to the desk. I settled in the chair and took a sip of my drink, setting the replacement glass next to my laptop as I tapped the space bar. Good thing the hotel provided four glasses.

I leaned back, hands in my lap, closed my eyes, and exhaled a cleansing breath.

I opened my eyes and sat up, staring at the monitor. "Cole Brennan" was already typed into the browser's search bar.

I pushed Enter.

CHAPTER SIXTY-SIX

Washington, DC

SINCE THE SHANE Tallent killing in Seattle, the CONFAB task force had moved to a major-case room at FBI HQ to signify the importance of the case and to accommodate the team's growing number of members. The space resembled a war room, with photographs, maps, sketches, and notations plastering the walls.

Jade faced the team from the front of the room, pictures of each of the known victims of TSK, in life and in death, on the large flat-panel screens behind her. Liz Holder's publicity photo was the latest addition. The agents sat in chairs spread out before her. Ethan stood by the door.

She gave him a slight nod. He nodded in return. His faith in her unwavering. Still.

She held up her hands. "Let's get started."

The room quieted. Jade outlined the security measures taken at Cole Brennan's home and office. Agents posed as employees at his employer, Patriot News.

"What do you have for me?"

Christian waved his hand.

"Using the facial composite, we were able to trace the

UNSUB's flight to Seattle. It originated in DC. He flew under the name Michael Brown."

Jade looked at Max, surprised. "This couldn't have anything to do with Ferguson could it?"

Max shrugged. "Who knows at this point? Maybe."

Jade turned back to Christian. "Connecting flight?"

Christian shook his head. "Not as far as we know."

Did the killer live here?

Other agents had minor information to report.

"I have something else," Jade said, nodding to an agent at the back of the room. The lights dimmed. "CNN sent us this iReport." Jade pressed a button on the remote and an image filled the large projection screen beside her. The picture was moving from side to side, as if the person holding the camera had Parkinson's disease or was striving for *The Blair Witch Project* effect. The camera's holder approached a parked car beside a drive-thru menu with a microphone in front of it. The camera turned. Inside the car, a woman with long, blonde hair was facing straight ahead, talking animatedly. As she turned toward the camera, something black filled the screen. A glint of metal flashed in the sunlight. The woman's head fell forward onto the steering wheel. The picture faded.

Jade glanced toward the back and waved her finger for the agent to turn on the lights.

Most of the agents' mouths were open.

"Man, that's sick!" Austin said, shaking his head back and forth.

"Was there audio? Did he send a note?" This from Christian.

"No," Jade said. She let the silence linger for a few moments. "Max?"

Max pushed up his glasses. "The murders are not only accelerating, but he is becoming bolder with each one."

"Do you think Brennan's next?" Austin asked.

"There's no doubt in my mind Cole Brennan is his next potential victim," Max said. "Every victim is more famous than the last." He paused. "But I want you to understand something. This guy won't go out in a blaze of glory, wanting the police to kill him after a standoff. No. He will kill Brennan and expect to get away with it. He believes he is doing the world a favor by eliminating their damaging rhetoric from our political discourse. Once Brennan is dead, his job is done. He wins. Liberals win. The country wins. He'll ride off into the sunset, finally attaining the respect he deserves."

Christian leaned forward to look at him. "So, what you're saying is he may knock off Brennan, go back to his life or leave the country, and we'll never find him."

Max nodded. "That's what I'm saying."

Jade glanced around the room.

"Everyone hang here for a few minutes while I give you your assignments. You may want to go home tonight and give your families a quick kiss, because you may not see them for a while."

❧

The next day, Jade reviewed interview reports from the Holder killing in her office at the Bureau. A witness reported he had been filling up his gas tank across the street from the Starbucks when he saw a man walking away from the scene with what he had described as a knife dripping with blood. She grabbed a photo showing a wide-angle shot of the crime scene and shook her head. Given the distance, a defense attorney would argue the witness wouldn't have been able to tell if the substance was blood or some other liquid—or whether he was holding a knife, for that matter.

Since the knife-wielding man seemed to be headed for the gas station, the witness got into his car and drove away, but not before seeing the man hop into what appeared to be a Ford Focus parked at the Wendy's. He was too far away to see the license plate number. After seeing the iReport of the killing on the news, the witness decided to perform his civic duty and report what he saw despite, he said, his feelings about the victim.

The Focus was traced to a Dollar Rent-A-Car located at the Westchester County airport. The car was rented by Eddie Cullen, who flew from DC on a direct flight from National Airport. Jade had sent a team of agents to interview the ticket agents and flight attendants for Cullen's flight and contacted the FBI New York Division to cover the rental car agency.

She presumed the name used for the Seattle flight, Michael Brown, and the name Eddie Cullen, were aliases. What was their significance? Jade racked her brain, but came up empty.

She set the reports aside and brought up some liberal blog sites. She had narrowed down the group of bloggers to ten. Some of them worked at MSNBC. Emulating the talking heads on television or online was easy enough. *We've become a society of talking points.*

A few hours later, Jade journeyed to the break room to refill her coffee. The sludge at the bottom of the pot looked uninviting and undrinkable. She poured the liquid to the brim of her cup and took a sip. *Nasty.*

She returned to her office, full cup in hand, and surveyed the organized stacks of paper on her desk. She kept TSK's manifesto on the corner of it, always within arm's reach. As she sat down, the document fell from the desk. Jade reacted without thinking and caught it without spilling her coffee. She smiled at her athleticism.

I've still got it.

She set the cup down and opened the manifesto to where her thumb held it. It was at the page of the drawing she had noticed before. Like before, she traced the caricature of congressmen and congresswomen standing on the Capitol Hill steps.

Her finger stopped.

Her pulse quickened. She had seen this drawing style before.

She called the main number for Chattenham College. After several transfers, someone answered, "WCCO."

"This is Special Agent Jade Harrington with the FBI. I visited your radio station five months ago and there was a mural on the station wall. Do you know who drew it?"

"No."

Jade waited for the person to continue. When he didn't, she snapped, "Can you find out?"

"Yeah. Hold on."

The student on the other end dropped the receiver without bothering to put her on hold. Jade monitored her breathing to give her something to do while she waited. In, out. In, out. After several excruciating minutes, the receiver was picked up.

"Ma'am?"

Jade exhaled a breath she didn't realize she was holding. *When did I become a ma'am?* "Yes, I'm here."

"His name was Hewitt. Caleb Hewitt."

"Thanks." Jade hung up.

Caleb Hewitt. The "C" in Kyle Williams's journal?

ꕥ

Jade didn't think she would ever visit Chattenham, Pennsylvania again in her lifetime.

Six hours had passed since she'd heard the name Caleb Hewitt for the first time, and now she and Max sat on a 1960s sofa covered in plastic in Hewitt's parents' living room. She wondered if Mrs. Hewitt knew this sofa was in style again. The Hewitts sat across from them on a matching sofa. Christian stood, arms crossed, near the window behind Jade.

Caleb no longer lived here.

After pleasantries and making the Hewitts feel at ease the FBI was in their home, Jade started the interview.

"When was the last time you saw your son?"

Mrs. Hewitt clasped her hands in her lap. She opened her mouth to answer, but closed it.

Mr. Hewitt had his arm around his wife, but not in a protective or comforting way. More as if he were playing a role in a performance.

"He left home about ten years ago," the father said. "After he graduated from college. We haven't seen or heard from him since."

Jade tried to hide her surprise. "Why?"

The mother examined her hands.

The father shrugged. "We don't know."

"What do you do, Mrs. Hewitt?"

"I'm the dean of the college."

Jade knew this. She had researched the Hewitts before she left DC. She turned to Mr. Hewitt.

"I'm a professor at the college," he said.

"He spends most of his time at the lab," Mrs. Hewitt added.

Mr. Hewitt glanced at his wife. His eyes narrowed and his jaw clenched. You didn't need to spend much time with this couple to realize that his time in the lab was a constant source of irritation in their marriage.

"I'm a scientist," Mr. Hewitt explained to Jade.

"Let's talk about Caleb."

The couple exchanged glances, but said nothing.

"What did he major in?"

"Philosophy." This from the husband.

"Did he participate in any extracurricular activities? Sports? Clubs?"

"The college radio station."

"Go on. What did he do there?"

"He was a disc jockey or commentator, whatever you call them. He had a weekly show in which he talked about politics."

"I saw a picture of the students who worked at the radio station. Your son wasn't in the photograph."

Mr. Hewitt glanced at his wife again. "That's because he . . . quit. After Hurricane Katrina and the federal government's reaction to the crisis, he sort of . . . lost it . . . on the air."

Caleb's mother looked up from her hands. "He was asked to leave the station."

No one spoke. The house was quiet, eerie. Jade wondered why Dante hadn't discovered all this during his investigation of the college yearbook. She knew the answer to her own question. He hadn't conducted an investigation. *Did he purposefully set her up for failure?*

Max spoke for the first time in his quiet way. "Mrs. Hewitt, do you know where your son is now?"

The woman's back straightened for the first time. "No, I don't."

ঌ

Jade stood and headed for the fireplace toward her left instead of the archway leading to the foyer on her right. Numerous pictures of a smiling, blond boy with a Beatles haircut dotted the mantle and a side table.

She picked one up and turned to Mrs. Hewitt. "Caleb seemed to be a happy boy."

For a brief, fleeting second, Mrs. Hewitt's eyes lit up. The Hewitts shared another look. Mrs. Hewitt wrung her hands. She opened her mouth to say something but nothing came out.

Mr. Hewitt hesitated, and said, "That's not Caleb."

"Oh?"

"That's our older son, James."

"Where is he now?"

"He . . . uh . . . died. When he was thirteen. A bicycle accident."

Jade replaced the frame on the mantel.

"Do you have any pictures of Caleb?"

Mrs. Hewitt nodded toward the pictures. "Such a happy boy, wasn't he? And he was smart and talented. An excellent athlete."

"What about Caleb, Mrs. Hewitt?" Max asked.

"Caleb was smart, too," Mrs. Hewitt said, "but he was quiet. Kept to himself. Spent a lot of time alone in his room. He didn't like sports much. He'd rather listen to the news." She gave Jade a feeble smile. "He was always . . . different."

Christian straightened from where he had been leaning against the window frame. "May we see his room?"

"You may," Mrs. Hewitt said, "but you won't find anything. I turned it into an office as soon as he left. My home office."

To prevent herself from pacing, Jade returned to the sofa and sat down. At her full height, she could be intimidating.

"Mrs. Hewitt, do you have any photographs of Caleb?"

The woman inspected her hands again. "I may. I'll need to check in the basement."

Jade stared into her eyes. "We'll wait."

ꟹ

Mrs. Hewitt returned with a photograph of Caleb with four other boys and two girls. The boys wore ill-fitting business suits, the girls, shirts and skirts. Caleb stood at the end. Long blond hair, a darker shade than his older brother's, leaning away from the others. Caleb appeared to be about fourteen.

This Career Day photograph was the most recent one Mrs. Hewitt had of her younger son.

The agents said good-bye to the Hewitts and walked toward their car parallel parked on the tree-lined street.

"Did you see how the mother's eyes lit up when she talked about her other son, James?" Christian said in a low voice.

"She couldn't wait to turn Caleb's room into an office for herself," Max added.

Jade pulled on the handle of the front door on the passenger side and looked across the top of the car at them.

"No wonder Caleb left and never came back."

CHAPTER SIXTY-SEVEN

Washington, DC

JADE SPENT THE next afternoon at the Bureau entering Christian's notes from the interview with the Hewitts into the database. She finished polishing off an Italiano sandwich from the Cosi across the street. At noon, swarms of agents left HQ for lunch at the many surrounding restaurants like kids sprinting out of an elementary school for recess. She avoided the rush by eating late.

She had given the photograph of Caleb Hewitt to Pat to analyze against the millions of faces kept on file and on the Internet. A nose, the width between the eyes, the chin, any aspect of the face could be matched and lead them to the suspect. Nothing had come back, yet. She also hadn't received any confirmed hits on the facial composite of the UNSUB.

Michael Brown.

Michael Brown, the name the UNSUB flew under from DC to Seattle.

Mrs. Hewitt had said Caleb had freaked out at the federal government's response to Hurricane Katrina. The person in charge of that operation worked for the Emergency

Preparedness and Response division of Homeland Security. His name was Michael Brown.

Coincidence?

Jade didn't believe in coincidences.

She stood, stretched, and paced her office before sitting back down again. Sometimes, when she wasn't making progress with a case, she started from the beginning. Jade pulled out a folder from the bottom of the stack containing the emails from TSK. She read the first one and leaned back in her chair.

Something about the first email bothered her. *What was it?*

She closed her eyes.

Something involving Zoe. She thought back to the time when she had been working at home and Zoe dropped by with dinner. They had talked about the Fairness Doctrine and the haves and have-nots. Zoe mentioned the online chat room and how its members discussed the email from TSK.

Something about that remark.

And it came to her.

Zoe's group had been discussing the email *before* it was released to the public.

She grabbed her cell phone, touched a button, and stood.

"Hey, you. Long time, no—"

"The guy in the chat room . . . what was his name?"

"You're not going to bother to say 'hello?'"

"Zoe, I don't have time. The guy."

"Which guy?"

"We were at my house. The chat room. Where you talk with like-minded individuals. You told me once about a guy in that room. You said he was intense. We talked about the TSK email. What was his name?"

"Oh. Him. He uses the name Oedipus."

"But what's his real name?"

"I don't remember. Hold on, hold on. You're making me nervous. Let me think."

Jade tightened the grip on her phone.

After a while, Zoe said, "Caleb. His real name is Caleb. I'm not supposed to know that, but he let it slip one—"

Jade hung up.

⁂

She put out an APB for Caleb Hewitt.

While waiting and without anything better to do, she reached over to a stack on her desk to pick up another report. Reading was more productive than pacing. The phone rang.

"Harrington."

Static. "Jade, it's Austin."

"What's up?"

"I may have something."

She sat up at the excitement in his voice. "What is it?"

More static.

"From the . . . three identical . . . voice—"

"What? You're breaking up. What about the three identical voices? Austin, are you there?"

"I'm going to move." He said nothing for thirty seconds. "Can you hear me—?"

The line went dead.

Jade speed-dialed Austin's number. The phone rang and rang and rang. She disconnected and tried again. And again.

Her calls kept going to his voicemail.

She tossed the phone on her desk and sat back hard.

She got up and started to pace and waited for Austin to call her back.

*

Jade placed her hand on the door handle.

Christian, a step behind her, said, "Where's Austin?"

"Not sure. He called me earlier and said he may have something. I haven't heard from him since. I've been trying to reach him all afternoon."

They walked in. Jade had had a liberal blogger named Evan Stevens brought in for questioning. Even though Caleb Hewitt was now the prime suspect, she decided not to cancel the interview.

Inside, sat a man, his posture excellent. He wore jeans and a button-down, black collared shirt. His hair was medium length and styled with gel, his short beard trimmed to perfection. His lawyer sat next to him, bent over a legal pad. Although the lawyer was in a suit, Evan Stevens appeared the better dressed of the two.

Jade went through the preliminaries of an interrogation.

"Tell me about your blogs."

"Have you read them?"

Jade didn't answer.

"What's there to tell? I write about injustice. Unfairness. Inequality."

"Is Evan Stevens your given name?"

"Yes."

She threw TSK's manifesto on the table. The document landed with a thud. Evan jumped.

"Did you write this?"

Evan leaned forward, peered at the cover. "No." He shifted

his eyes to his lawyer and back at Jade, his eyes boring into hers. "I discuss ideas. I don't need to kill anyone to get my point across."

"Your writing style is similar."

"A lot of people believe in an equitable and tolerant society."

Jade hesitated. This wasn't going well. She wished she could see Max's face through the interrogation window. She was wasting her time.

A knock on the door. Her boss, Ethan Lawson, leaned his head around the door frame.

What was he doing here?

"I need to talk to you," Ethan said. "Both of you."

Jade and Christian glanced at each other, and followed him out.

From behind her, Evan asked, "What about me?"

"I'll be back," Jade said, over her shoulder and shut the door.

Max and Pat were standing in the hallway.

"Ethan, I'm busy. What's up?"

The somberness on Ethan's face surprised her. She had never seen this expression on his face before.

"What happened?" Jade asked. "Another killing?"

He spun his wedding ring. Once. Twice. "Yes."

"Dammit!" Jade slapped the wall. "Brennan?"

"No," he said. "It wasn't Brennan."

"No? Who else could it be?"

"Jade," Ethan said, placing his hands on her shoulders. His eyes searched hers. "It was Austin."

A knot started to form in her stomach. "What about Austin?"

"He's dead, Jade."

Her legs failed her. She sagged against the wall, as if someone had punched her. Christian's strong hand gripped the back of her upper arm holding her up.

❧

Jade took two dribbles to the right, stopped on a dime, and went into her fluid shooting motion. The ball swished through the basket eighteen feet away, nothing but net.

Ordinarily, there was no sweeter sound.

Austin had discovered something and decided to check out his own lead. She still didn't know what he had found out.

His body was found by a couple of kids on an outdoor basketball court in Springfield, Virginia. Austin had stab wounds on the right side of his body. His tongue was left intact.

Austin wasn't a talk-show host.

After the crime-scene technicians had finished yesterday, she pushed her way through two agents as she used to bust through double picks during her basketball career. Despite the protests, she cradled Austin's head in her lap. Surrounded by agents, police officers, techs, photographers, and reporters, she held her rookie agent. *Her* rookie agent. She gazed at him. He appeared peaceful. She took in the freckles from the bridge of his nose to his cheeks.

A note was pinned to the lapel on his suit jacket.

Dear Special Agent Jade Harrington,

I'm sorry about this. It was an accident. He was in the wrong place at the wrong time. He seemed like a nice kid. My battle is not with him. Or you.

I have a job to do. Let me do it.

Your Friend,

TSK

P.S. I thought this would be an appropriate place to leave him.

After slicing through the net, the ball hit the ground and spun back toward her. The sign of an excellent shooter was one who didn't need a rebounder. She dribbled back to her original spot and took the same shot going to her left. She shot like a machine for a half an hour. She rarely missed.

She continued to shoot and think about Austin. How he balked at the beginning of his assignment to listen to the radio broadcasts. How he didn't quit. His passion. His enthusiasm. How his freckles seemed to multiply when he became excited.

No one had protected her when she was a kid. And, now, she had failed to protect Austin. She should have tried harder to call him back.

She shot an air ball.

The ball sailed out of bounds and rolled to a stop under a tree.

She thought about LaKeisha, the middle-school basketball player she had coached last year. LaKeisha told her life was hard, but with Jade she felt safe.

Jade sank slowly, ignoring the pain as her knees hit the asphalt. She looked up to the sky searching for a God she never thought much about and yelled.

"Why?"

After several minutes and hearing no answer from above, she started to cry. And cry. Her head fell to the ground with the weight of her tears.

She didn't know how long she lay there, but eventually felt a hand of comfort and strength on her shoulder. She looked up, expecting to see either Max or Christian.

"He was a good kid," Dante said.

PART III

CHAPTER SIXTY-EIGHT

Arlington, Virginia

"HOW LONG WERE you standing there?"

"A while."

Jade never wanted anyone to see her cry. Ever. Especially Dante. She shifted in her seat, uncomfortable.

"My father played professional basketball," he said.

Jade took a sip of her latte and swallowed. "I know who your father is."

Marco Carlucci was a long-time professional Italian basketball player who spent his twilight years in the NBA.

"You have no idea what it was like."

Jade glanced around the near-empty coffee shop. "Tell me."

"I was tall," Dante said, a bashful, charming smile spread across his face, "and I was awful. My dad put a ball in my hands when I was three years old. I couldn't hang on to it to save my life. I was so uncoordinated. I thought it would kill my father." He sipped his espresso. "Later, I tried soccer. To placate him." He laughed. "I couldn't play that either."

Jade sipped her latte, watching him over the rim of her cup.

"My whole life. Everyone told me how great my dad was."

He pitched his voice an octave higher. "'Are you going to be a baller like your dad?' I got so sick of being compared to him. I still am. I joined the FBI over his objections. I did pretty well at the Academy. My first few years here were going well. I thought I would be promoted." He looked across at her. "And then you came along. You were great. You are great. At everything. People talk about you all the time. You have no clue how you come across. Like you're better than us. Better than me." He looked down into his cup. "You remind me of him."

They each sipped their coffee, lost in their own thoughts.

"There's more to life than basketball," Jade said. "No matter how great of an athlete you are, it ends someday, and most of your life is spent doing something else." She set her cup down. "What's your passion? Outside of work."

He gave her an embarrassed smile. "Cooking."

"Italian?"

A shake of the head. "French."

"I read in a book once," Jade said, "that athletes grow up later in life than everyone else."

"That makes two of us."

They eyed each other, before they both burst out laughing.

ঌ

A few days after Austin's funeral, Jade sat at her desk at the Bureau staring—unseeing—at the 302 form for the aborted Evan Stevens interview. She dropped the document on her desk. She couldn't concentrate. Besides, she had a hard time deciphering Christian's handwriting on a good day.

The funeral had been a solemn affair with over a thousand people in attendance: FBI agents, police officers from Maryland, DC, and Virginia, Austin's family, as well as

President-Elect Whitney Fairchild. She exchanged nods with Fairchild, but did not have a chance to speak with her.

When Jade's turn came to offer condolences to Austin's mother, Jade had trouble looking her in the eye. What do you say to a mother who has to bury her youngest son a week before Thanksgiving?

While she mourned her agent, TSK always seemed to be one step ahead of them. Jade was sick of waiting and reacting.

Enough!

She typed "Cole Brennan" into her browser. Millions of hits came up. She did a quick scan of his Wikipedia page. Most of the information she already knew. She clicked the link for his radio show's website. No, she didn't want to order his latest book or a t-shirt, thank you very much. After rifling through a few pages, she stopped at a link midway down the page of Upcoming Events. It read American Values Conference.

She clicked on the link and the screen filled with the conference's home page. The annual American Values Conference brought together conservative luminaries from across the country. The conference promised speeches on traditional family values, pro-life, gun rights, and protecting Americans from their government and illegal immigrants.

Cole Brennan was the keynote speaker.

Jade's pulse accelerated. She scrolled down to the bottom of the page to find out where and when the conference would take place. Three days from now at The Washington Convention Center.

Here.

What better place for TSK to strike?

ை

The task force gathered in the conference room, but the mood today was different. Earlier, she had met with Christian, Max, and Pat to go over her idea. If they were surprised at Dante's presence in the room now, they didn't show it. She outlined her plan to them, and they went over the logistics.

This time they would be preemptive.

She scanned the room and stopped at the empty chair. Austin's chair. Jade walked over and stood behind it, facing Dante sitting up straight in his chair instead of the usual slouch.

He searched her face, uncertain.

"Welcome back to the task force. I want you to finish what Austin started. Find out why he died."

CHAPTER SIXTY-NINE

Bethesda, Maryland

COLE BRENNAN OPENED the front door to his home. The younger kids ran past him and down the hall toward the family room. He and Ashley and the older kids followed. Everyone, except for Kaitlin and Cole Jr., was stoked; an animated conversation ensued throughout the ride home from the conference. His speech was a big hit, and TSK didn't appear. The younger children didn't realize how many people loved their daddy, outside the Beltway anyway.

Cole Jr. turned on the TV set, as Cole sat on the sofa. Ashley left and returned with cognac. He smiled and held his hand out, accepting the drink. He patted the seat next to him. She laid her head on his shoulder. The family viewed sound bites of his speech on the news.

Cole beamed. "Daddy looks good!"

The doorbell rang.

Cole Jr. left to answer it. A few moments later, he reappeared with one of the FBI agents wearing the regulation blue jacket and sunglasses. Cole let out a breath, relieved. But his relief soon turned to anger. He hated feeling afraid in his own home.

The agent looked at him. "I wanted to make sure everything was okay in here."

"Never better. In fact, if you've got a little time, sit down. I'm on TV."

The agent shook his head. "No, thank you." He did not turn to leave, but instead removed his glasses. He stared out the large window and scanned the room's interior, taking in each of the children. His eyes rested on Ryan. He smiled the indulgent smile that adults tended to give children. Cole's attention drifted back toward the television.

Ryan smiled back at the agent. "Thanks for my soccer ball."

Cole froze. The glass slipped from his hand, as if in slow motion, the thick carpet muffling its landing. The amber liquid spread, seeping into the beige carpet.

The agent whipped a gun out from under his FBI coat. "Everyone freeze. Do not scream or I will start shooting."

Three of the kids started crying. The others appeared confused, not sure whether this was for real or they were being punked on a reality-TV show.

The agent pointed to another couch.

"Kids, I want you to go sit over there." He jerked his head at Ashley. "You, too."

"I'm not leaving my husband," Ashley said, her tears not masking her resolve.

"Madam, this is between your husband and me. I don't want to hurt you. Your children will need you."

Ashley, puzzled at first, understood. She glanced at Cole. He nodded. She kissed him on the cheek and moved toward her children. She opened her arms and held as many of them as she could.

Cole's initial fear was gone. He was angry. "You come into my house and scare my family—" He started to rise.

The agent waved Cole down with his gun. "Sit down, old man. As always, you talk a good game, but you never *do* anything. I know you. I know everything about you."

"You don't know me. Why don't we go into my office? We can talk in there. Man to man."

"I know this is your favorite room in the house. So, I think I want to sit right here. I have some things to say to you and I wouldn't mind an audience."

CHAPTER SEVENTY

Bethesda, Maryland

CHRISTIAN PARKED THE car at the curb.

Jade glanced at him. "I feel like I need to take a shower."

"Come on, now, it wasn't that bad."

She threw him a look and moved her hand to the door handle. "We don't need waterboarding. Let's force terrorists to listen to Cole Brennan for a few hours. They'll talk."

Christian laughed. They got out and strolled down the street toward the agent in charge standing near a Suburban SUV parked in front of Cole Brennan's house. Christian and Jade had come here to conduct a routine check on the surveillance.

Jade surveyed Brennan's expansive lawn, stopping at the red front door in the distance. She eyed the agent. "Anything?"

The special agent in charge said, "Nah, it's been quiet," he hesitated, "but—"

Christian stepped forward, invading his space. "But what?"

"After the family returned from the conference, an agent told me he was going to check on them. I was on the phone with HQ, not paying attention. I didn't even see who it was. That was twenty minutes ago."

"And he hasn't come back out," Christian said.

The agent shook his head.

Jade gazed up at the red door again. "He's here."

CHAPTER SEVENTY-ONE

Bethesda, Maryland

THE FAKE FBI agent sat in a chair opposite Cole. Legs crossed, his pants were creased in the right places. With one hand, he smoothed a nonexistent wrinkle. The gun rested on his leg, the finger in the trigger, a casual gesture. If not for the weapon, an outside observer would surmise the two of them were having a normal conversation. Cole couldn't ignore the queasiness in his stomach. He shouldn't have goaded this killer into coming into his home and terrorizing his family.

The agent bestowed on him a condescending smile. "Do you believe all the shit that you say?"

"Yes, I do," Cole said. "And watch your language."

The agent raised an eyebrow, surprised. "My language? Do you realize how many hurtful things you say on any given day?"

"It's the truth. If some people find it hurtful, they have the right to listen to another station."

"You talk about circumstances about which you know nothing. You do not understand what it is like to be a minority or a pregnant woman or gay."

Cole laughed, a harsh sound. "And you do?"

"At least, I can empathize with them. Try to put myself in their place. Would you oppose marriage equality if you were gay?"

"Gay marriage has nothing to do with equality. Two people of the same sex shouldn't be together. It's in the Bible. That's just another politically correct term dreamed up by liberals to get public acceptance."

The agent ran his fingers through his hair. "Will you please answer the question?"

"What was the question again?"

"Would you oppose gay marriage if you were gay?"

"But I'm not."

"But what if you were?"

"I wouldn't be."

"So, you think your sexual orientation is a choice."

"Yes."

"And you choose to be heterosexual?"

Cole wanted to wipe that smile off his face. "No! It's what I am!"

The agent considered Cole, disdain written all over his face, as if Cole weren't his intellectual equal.

"You proved my point. Gays do not have a choice, either, and should have the same rights we do."

"Marriage is between a man and a woman."

"I guess if you repeat that often enough, it must be true."

The smugness of this guy wore on Cole's nerves. He couldn't stand these intellectual-elite types, always trying to show off how smart they were. Cole took in the agent's good looks. Something about him seemed familiar. Was he in the business? "Do I know you?"

From the couch, a male voice, which only a couple of years ago was one octave higher, spoke up.

"I don't think there's anything wrong with gay marriage."

Cole forgot about the killer sitting across from him for the moment and flashed a look at his namesake. "What's that, son?"

Cole Jr. regarded him. His hair, longer than it should be, brushed his shoulders.

"Why shouldn't gays be allowed to marry whom they love? How does that hurt you, Dad?"

Cole's emotions, shaken by the presence of a killer in his home, now roiled with the realization his son might be a liberal. Or worse. *Please, God, don't let him be gay.* He shook his head, exasperated. "Please tell me this isn't happening."

The agent laughed at Cole's discomfort.

Cole wanted to kill him.

After a beat, the agent stared up at the ceiling. "Are you willing to die for your country?"

A few of the kids began bawling.

Cole glanced over at his children. At Ashley.

The agent turned toward the kids. "Shut up!"

Cole started to rise. "This is my home. Don't you dare talk—"

The agent waved his gun again for Cole to stay seated. "Answer the question."

"Yes," Cole said. He studied his large hands. "No." He didn't care he was crying in front of his children and his wife or that snot was running over his lips or he was about to plead for his life to a liberal madman. "Man, I just want to be with my family."

The agent leaned forward. He smiled at Cole, his eyes fixed, unblinking. "Then, don't speak."

"What?"

"Don't speak."

"What do you mean? Now? I don't get it."

"I will let you live if you promise to cancel your show and stop writing your incendiary books."

CHAPTER SEVENTY-TWO

Bethesda, Maryland

JADE STOOD WITH the members of CIRG—the FBI's Critical Incident Response Group—as they congregated around a Suburban, an architectural layout of Cole Brennan's home and its surroundings on its hood. After several minutes of quiet discussion, the CIRG team broke off running toward the radio host's house in different choreographed directions. She started to follow.

Christian put a hand on her forearm. "They've got this."

She tensed at his firm touch, ready to argue. This was her case. Her perp. Her agent. This was for Austin. She wanted to be the one to bring this guy down. She glanced at Christian and stared at his hand on her arm. She gave him a crisp nod. He removed his hand.

Another agent handed her a headset so she could listen to the CIRG leader.

She heard nothing for a few minutes. Then, a hushed voice said, "The family is in the great room. I have a visual on our suspect. He's sitting on a chair across from them. Armed. Handgun. They seem to be"—the CIRG leader's voice ringed with amazement—"having a conversation." Silence. More minutes passed. "Brennan appears as if he's trying to stand up. The UNSUB's waving the gun around." Silence. "Our sniper has a clear shot."

Jade didn't hesitate. "Go."

A minute later, breaking glass.

And another shot.

Jade threw her headset on the ground. She, Christian, and the rest of the agents ran toward the back of the house. Jade arrived first. The large bay window overlooking the back yard now had a big, jagged hole in it. Jade jumped from the lawn to the brick patio and through the window, ignoring the shards of glass stuck to her clothing. She took in the situation. Brennan's kids were screaming. Cole Brennan and his wife held one of their daughters, tears streaming down their faces.

Brennan didn't take his eyes off his daughter. "He missed." He was crying. "He missed her by inches."

Ashley peeked up at Jade. "When the window exploded, the man's hand jerked and his gun went off."

Jade crouched next to them. She reached her hand out toward the girl but placed it on her own lap instead. She whispered to no one in particular. "Where did he go?"

Brennan cocked his head to the left but continued to stare at his daughter. "There's a side door off the kitchen. He went that way."

"Radio an ambulance," Jade said to Christian. She sprinted in the direction of the kitchen.

Christian called after her. "Jade, wait!"

The door had been left open. She didn't break stride as she went out the door and back into the night.

৵

For once, Jade was grateful for the big yellow FBI lettering on the back of their jackets. It made following him easier. TSK sprinted toward the woods bordering Cole Brennan's large backyard. Jade figured he had a hundred yards on her.

As she entered the forest, she slowed down, fearful she would sprain an ankle on a tree root or the uneven terrain. She didn't want to risk losing him, though.

The killer didn't slow down. He had been here before.

After what seemed like a mile, the woods gave way to grass and, beyond, the parking lot of a sizable, suburban shopping center.

She was gaining on him.

Signs for Macy's, Nordstrom, and Bloomingdale's were alight in large letters. The shopping center was closed at this time of night. Her suspect sprinted up the outside stairs to the second floor and jumped with ease over the sagging, useless chain at the top of the stairs.

She followed.

She ended up on the wide terrace of a restaurant. Tables, with chairs stacked on them, were pushed against the wall. The commingled aromas of steak, chicken, and fish permeated the air.

He was waiting for her.

He stood in the shadows, leaning against a table, his hands clasped in front of him. He had removed the FBI jacket. It lay on the floor nearby. Dressed in all black, he now wore a balaclava with only his eyes and mouth showing.

"Hello, Jade," said a soft, familiar voice, but she couldn't place it.

Jade said nothing.

After all the long months, thinking about this guy and

talking about this guy and visualizing catching this guy, it felt surreal coming face to face with him.

"You are wondering why I did it," he said.

"I know why."

"Oh, you do? Sometimes, there is more to a situation than what meets the eye."

"I'm listening."

"Those conservatives were such horrible human beings."

"Does that mean they had to die?"

He smiled. "Yes . . . and no."

He lifted a Glock 23 in front of him with the barrel pointed up at a ninety-degree angle. FBI-issued. One of theirs. He caught her staring at it.

"A gift," he said, "from Austin."

The blood rushed through her veins. She took a step toward him, gun or no gun.

He held his hand up. "Don't. I don't want to shoot you, but I will."

She stopped.

He paused, and then placed the gun on the table next to him. He strode toward Jade and started circling her.

She still did not move.

"They were despicable creatures and our country is better off without them. You cannot disagree with me on that."

"If I disagreed with their points of view, it wouldn't mean I would want them to die. What about freedom of speech?"

"Ah . . . but what choice did I have? Their vitriol gets worse every year. You cannot debate someone who argues only with emotion, irrationality, or outright lies."

"You can use your vote."

"Yes, but you know as well as I that the Super PACS and

corporations control elections today. No"—he tilted his head, a brief thought—"this was the only way. Besides, don't you want a woman president?"

"Not at any cost." She paused. "Is that what this is all about?"

After he completed his 360-degree examination, he stopped in front of her. The Brennan boy was right. He was tall. She continued to stare at the killer.

He crouched into a martial-arts sparring stance.

Jade hid her surprise. *Does he want to fight me?*

His eyes bored into hers. "I like this. Mano y womano. This is how it should be. Come now, Agent Harrington. You have trained and competed in tournaments for all these years. It is time to fight for real."

How did he know? Max's assessment came back to her. *The UNSUB is a planner. He studies his victims' daily patterns and knows when they'll be alone. He has some degree of superior intelligence.*

Why wouldn't he have studied her as well?

She didn't see the round kick coming.

Too late, she lifted her forearm to block it. His foot grazed up her arm and landed on her temple. She stumbled, before dropping to the designer concrete floor, dazed. On instinct, she shot back up on her feet.

She tried to steady her breathing, while calculating if she could draw her weapon before he neutralized her.

She went into her sparring stance.

He smiled again. A hideous smile, made more so by the balaclava. "You are not the only one with martial arts skills. Fifth degree. Jiu-Jitsu."

Her instinct to get off the ground had been correct. Jiu-Jitsu was a grappling martial art.

They circled each other.

He moved in to tackle her. She lifted her leg straight up for an inside crescent kick, bringing it down on his collarbone. In the still of the night, the crack of the bone was audible.

He bent over, holding his shoulder. He gritted his teeth. "Very good."

She stood over him, reaching for her handcuffs.

He shot up, still grabbing his shoulder, and punched her in the nose.

As her head popped back, he tackled her, knocking the wind out of her.

The pressure increased as he straddled her chest with all his weight.

Groggy from the kick and the punch, blood poured from her nose. The killer loomed over her. His face came into focus, tinged with pity.

"I know you're only trying to do the right thing. 'Fidelity, Bravery, Integrity,' and all that. But I'm sorry, Agent Jade Harrington. Despite your athletic exploits, your life will be a footnote in history. A casualty of freedom."

Jade spit out the blood that had seeped into her mouth. She held his eyes with hers. "You've got one thing right. You will be sorry."

He laughed. "I like you. And I love your confidence."

He encircled her neck with his hands, cringing as if he did not like her blood touching his skin. He squeezed.

She couldn't breathe.

Pinpricks of light darted behind her eyelids. Her brain was going to explode. *Where was Christian? The rest of CIRG?*

No one was there for her. Again.

Darkness started to descend. She thought of Austin. Zoe. Card. Max. Her parents.

The hand on the side of his body with the broken collarbone struggled to maintain its grip.

A calmness came over her, overriding the strong beating of her heart and her need for oxygen.

She had one chance.

Jade summoned all of her energy and lifted up her chest as high as she could. She slithered her arms through the opening of his legs, clasped her hands together, and brought them down on his injured shoulder.

He screamed in pain as he fell off her.

Jade scrambled away, coughing and holding her throat with one hand. They stared at each other, she clutching her throat, he clutching his shoulder.

They both rose and faced each other.

She relaxed every muscle as Master Ho had taught her. Control. *Trust your training.*

Jade struck him with a left knife-hand strike to his right temple, followed by a right knife-hand strike to his left temple. Before he reacted, her body coiled, twisted, and lifted higher and higher into a spinning hook kick. She hit his left temple again with her left heel, the same kick she had used at her fourth-degree black belt testing a lifetime ago.

The killer staggered backward, his lower back hitting the railing. He tumbled over it, out of sight. Jade clutched the railing with one hand, her throat with the other, and peered down.

The man was sprawled on the asphalt, his body positioned like an old police chalk outline. Light from the tall parking lot pole illuminated the dark liquid seeping from his head.

Jade ran down the stairs and over to the stilled form. She stood over the body. His neck was tilted at an unnatural angle.

He stared up at her, eyes unseeing through the mask.

Christian rushed up to her, followed by other agents, Glocks drawn.

She didn't bother to look at him. "You're late."

Christian said nothing.

Jade touched her nose. It still hurt, but the bleeding had stopped, and it didn't feel broken. She dropped her hand and kneeled next to the body.

She glanced at Christian once more before removing the balaclava.

Staring back at her were the lifeless eyes of Landon Phillips.

CHAPTER SEVENTY-THREE

Crystal City, Virginia

THE NEXT DAY dawned cold and quiet.

Jade and Christian, in their dark blue FBI coats, braced themselves on either side of the front door to an apartment in a high-rise building in Crystal City. She had called earlier and no one had answered.

She knocked.

No answer.

She eyed Christian. He had his game face on. He nodded. She moved to allow Dante to insert a key obtained from the building's management company. Dante opened the door and stepped back as well. Bomb-sniffing dogs entered first to make sure Landon Phillips's apartment wasn't booby-trapped. Members of the Critical Incident Response Group followed the dogs.

After five minutes, "Clear" came from someone inside.

Jade, Christian, and Dante entered. The vast apartment seemed larger with floor-to-ceiling windows on two sides. The sleek, modern furniture appeared brand new.

She peeked into the apartment's sole bedroom off the kitchen. Queen-size bed, a dresser, and a nightstand with a lamp on one side and a pile of books on the other. The walls were devoid of pictures and there was no television. Landon Phillips had not spent much time here.

It was weird being inside his home. His room. That he had never invited her over was not lost on her. She felt sick to her stomach that she allowed him to kiss her.

She checked out the closet, small for an apartment of this size. Pulling on gloves, she knelt and examined the bottom of a pair of hiking boots. They had been cleaned, but she bet the tread would match the shoeprint found at the Liz Holder crime scene. She searched the rest of the closet, but didn't uncover any obvious evidence. She returned to the living room.

A team of forensic analysts collected fingerprints. One analyst began vacuuming. Another cut out a small section of the carpet to take back to the lab to compare with the trace evidence collected from the crime scenes.

She mentioned the boots to an analyst and walked over to a bookcase bulging with books. She peered closer. The books, arranged in alphabetical order, aligned with the edge of the shelf as in a library. Like hers at home. *OCD.*

That's why we got along so well.

Most of the books were political or philosophical: Hitler, Churchill, Roosevelt, Marx, Machiavelli, Locke, Sartre, Nietzsche. True crime and a few novels, predominately thrillers, also graced the shelves. Jade no longer read thrillers.

She lived them.

She pulled out one of Nietzsche's books, *Thus Spoke Zarathustra.* A hole gaped in the center of the cover, made by a knife or a pair of scissors. Landon probably hadn't recommended this one on Goodreads.

An electric guitar stood on a stand in the corner.

She walked to where Christian and Dante stood by a wall covered with pictures and newspaper articles, presumably of the victims and Landon's exploits.

As she got closer, Dante and Christian exchanged a look before parting for her. Puzzled, she glanced at each of them and then at the wall.

Her lips parted.

The entire wall was a shrine to President-Elect Whitney Fairchild.

At all stages of her life. The newspaper article of her wedding announcement to Grayson Fairchild. The birth of her two children. The announcements for her candidacy for the House, Senate, and presidency. Campaigning.

She looked at Christian, unbelieving, and back to the wall. She leaned forward, scrutinizing a sketch of the president-elect, the likeness unmistakable. The signature was in charcoal. *Landon Phillips.*

Confused, she glanced over her shoulder at Christian. "What the hell?"

Christian, arms crossed in front of his chest, scanned the wall. "Maybe he was in love with his boss. What if these murders were all for her?"

"Like John Hinckley and Jodie Foster?" Dante asked, laughing. "Isn't she a little old for him?"

Christian shrugged his shoulders. "Maybe it's a cougar thing."

"Or to help her get elected," Jade said.

After surveying the wall for several minutes, they ambled over to the corner of the living room set up as an office. Three flat-screen monitors connected to a laptop still nestled in its docking station. A forensic examiner from the FBI's Computer Analysis and Response Team worked on the laptop.

Dante gestured toward the large flat-screen television and the computers. He whistled. "Nice setup."

"I wonder why he didn't take the laptop," Christian said.

The technician tapped the touch pad. "I'm not sure, but lucky for us he didn't." All three monitors sprang to life. The technician glanced back at them. "He also never set up a password. Guess living alone, he thought he didn't need to. Today must be our lucky day."

Jade, Christian, and Dante peered over the technician's shoulder. One screen was filled with numerous Internet pages about Cole Brennan: his politics, his life story, and even an *Architectural Digest* article on his home. On another monitor appeared to be a transcript of a conversation or a chat. The last screen displayed the website for the American Values Conference. *Had Landon been there?*

Jade, Christian, and Dante left to allow the technician to finish his work.

As they walked down the hallway toward the elevator, she stopped. "Wait."

She sprinted back to the apartment and straight to the desk. She stared at the screen with the transcript. Something about it nagged at her. She bent closer to read it. The technician got up from the chair without a word so she could sit down.

SusanB: *It's another example of big corporations squeezing out the little guy.*

PittFan: *Fuck yeah. The only welfare that matters is corporate welfare.*

Oedipus: *'Corporations are people, too, my friend.'*

SusanB: *<Groan.> Caleb, please don't start with the Mitt Romney quotes.*

Oedipus: *Please call me Oedipus.*

JoanofArc: *Did you all catch any of Cole's show tonight? Scary. And I'm not talking about the Talk Show Killer.*

PittFan: *Cole's a fucking idiot.*

AlextheGreat: *Guys, we listen to him so that we know what we're up against.*

Oedipus: *I went to Cole's speech in Philadelphia last month. It was horrible. He wants to eliminate all federal agencies and move their functions to the states or privatize them.*

SusanB: *The other party isn't going to be happy until all minorities and poor people die or go away. I wouldn't put it past them to be behind the killings.*

JoanofArc: *Why would they do that?*

SusanB: *To gain sympathy to win the election.*

JoanofArc: *That sounds a little farfetched. And we're the ones always blaming them for concocting conspiracy theories.*

PittFan: *The killer deserves a goddamn medal if you ask me.*

AlextheGreat: *Violence isn't the answer, PittFan.*

Oedipus: Maybe for Cole Brennan it is.

Jade stopped reading. No question Landon was Oedipus. The cursor blinked next to "Oedipus" at the bottom of the screen. She remembered Zoe was SusanB.

Jade's blood ran cold.

Did Zoe know Caleb was a killer? Did Zoe know Landon was Caleb?

CHAPTER SEVENTY-FOUR

Washington, DC

IN THE SENATE Radio-Television Gallery room in the US Capitol, President-Elect Whitney Fairchild stood alone at the podium. She scanned the audience of reporters. She glanced at her notes and took a deep breath.

"Ladies and gentlemen of the press and everyone else who may be watching, through the efforts of law enforcement in several jurisdictions, but especially our Federal Bureau of Investigation, the perpetrator of the heinous crimes attributed to the TSK killer is now dead.

"Nothing can bring comfort to the families of the victims at this time, but I hope Landon Phillips's death will provide them with at least a sense of justice and some measure of peace. I shall continue to keep these families in my thoughts and prayers and I ask all of you to do the same."

She peered down at the papers on the podium without seeing them. All she wanted to do was cry, but she would not. Female politicians could not cry. A crying male politician displayed his sensitivity. A crying female politician revealed her weakness. A president—even a future president—could not be weak.

"How does it feel knowing that you've been working side by side with a killer for years?" a voice shouted from the back of the room.

"Devastating. Landon was hardworking, intelligent, and loyal. He would be the last person I would think capable of committing these heinous crimes."

"A little too loyal, if you ask me," a reporter commented. This elicited some nervous laughs.

"Why do you think he did it?" cried out another reporter.

"Who knows why? Who knows what demons he faced? Perhaps, in some misguided way, he believed he was helping me or the causes of our party by silencing the opposition, but that is not the way to prevail. We win by the validity and effectiveness of our ideals, ideas, and implementation of our policies. As a country, we win when two sides oppose each other, find common ground, and come up with the best solution.

"I, too, have many questions. Could these senseless deaths have been prevented? Is there any way I could have stopped them? How can we prevent this situation from happening again? But today is not the day for questions. Today is a day for healing. I will not take any more questions. Thank you."

She picked up her notes and walked briskly off the stage, leaving behind an unusually quiet press corps.

CHAPTER SEVENTY-FIVE

Washington, DC

DANTE PUSHED ASIDE piles of transcripts stacked on the conference-room table at the Bureau. He placed a laptop in front of him and connected tiny speakers.

"I backtracked what Austin did. I listened to these recordings for weeks. Listen to this. Here's a call to the victim—Sells—in Pittsburgh." He clicked the play button.

". . . Income and wealth inequality have increased significantly over the last thirty-five years. What do you propose we do about it?" came a voice from the speakers.

He stopped the recording, clicked on another audio file, and pressed play. "Tallent in Seattle."

"Income and wealth inequality have increased significantly over the last thirty-five years. What do you propose we do about it?" said the same voice.

He pressed another. "Holder in New York." The same sentence was asked word for word. Dante pushed stop, an expectant expression on his face.

Jade thought for a moment. "Sounds like the same voice. From the Northeast. Like the witness from Seattle said. I'd say

Philadelphia. I had a teammate in college from Philly and she had that same distinct accent."

"Confirmed by Linguistics. It's definitely a Philadelphian dialect and it belongs to Landon Phillips."

Jade looked doubtful. "He didn't sound like that in person."

Dante shrugged. "Maybe he disguised his voice. All three calls originated from Phillips's cell phone number." He hesitated. "This is what Austin discovered. This is why he died."

A quietness descended around the table. Pat stopped clicking. Max stared at the wall. Christian's head was bowed, as if in prayer.

Jade allowed the silence to continue for a few moments. "Good work, Dante. Okay. We're not done. Talk to me about Phillips."

Pat brought up a file on her computer. "Adopted by Addison and Maddy Hewitt when he was a baby, who christened him Caleb. Birth name, birthplace, and birth parents are all still unknown. We're working on it. The Hewitts had a biological son named James, who died at thirteen. He was killed while riding a bicycle on a street near his home. The Hewitts adopted Caleb shortly thereafter. They had no other children."

Max appeared thoughtful. "The Hewitts adopted Caleb to replace their dead child. You saw their living room. No wonder Caleb never measured up."

Jade recalled the photographs of James Hewitt scattered throughout the living room. Not one picture of Caleb. The mother had to hunt around in the basement for a picture of him.

Christian stood and turned his chair around. He placed

his forearms on the top of the chair. "Probably didn't help the kid's confidence growing up."

Jade said to Christian, "The house was so quiet, remember? The dead son was still present."

Max pushed up his glasses. "And Caleb was waiting in that house, year after year, for his birth parents to come back for him."

"Sad," Pat said. The way she always hunched over her computer reminded Jade of Schroeder from the old *Peanuts* cartoon hunched over his piano.

Dante leaned his chair back. "Why did he do this? To get his parents' attention?"

"Maybe to hurt them," Max said.

He lied about having a sister. He lied to my face about his mother's bout with cancer, what his parents did for a living. He lied about everything. Except the guitar.

"He probably didn't even like craft beer," she said.

"Craft beer?" Dante asked, bewildered.

"Never mind," Jade said. She shook her head, disgusted with herself. She thought back to the Holder murder. Phillips had called her the day after. She shivered. *What kind of FBI agent am I?*

"Are you all right?" Christian asked.

"Yeah. Just felt a chill."

Pat continued her briefing. "Caleb Hewitt, a bright and gifted child, finished in the top of his class in high school. Family, friends, and neighbors described Hewitt as friendly but quiet. He preferred being alone with his books and his ideas.

"He was also a page for Representative Fairchild when he was a junior in high school," she added. "I wonder if Fairchild remembered him from back then."

"I wonder if his fascination with her started then," Max said. He made a note.

Some people that knew Caleb said the US invasion of Iraq infuriated him and propelled him into politics. He attended Chattenham College, which boasted a history of political activism. He also worked at the college radio station. This morning, Jade had spoken to the station manager during that time who told her Caleb was unhappy when the station launched a conservative program and confirmed that Caleb knew the first known TSK victim, the student conservative talk-show host Kyle Williams.

Cole Brennan was an on-air personality in Philadelphia at the time. The task force presumed Hewitt had listened to Cole's broadcasts, which would have enraged him further.

Caleb Hewitt received his BA in philosophy from Chattenham. He left the school and the town and was never heard from again.

"Over ten years ago," Christian said. "Maybe that's why he lost his accent or pretended to anyway."

A gap existed in Hewitt's history until three years later, when Landon Phillips joined Representative Whitney Fairchild's staff. Gone were the long, shaggy blond locks, jeans, and t-shirts. They were replaced by business suits, contacts that changed his brown eyes to green, nose job, and age-darkened light brown hair. He looked like a different person. Because he was.

The Hewitts had no idea their son worked for the woman who would one day become president. They wouldn't have recognized him anyway.

~

Evidence proving that Caleb Hewitt, aka Landon Phillips, committed the murders began to come together. Analysts confirmed the carpet fibers found at the Taylor LeBlanc (Baton Rouge) and Shane Tallent (Seattle) scenes matched the carpet in Phillips's apartment. The carpet fibers found in the Pete Paxson (Houston) scene did not match. Pat found out Phillips had moved into his apartment after the Paxson murder. A baseball bat hidden underneath a floorboard in the living room was determined to be the murder weapon of his earlier victims. The bat had been wiped clean, but Forensics matched the blood residue, invisible to the naked eye, to the victims. So far, they hadn't discovered any more victims.

And, of course, Phillips wasn't talking.

"Oh," Dante said, "and the reports came back on the contents of his medicine cabinet. Guess what they found?" He smiled at her. "Rohypnol."

Her brow furrowed. "The date-rape drug used in the LeBlanc killing?"

"Yeah! The drug can also be taken to treat anxiety and insomnia. Phillips suffered from insomnia big time. We're still trying to track down how he got it."

She thought for a long moment. "Nate, the security guard at the college, told me they had had huge problems with date rape at the time Kyle Williams was killed. Dante, call him. Find out if any of the victims can identify Caleb Hewitt. Perhaps, we can provide them some closure."

Dante nodded. No smirk this time.

She squinted her eyes at him, but said nothing.

Christian examined a file. "Living in Crystal City was convenient. He could walk to Reagan National airport."

"Fairchild was traveling so often," Jade said, "she may not

have noticed his personal side trips. We need to check out his travel records."

"On it," Pat said.

"By the way," Christian said, "they found detailed dossiers on his computer on all of his victims, plus the top fifty broadcasters in the country."

"Insomnia can be a blessing for a workaholic," Pat said. "He should have worked for us."

Christian continued. "There was also a dossier on Fairchild." He hesitated, and turned to Jade. "And you."

I'll bet.

She thought about their dinner together. Playing basketball. That kiss. She tried not to shiver.

"Also, CART found a list," Christian said.

"Of potential victims?" Max asked.

"No. It appears to be a list of everyone who had ever offended him or hurt him in his life. It's a long list. A lot of names I don't recognize, but his parents are on the list. Some famous people, too, including our future president." He looked at Jade. "And you again."

Because I wouldn't let him walk me back to the office? Because I stopped seeing him? Stop! Focus!

Dante shook his head. "Fairchild? She gave him a great opportunity. He worked for the soon-to-be most powerful person in the world. Crazy."

Jade looked at Max. "What about the shrine to her we found in his apartment?"

Max paused. "Hard to say. Could be an obsession, like Hinckley." He nodded at Dante. "Could be something else. We haven't uncovered any romantic correspondence to her, but it is certainly something we should look into."

"Perhaps, we should ask her," Pat said.

"But what about the Oedipus nickname?" Christian asked. "Was he in love with his mother? And, if so, why didn't he visit her after all this time?"

"I guess this means we need to pay the Hewitts another visit," Jade said.

Christian groaned. "Do we have to?"

"We have to go to Chattenham anyway," Jade said. "I made a promise." She hadn't forgotten the promise she made to Kyle Williams's mother to bring home her son's journal and college yearbook.

Christian closed the file he had been reading. "CART found the manifesto and hundreds of articles written by Phillips on his computer. They also found a cryptic note. Almost like a suicide note, but no mention of suicide. He ended it with 'She never mentioned me.' No signature."

Dante dropped his chair on its front two legs. "Probably his mother."

"Or maybe Fairchild," Christian said. "Maybe he was pissed that she didn't thank him in her acceptance speech or something."

"Interesting ideas," Max said. "Worth pursuing."

Jade was still kicking herself that she hadn't matched Phillips's online articles with the manifesto. He had even suggested that she do so. She felt like an idiot.

A silence fell over the group. One by one each head turned to Austin's empty chair.

Dante interrupted the silence. "How's the kid?"

"Kaitlin's going to be fine," Christian said. "She was shaken up, but Brennan says she's almost back to normal. She started questioning his conservative politics again."

Jade joined in the laughter. It felt good.

CHAPTER SEVENTY-SIX

Washington, DC

COLE BRENNAN BEGAN his first broadcast after his encounter with the Talk Show Killer.

He boomed into the microphone. "'Free at last! Free at last! Thank God, Almighty, I'm free at last!' Never thought I would be quoting Martin Luther King. Yes, I'm back, folks. Safe and sound after staring down my would-be murderer. Before I forget, I owe a lot of thanks to a little lady from the FBI."

He wiped his brow. Despite the freezing cold December day, he was sweating. Maybe this attempt on his life was a wake-up call from God to start losing weight.

"Yes, folks, I had a scare, but that won't stop me. No one can stop the truth. And I am the truth! But enough about me. Let's take some calls. Josh from Arkansas. Go!"

"Hey, Cole. Love your show. I'm glad you're all right. Me and the Mrs. have been praying for you, man."

"Thank you, thank you. What's your question?"

"Next month, we'll have our first lady president ever. How will she change the office?"

"Besides painting the Oval Office pink, you mean? Ha!

Well, my hope is she and this divided Congress will work on a plan for serious budget deficit reduction, but I also hope Marilyn Monroe comes back to life and asks me to be her fourth husband. Just kidding, Ashley! What I'm saying is, it's not going to happen, Josh. My guess is the first piece of legislation coming out of this Congress and this president will be an amendment for gay marriage and any other kind of marriage you can think of: man and beast; woman and beast; beast and beast; woman, man, and beast. The possibilities are endless!"

"That's scary, man."

"You're telling me. Mark my words . . ." Cole stopped. What was he saying? Sometimes, he lost track. He said the same things over and over without thinking. He thought of his son, Cole Jr. What if he turned out to be gay? Would that change how Cole felt about him? It didn't take long for him to answer the question.

No. He loved his son.

What had Landon Phillips asked him?

Do you believe all the shit that you say?

He had lost his train of thought. He stared at the monitor, trying to locate the caller's name.

"Thanks for calling . . . Josh. Next caller, Michelle from Iowa."

"Thanks for taking my call, Cole. I've been praying for you and your family ever since this tragedy happened. That girl didn't save you. God saved you."

"That may be true, Michelle, but I was there. She helped a lot. How can I help you?"

"What do you think is going to happen to the pro-life movement under this woman's presidency?"

"Good question. The liberals here in Washington are

going to try to push back the term in which a woman can kill her baby. The number of abortions will go up. We'll probably see burning bras again as well. Morality will go in the toilet. Soon, we'll be back to LSD and free love, man!"

"Say it isn't so, Cole. What about illegal immigration?"

"The Commiecrats will open up the borders and illegals will scatter all over the place. You'd better learn Spanish, Michelle!" Cole started to continue and then stopped. "Wait a minute . . . ."

He had put his family in jeopardy by his egomania and stubborn hubris. He thought about his daughter, Kaitlin, and her disapproving glances and challenging questions about his politics. Despite them, he loved her for it. He was blessed and grateful she was still alive.

His heart wasn't in it tonight.

Do you believe all the shit that you say?

Cole breathed, a deep, cleansing breath.

"Hold on, folks. I want to say something."

His producer waved at him, indicating a new caller was on the line. Cole ignored him.

"Listen to me. Even though I don't agree with most of her political positions and I fought with all the strength I had to re-elect President Ellison"—he hesitated—"I ask you, my listeners, to come together as Americans and support our new leader, President Whitney Fairchild."

"Cole, you don't mean it."

"Yes, I do." Cole smiled. He hung up on Michelle from Iowa. "Yes, I do. This is Cole Brennan for life, liberty, and the pursuit of happiness. Come back after the break for more of 'The Conservative Voice.'"

Cole pushed a button and took off his headphones. He sat

for a moment thinking about what he had said. His listeners and sponsors wouldn't be happy.

For once, Cole Brennan didn't care.

◆

After the show, Cole returned to his office and sank into the comfortable leather executive chair behind his desk.

The phone rang.

Uh, oh . . . it's starting already.

His assistant's voice came through the speakerphone. "Mr. Brennan, the president of the United States is on the line."

Cole, surprised, picked up the handset. He hadn't spoken to Richard Ellison in several weeks. And the president never called him.

"Yes, Mr. President."

"I listened to your broadcast. I'm calling to congratulate you. That took courage."

"Thank you, Mr. President."

"If you move toward the center, you could have greater influence. A positive one for the whole country."

"I'm not sure I want to go *that* far."

"Anyway, I haven't always agreed with your views, but I do want to thank you for your support over the years."

Cole waited for the president's usual snide comment. After a few seconds, he realized none was forthcoming.

"Thank you, sir. What's next for you?"

"Not sure, yet. I do know there's a lot of open land and clear blue skies in my immediate future. What about you?"

"I'm not sure either, but tonight I'll be going to a musical recital." Cole's chest swelled with pride. "My son's in the glee club. He's pretty good."

"That's nice."

The president sounded genuine. Cole again waited for a sarcastic follow-up. None came. "Good luck in Wyoming, sir. I wish you well in private life."

"I'm glad your little girl's okay. Take care of yourself, Cole."

CHAPTER SEVENTY-SEVEN

Washington, DC

JADE SURVEYED THE beer mugs raised in front of her and the faces of the individuals around the table holding them: Ethan, Christian, Dante, Pat, Max, and even Detective Miles Thomas from Baton Rouge. He was in DC to provide testimony to Congress supporting the Fairness Doctrine, the last act of legislation sponsored by Senator—now President-Elect—Whitney Fairchild.

"I want to thank everyone for all of your hard work," Jade said. "I wasn't always easy on you, and there were many nights away from your families, but—"

"Chief, can you hurry up? My arm's getting tired," said Dante. Everyone laughed.

"Anyway, thanks. To the good guys!"

"To the good guys!" the group responded.

The agents and Thomas clinked glasses all around and took long swigs of their beers. They sat at two tables pushed together at a sports bar across the street from the Bureau. The place was empty, a weeknight without the Redskins, Caps, or Wizards playing.

She hesitated and raised her mug again. Her breath caught. "To Austin."

A subdued cheer this time. "To Austin!"

She set her beer down. Everyone became quiet, as they thought about the freckle-faced kid who had grown up with the dream of being an FBI agent.

One mug still hung in the air. She peeked at its holder, surprised. Dante smiled at her. "You did good, Chief."

"Hear, hear!" The group yelled and clinked glasses again.

Two servers arrived and passed out their orders of burgers, wings, and French fries. Jade was glad Zoe couldn't make it. No healthy eating tonight. She eyed the waitress and twirled her finger for another round of beers. Everyone attacked their food.

"Miles," Christian said, in between bites of his burger. "You should have been here, man. She's tough. She kicked Phillips's butt. I'm sorry we got there too late to witness it."

"Oh, yeah? She's not that tough. I couldn't get her to eat alligator when she came to Baton Rouge."

Dante was stunned. "You eat alligator?"

Inevitably, talk turned to the case. They discussed the long hours, the ups and downs, the funny moments.

Christian tapped his fingers against his temple several times. "Did he really think he was going to get away with it? Silencing everyone?"

Max nodded. "Yes, he did."

Jade remained silent. Talking about him still hurt. No one, except Zoe, had found out about her budding relationship with Phillips. She wanted to keep it that way.

Dante leaned back in his chair. "Yeah, Landon Phillips had it all. Great job, great apartment, the women all probably thought he was so smart and handsome." He eyed Christian. "He was a goody-goody like you. Well, except for the fact he killed people."

Christian frowned. "I'm not a goody-goody."

"Yeah, right. Prove it."

Christian hesitated. "Okay." He drained his beer. He grabbed the mug off the serving tray the waitress had brought and downed that one, too. He got up and shot Dante a look, popping his shirt cuffs as he went.

Jade called after him. "Christian, what are you doing? Don't listen to him."

Christian stepped on a chair and onto a table next to theirs. He began to gyrate his hips, unbuttoning his shirt, stripping to his waist. Flexing his pectoral muscles back and forth, he never took his eyes off Dante. The group started hollering and catcalling.

Jade's lips parted, not believing what she was seeing. After a while, she started hollering, catcalling, and laughing with the rest of them.

She called out, "Christian, get down!"

Pat Turner, their surrogate mother, yelled out: "How much do you charge by the hour?"

Christian gyrated once more, raised his arms in victory, bowed, and jumped off the table.

"Where did you learn to do that?" Jade asked him.

Christian shrugged. "I had to pay for college somehow."

Dante threw a dollar at Christian. "You win."

The group broke up into laughter.

Max leaned over to her. "I need to go."

"I'll walk you out."

The frigid night was refreshing after the overpowering scent of fried food and beer.

"Thanks for everything," Jade said.

Max stood before her, his hands in the front pockets of his slacks.

"Like Dante said . . . you've done well, Harrington."

He lied to me. He lied to my face. "I missed so much."

Max peered at her over his glasses.

"Will you ever learn to take a compliment and just say 'thank you?' You just met up with a formidable opponent this time. It won't be your last." He took her chin in his hand. "You're a great FBI agent. One of the best we have. And notice I didn't use the adjective 'female.'"

He leaned in as if to give her a hug, but decided against it. Instead, he gave her chin a soft squeeze and walked away.

"Thank you," she said to his retreating back.

He didn't hear her.

CHAPTER SEVENTY-EIGHT

Washington, DC

JADE WAS ACCUSTOMED to the extremes of the DC-area weather. Last Wednesday, it snowed, accompanied by cold, unbearable temperatures. Today dawned sunny and a record-breaking seventy-five degrees. Global warming had its advantages.

She strode down the sidewalk alongside Independence Avenue in Southwest Washington, DC. She turned left into the entrance of the Martin Luther King Jr. Memorial. She spotted Zoe among the sightseers, staring up at the statue of the great man himself.

Zoe turned at Jade's footsteps. "Hey, you. Great news about the ERA, huh?"

Congress finally repealed the deadline. Soon thereafter, Florida, Virginia, and Missouri ratified the Equal Rights Amendment.

"Yeah. Great news."

"Huh! I thought you would be more excited."

Jade gazed at the statue for a moment. It never failed to give her strength, a sense of purpose. She cocked her head for Zoe to follow her away from the small crowd. They sauntered along the memorial stopping on occasion to read the inscriptions on the granite wall.

When they reached the end of the wall, Zoe stopped and faced her. "What's wrong with you? You're not one to take an afternoon off to go sightseeing."

"It's about Caleb."

Zoe's eyes widened, but she said nothing.

Jade handed her a sheet of paper.

Zoe read the document, her eyes blinking faster as she read. "I can explain."

"Then explain. I have all afternoon."

She examined the sheet again—a transcript of one of their chat conversations—and handed it back to Jade.

"It started out as something to do. I liked talking to other liberals without being careful of what I said. It was fun and totally anonymous." She shook her head. "Or so I thought. We were only chatting." She stared at Jade. "I had no idea he was going to *do* anything."

"You gave me a clue without realizing it," Jade said. "The night you came over to my house, and I was working. You brought dinner. You mentioned the first TSK email before he had sent it to the network."

"He must have told us about it in the chat room. I thought the whole thing was intense, but harmless. Those guys display such bravado. I call them ATNA—All Talk, No Action."

"And it never crossed your mind to talk to me about it? The lead investigator on the case?"

Zoe walked a few paces away. She sighed. "I fucked up. I didn't realize the significance of the email."

"He was killing people, for God's sakes!"

Zoe turned, her eyes blazed, her chest heaving. "Do you

think I knew that? Do you think I would continue chatting with him and not tell you? Give me some credit. Fuck!"

Jade peered out over the Tidal Basin at the Thomas Jefferson Memorial. She was silent for several minutes. The nearby sightseers, who had stopped reading the inscriptions to eavesdrop, lost interest.

"Say something," Zoe said. "I hate when you get angry. You shut down. Yell at me or something."

"Did you know Phillips had a website? At aliberaltruth.com? He had about ten thousand followers."

"I didn't realize it was Landon's, but sure, I visited the site." Zoe paused. "I loved his blogs."

Jade whispered, almost to herself. "I read his blogs, too. I should have realized the similarities with the manifesto and the emails."

Zoe closed the distance between them. "It's not your fault. A lot of people missed it. You don't always need to be perfect, you know."

Jade continued to stare across the water, her arms crossed, protecting herself from the cooling late afternoon.

"I remember in college, you slept with one arm across your eyes, always protecting yourself."

Jade smiled. "Still do."

Zoe came and stood in front of Jade. "For a psych major, you have never taken the time to analyze yourself. Is that why you're always trying to solve other people's problems?"

Jade shrugged.

"Do you remember the first time we met?" Zoe asked.

Jade hesitated, and then nodded.

"When I realized you were sitting across the table from me in the campus library, I had to introduce myself. Did you really think my pen stopped working so I had to borrow one of yours? I had thrown it under the table, giving me an excuse to meet you. You introduced yourself as if I didn't know you were the best point guard in Stanford history since Jennifer Azzi."

Jade's face grew hot, embarrassed. She remained silent. She had no idea where this was going.

"Do you know why I did that?"

Jade shook her head, a slow, cautious movement.

"Because I knew underneath that tough-jock exterior, you needed me."

She reached up with her right hand and caressed Jade's cheek. The display of physical affection made Jade uncomfortable. She wasn't the touchy-feely type. Zoe, her beautiful best friend for the last ten years, knew this.

Zoe reached up with her other hand, cradling Jade's face. "I'm sorry. I should've suspected him. And I should have told you."

Before Jade could react, Zoe planted an exaggerated loud kiss on her lips.

Jade wiped her mouth. "Shit!" She cast a glance at the sightseers staring over at them again, amused smiles on their faces. Through clenched teeth, she said, "What're you doing?"

"Begging for forgiveness. You solved your case. Let's go celebrate it and the historic passage of the ERA. I know the perfect place in Dupont Circle."

EPILOGUE

The White House, Washington, DC

AFTER EIGHT INAUGURAL balls, President Whitney Fairchild stepped into the Oval Office, alone, and kicked off her high heels. *My feet hurt. And, besides, who's going to stop me?* In her stockings, she padded around the room, gazing at the wall paintings. She allowed her hand to trail along the softness of the sofas and chairs as she made her way to the most famous desk in the world, the nineteenth-century *Resolute* desk, a gift from Queen Victoria to President Rutherford B. Hayes in 1880. President John F. Kennedy was the first to use the desk in the Oval Office, as had many of the presidents since. She sat in the presidential chair and placed both hands on the top of the desk.

She thought about the swearing-in ceremony earlier that day at noon on the west steps of the US Capitol, when she tried to keep the dignified smile on her face despite the biting, freezing cold of Washington, DC, in January. The proud faces of her husband, Grayson, her two children, and her parents as they stood by her side. She was grateful to all of them for their support and sacrifices over the years. With her hand gracing the same Bible used in Abraham Lincoln's inauguration in

1861, she scanned the crowd on the Mall, the largest ever to witness the swearing in of a US president.

Next, the drive down Pennsylvania Avenue. The consternation of her advisors and the Secret Service when she and Grayson got out of the bullet-proof Lincoln Town Car and walked hand in hand down the street waving to the massive crowd. She had lunch with her former colleagues in the Senate and House and attended meetings and briefings the rest of the afternoon, because the president never had a day off. The amount of information was overwhelming. For all the consideration she'd given it, she still had managed to underestimate the awesome responsibility she had assumed until she read her first President's Daily Brief.

She thought again of the balls earlier that evening and hoped she didn't appear too foolish dancing. She had practiced during the last few weeks, but it had been years since she and Grayson had gone dancing. She cringed now, thinking about some of their more awkward dance moves.

She had run into Blake Haynes at one of the balls. Her interview with him last week had been such a success that MSNBC had given him his own show. Needless to say, he was happy to see her. FOW indeed.

Leaning back in her—*her!*—chair, she reflected on the campaign and all the people she had talked to, the hands she had shaken, the late-night strategy sessions, and trying to find healthy food in some of the towns she had visited.

She thought of Ted and everyone on her legislative and campaign staffs. She remembered the scandals with her husband's company and his mistake with their neighbor. She was fortunate these scandals had not derailed her campaign. The other side had tried and failed. She let out a contented sigh. She was blessed.

When she and Grayson toasted, "To us!" with champagne in the private residence earlier in the evening, it felt like a new beginning. Not only for her term as president, but for their relationship as well.

An envelope addressed to her was positioned in the center of the desk. She recognized Richard Ellison's large, sloping scrawl. She opened it.

Dear Whitney,

By the time you read this, you will be president. Although our interactions going forward will be few, please know I'm rooting for you.

Respectfully,

Richard

Whitney smiled, touched, even though she knew Reagan had started the tradition with H.W. Every president since had left a note for his successor.

A gift sat on the corner of the desk. It was in the shape of a book. At first, she guessed that it, too, was from the former president, but now remembered it was a gift from Landon. In the confusion of the transition, she had never opened it. She hesitated, wondering whether she should do so now.

Whitney read the note scribbled on the decorative paper. *Please don't open until after the election.*

She opened it.

In her hand, she held a first edition of Louisa May Alcott's *Little Women*. The brown and white cover was well preserved. She flipped through the pages; none seemed to be missing or damaged. The book appeared as if it had never been read. A page of expensive beige parchment paper was tucked inside the front book cover.

Dear Senator,

I'm sure you already own this classic, but this volume is in pristine condition and, I am told, one of a kind. I've enjoyed our reading challenge, and since I'm so far ahead, I wanted to give you a chance to catch up.

Seriously, I want to thank you for the opportunity to work for you and alongside you all these years. Every day has been a joy.

I am proud of what we've accomplished and look forward to what we'll accomplish over the next eight years (yes, I said eight!). I know you will win.

I want to have one of our talks after you read this. I believe we'll have much to say to each other.

You have no idea how much I love you.

Your son,

Landon

The End

AFTERWORD

The Equal Rights Amendment was introduced into Congress in 1923, passed both houses in 1972, and was ratified by thirty-five states that same year. It failed to become law by just three states. The amendment has been reintroduced in every Congress since 1982.

ACKNOWLEDGEMENTS

If it takes a village to raise a child, then it takes a team to write a book. Although I was the one who first put fingers to keyboard, this book would not have been published without the support, guidance, morale boosts, and constructive criticism I received along the way. I want to thank my editors, Alan Rinzler and Jim Thomsen. You both made this a better book. In addition, thank you, Jim, for helping me to assemble #TeamJLBrownauthor. Thanks to web designer, Anne Clermont, Damonza, who created an awesome cover design, and my proofreader, Christina Tinling.

Thanks to Darcia Davis Photography, who tried to make a model out of me. Special shout out to an early reader, Sherron Bates (the book has changed a little since then), and fellow writers on Twitter who encouraged and cheered me on.

I am also grateful to the following writers: Renee Flagler and Lissa Woodson, who took the time to help a sistah out, Kathleen Antrim for her support and guidance, Christina Katz for her uncompromising honesty, and Dan Schlosser for always being there to answer my questions.

To my parents who never let me settle and instilled the work ethic in me I would need to become an author. To my mother, who put a book in my hand at the age of three; I have had one in my hand ever since.

To my sons, Travis and Brandon, for all of their love and support, and my daughter and marketing strategist, Jasmine, for her love, support, creativity, and enthusiasm.

To my cat and constant companion, Duke, who spent many hours on my lap as I wrote this novel. I miss you every day.

To my amazing wife and manager, Audi, who encouraged me to write this novel in the first place, read and commented on every draft, and supported me throughout the entire project. I found my beach. I love you.

Reading Group Questions

1. Why is Jade so driven?
2. How would you describe Whitney and Grayson's marriage? What does it look like from outward appearances? How does it work for them? What do you think about Grayson not joining her on the campaign trail?
3. Some people may consider Cole disagreeable. What are his good qualities?
4. What is the significance of the killer cutting out the victims' tongues?
5. How did your personal political affiliation help you to identify with one character versus another? What commonality did you find with any of the characters from the other party?
6. How did this novel help you see any issue from a different perspective? Which of your views, if any, changed because of what you read in this book?
7. Whitney tries to be an ethical politician, but doesn't hesitate to cross the line when it suits her. How important is honesty in a politician to you? How have the politicians through history measured up to that?

8. When did you figure out who the killer was? What clues gave it away?
9. How do you feel about TSK's position that the media should air both sides of the issues?
10. What do Whitney and Jade have in common? What are their differences?
11. What did you think of the revelation at the end of Landon's letter? What about your opinion of his character did it change?
12. How was Landon able to work alongside Whitney every day?
13. Why does Jade eat only one M&M at a time?
14. How does it feel to know that women are not entitled to equal rights under the US Constitution?
15. On what issues do you think the two major political parties should be able to find common ground?
16. What would you say to Jade after how she treated Dante?
17. How does the use of language ("pro-choice" versus "abortion," "gay marriage" versus "marriage equality," etc.) frame political discourse?
18. What do you think about the fact that no one witnessed the Starbucks murder because they were all on their cell phones?
19. How did you feel when Cole disrespected Jade?
20. Some people believe that you should never discuss religion and politics with others. Do you agree? If so,

how do you think we can solve some of the significant differences of opinion in this country on gun control, abortion rights, immigration, climate change, etc.?

The next installment in the Jade Harrington series...

RULE OF LAW

A JADE HARRINGTON NOVEL

J. L. BROWN

ISBN 978-0-9969772-3-4 (paperback)
ISBN 978-0-9969772-4-1 (ebook)

PROLOGUE

WASHINGTON, DC - ONE MONTH AGO

SHE SHOULD HAVE thrown the letter away.

Or shredded it.

She knelt before the altar of the small, quaint Presbyterian church near the White House. The nave was empty. Easter services had just ended. Her husband, Grayson, and the children waited outside. Lead Secret Service agent, Josh McPherson, stood alone by the entryway at the front of the church.

Although her hands were clasped together and relaxed, her head bowed in supplication, President Whitney Fairchild was not praying.

Instead, she was reading.

The expensive parchment paper, creased horizontally into two sections, lay on the raised carpeted step, worn from her reading it every day since her inauguration two months ago when she had first opened the envelope.

She needn't have bothered.

She had memorized every word.

Dear Senator,

I'm sure you already own this classic, but this volume is in pristine condition and, I am told, one of a kind. I've enjoyed our reading challenge, and since I'm so far ahead, I wanted to give you a chance to catch up.

Seriously, I want to thank you for the opportunity to work for you and alongside you all these years. Every day has been a joy.

I am proud of what we've accomplished and look forward to what we'll accomplish over the next eight years (yes, I said eight!). I know you will win.

I want to have one of our talks after you read this. I believe we'll have much to say to each other.

You have no idea how much I love you.

Your son,

Landon

Despite his sins, she still missed Landon Phillips.

"Mom?"

Whitney started at the sound of her son's voice.

Snatching the letter with reflexes she didn't realize she possessed, she stuffed it back into her purse.

Her son, Chandler, stood beside her, wearing a jacket, shirt, and slacks.

"What are you doing?" he asked.

"Working."

"Working and praying at the same time?"

She rose. "In this job, I do that often."

"Dad sent me in to get you. He's hungry."

She brushed the bangs off his forehead. His face was like looking at a mirror. "Dad, huh?" She looped her arm through his. "Did I tell you how handsome you look today, my favorite son?"

He grinned. "I'm your only son, Mom."

Whitney's smile faltered. "That is true."

They walked down the aisle past the stained-glass windows to the front of the church. As he chatted about the action movie they had watched last night in the theater room in the White House, her thoughts wandered.

She chastised herself for being careless. She was not ready to share the truth about Landon with anyone yet. Particularly her husband and her children.

That was close. I need to be more careful.

PART I

CHAPTER ONE

FAIRFAX, VIRGINIA

YOU HEARD THE breathing first.

Heavy breathing from one. Quick breaths through the nose from the one accustomed to fighting.

Next, you heard the whack, whack, whack as gloves met flesh.

Then, the smell: the overwhelming musk of teenage sweat.

There were no lights.

The "spectators" used the flashlights on their iPhones to illuminate the area. Some shone real ones.

The two boys in the cage wore MMA gloves, but no headgear or pads. No shirts. No shoes. But—oddly—they both wore baseball pants. One was in pro-style knickers.

Those were the rules.

Blood speckled the fighter's knickers like an impressionist painting.

Not his blood.

Watching the fight, a boy clung to the netting outside the

cage. He held it tight to hold himself up. His knuckles stuck out like small stones in the dark.

Every punch made him sick.

He didn't want to be here. If it were up to him, he would rather be anywhere else. Even home, doing homework. Or at the dentist, having a cavity filled.

But he had no choice. Attendance was required.

The fight would be over soon. The boy in the regular baseball pants was pinned against one of the poles. Each time he slipped off the pole from the sweat on his back and fell against the netting, the guy in the knickers would grab him, right him in front of the pole again, and pummel him some more. In the face. In the stomach. In the ribs.

In between punches and exhalations, the guy in the knickers shouted, "That's poppin'! That's poppin'!"

The spectators—also shirtless and in baseball pants—wore baseball caps. They chanted: *"Poppin'! Poppin'! Poppin'! Poppin'! Poppin'! Poppin'! Poppin'! Poppin'! Poppin'!"*

The gladiatorial dogfight atmosphere intensified as the fight went on. The punches landed harder. The cheering louder. The sweat shinier.

When the fighter against the pole finally faltered, the boy in the knickers threw him down and then lifted him by both ears and slammed his head to the turf.

No one made a move to help the loser.

Knickers started kicking him with the instep of his foot. "That's hot!"

The spectators chanted: *"Hot! Hot! Hot! Hot! Hot! Hot! Hot! Hot! Hot!"*

The presumptive victor mounted the prone boy, pummeling his head with vicious punches: his left ear, then right.

"Loser!" he screamed.

A regulation fight would have been declared over.

"Loser! Loser! Loser! Loser! Loser! Loser! Loser! Loser! Loser!"

"Tap out, man!" yelled one of the spectators.

"Yeah!" said another.

"Do it!" said an opposing voice.

"Fuck him up!"

"Queer bait!"

"Kill him!"

"Let him die!"

The victor's arm rose high in the air to deliver the coup de grâce, the ensuing punch anticlimactic. Blood flew from the nose and mouth of the boy on the ground, drops spraying those who were watching.

The vanquished fighter stopped moving, his long legs still. His arms extended perpendicular to his body. A crucifix without the cross. Even in the artificial light, the boy outside the cage saw the blood running freely from the prone boy's nose and mouth. Both of his eyes, blackening.

He looked dead.

The boy outside still clung to the netting. His arms shook.

He couldn't hold it in any longer.

A grumbling roiled in the pit of his stomach. The bile rose.

Leaning forward, his head between his arms, he threw up on the ground. Teammates near him jumped out of the way.

"Gross!"

"That shit better not be on my pants, man!"

"Wimp!"

"Idiot!"

"Faggot!"

The name calling hurt the boy, although he should be used to it. He battled the tears trying to escape his eyes.

He lost the fight.

He wiped his mouth with the back of his hand. Made sure his baseball cap was on tight.

And then he ran.

*

With his arms around their shoulders, to an observer, he appeared drunk. Good friends were helping him get home safely. The illusion ended when they dumped him on the front lawn of his parents' home, his head barely missing the sidewalk.

"That'll teach you," one boy said, kicking him.

"Warriors don't run," said the other.

The two ran back to the car, their sneakers loud in the quiet of the neighborhood.

Every bone and muscle in his body ached. He scarcely registered the squeal of the tires as their car sped away.

His chest rose and fell as he breathed. The only movement he was capable of.

The stars burned bright against the black sky. The Little Dipper. The Big Dipper. Perseus—or was it Gemini? He had learned about constellations during a class field trip to a planetarium three years ago. Life had been great then. When he was young.

Running away had been stupid. Where could he hide? He saw these guys every day. Two of them had grabbed him before he made it off campus. Tossing him into a car like a crumpled piece of paper, they had driven to a three-sided section of the main building. Back in the day, it had served as the student smoking lounge, if you could believe that. Now, just an area the high overhead night-lights and security cameras missed.

Two other guys had joined them—one, the fighter in the knickers—and beaten the shit out of him until he passed out.

Dew began to soak through his shirt. He wasn't sure how long he'd been lying here. The grass, mowed to the perfection of a baseball field, smelled as the boy imagined heaven would. His dad took enormous pride in his lawn.

He could lie here forever.

Turning his head, he spotted it in the moonlight. "I thought I'd lost you."

He pushed himself up, picked up his cap, placed it on his head, and gingerly made his way to the front door. Pain shot through his hand as he extracted the key from his back pocket.

Inside, quietly and painfully, he climbed the stairs. The noise of a television behind his parents' closed bedroom door masked his footsteps as he tiptoed by. Some reality show that offered a different reality than their own.

The boy entered his room at the end of the hall. Not bothering to pull off his pants or brush his teeth, he crawled into bed.

An hour later, sleep still eluded him. He reached for his nightstand and removed a bottle of pain-relief pills hidden in the drawer.

He'd taken a lot of them over the past two years.

Shaking out four pills, he swallowed them dry and lay down and waited for them to work.

As he drifted off to sleep, he remembered the name of the constellation.

Perseus. The hero.

CPSIA information can be obtained
at www.ICGtesting.com
Printed in the USA
FSHW011625120419
57201FS